A LEAP INTO THE UNKNOWN

RICHARD A. J. MORLEY

A fictional tale

British Library Cataloguing In Publication Data
A Record of this Publication is available
from the British Library

ISBN 1846850916
978-1-84685-091-2

First Published February 2006 by

Exposure Publishing, an imprint of Diggory Press,
Three Rivers, Minions, Liskeard, Cornwall, PL14 5LE, UK
WWW.DIGGORYPRESS.COM

'If I have seen further than other men,
it is because I have stood upon the shoulders of giants.'

Isaac Newton

For the greatest giants I know. For my parents.

PART ONE

THE LARGER THE ISLAND OF KNOWLEDGE,
THE LONGER THE SHORELINE OF WONDER.
EVERY ANSWER HAS TWO QUESTIONS.

THE STRANGEST OF MEETINGS

I FIRST met M.J when I walked into a shitty little backpackers hostel in Bondi. I'd stumbled in off the street originally thankful for the brief respite until I saw the state of this place. Trust me, it was a hole. It didn't help that I already wasn't in the best of moods. You see, me being me, meant that I had decided to walk from the bus station for some bizarre reason. I think there was method to my madness, but then again, I always think that.

So I'd wandered around aimlessly looking for some golden oasis that seemed to exist in my backpackers' guide, but not in reality. What didn't help was the fact that I'd deemed it essential to pack the whole world it seemed, onto my back. I mean really, come on, I've decided to travel half way around the world for a considerable amount of time, and I've packed such items as a travel iron. Hmm, right, why had I done that again? Oh yes, that was it, at some point I was going to be trekking through the jungles of Thailand, but everything would be fine, all possible situations would be catered for, because I'd be wearing a freshly ironed shirt.

In a very short space of time I'd quickly realised I was a world apart from the life I had known back home.

So I'd ended up stumbling into the first open door I'd seen. My back was killing me; I was sweating like I'd been masturbating continuously for a month, and my CK shirt was badly creased.

A number of cockroaches scuttled out of the door as I entered. It's never a great sign when even the insect clientele are abandoning a place in a desperate search for a classier establishment. However I was just too tired to try anywhere else.

Anyway, what was I saying? Don't you just hate it when your mind just wanders off somewhere without you. I should probably apologise right up front, because I'm always doing it.

Oh yeah, that was it.

So I reached my room, hesitating briefly at the door as I mused upon how to open it without touching the handle. You see there were some rather questionable stains on it, and call me old fashioned, but I prefer not to touch dried blood, vomit, and what could only have been bees wax (?) residue. It was alright, I needn't have worried, the lock proceeded to drop off as I looked on at my little puzzle, and the door just fell open. And that's the first time I saw M.J.

Well, semi-saw, because when the door opened a huge billow of cannabis smoke hit me like a cannon ball. I walked gingerly to my bed and became slowly aware that through the mist, 3 sets of eyes were visible, watching me. I thought I'd risk it.

'Hi, I'm _____.'

Apparently the three sets of eyes belonged to a blond-haired, dreadlocked fellow by the name of M.J, and two girls, possibly Dutch, Jetske and Yeldow.

'So, where are you from?' I ventured.

Silence.

This was not going at all well. Back home I was a 24-year-old trainee lawyer. I would soon be standing in court and demanding justice. I would be feared and respected by all and no one would dare withstand my questioning.

Yet in a single second I was once again a timid, shy and scared, 9 year old schoolboy, standing in the playground begging for someone to talk to me, begging for someone to be my friend.

Still silence.

M.J tilted his head, looked at me, and then thank goodness, he opened his mouth and I knew the dreadful silence would be broken, and everything would be fine.

'Are you gay?'

Now, this response was not exactly what I had been anticipating, and I must confess as to being just a little taken aback.

'No,' I stammered. 'I'm actually engaged,' and pointed to the thin platinum band on my finger.

'Would you die for her?'

My response this time was not stammered. It was bold and true. 'Yeah, I would.'

'Nice one mate. Smoke?' and the dregs of the untapped joint he was smoking was thrust towards me.

The sudden movement caused the ash to fall upon the floor but no one bothered to clear it up. Obviously the ashtray was the stained carpet. In fact, on closer inspection, it seemed to be the dustbin as well. The way you could see tiny entities moving in your peripheral vision was also of particular interest I noted.

'No thank you, I don't smoke,' I replied.

'No worries mate,' and with that M.J turned back to a previous conversation he and the girls must have been having.

Now, at the time, such behaviour seemed rather strange to me. Our conversation had obviously been concluded, and so I decided to lie down and recuperate for a while.

All in all, it had been a very long, very bizarre day. Little did I know, it was merely a hint of what was to come.

The 14-hour flight had taken a lot out of me, and the walk and talk had finished me off. After rummaging through my huge rucksack, I eventually gave up on trying to find the book I was looking for, (I did come across my highly classy and extremely useful travel iron a number of times. How many of these things did I bring again?) and I just laid down.

For once since I arrived, things went my way. A book wasn't required after all, as someone had gone to great lengths to provide reading material for me. Staring up at the underside of the bunk above me were several items of graffiti. 'Whoever sleeps here tonight will be raped and murdered, trust me, you can't stay awake forever, and I will get you. Didn't you see the stains on the door handle, they're from my last victim?'

Hmmm, oh good. Always a pleasant thing to be made to ponder upon. Either it was true and this was to be my last night on earth, or some wanker with the strangest and sickest sense of humour around was present. My gaze once again fell upon M.J.

This dude was blatantly not your stereotypical kind of guy. His dress sense was interesting. Far different from my own, and yet I must confess, I found something compellingly cool about it all. He had no shoes, socks, or top on for that matter. In fact his entire garb merely consisted of a plain black sarong wrapped around his waist, with what I recognised as Japanese writing dabbed in red around the fringes. He had a number of tattoos on his bare, tanned, toned torso, and as he talked to the girls he stroked a bushy goatee with his dirtied, bitten nails. Blond dreadlocks fell to his shoulders and the thinnest nose ring twinkled away every time it caught the light.

I remember thinking, what kind of man is this? Who can have the confidence to wander around half naked, meeting complete and utter strangers, dressed exactly as they wish?

Perhaps because of my school life, I mean, I wasn't exactly bullied, but the other kids did use to pick on me a bit, I was now the kind of guy who carries a travel iron around with him.

You see, I remember when I was younger, I figured if I looked exactly like I was supposed to, how society and the other kids expected me to, it would give people less opportunity to mock me.

I remember this one time, I must have been perhaps 8 or so, I wore a grey shirt to school. We didn't have a lot of money when I was growing up, and for whatever reason, grey shirts were cheaper than white ones. My mother bought me one for the new school year and so I turned up to school in a grey shirt.

Every one else wore white shirts, everyone else bar one other kid. Unfortunately that one other kid was 'Flee-Bag Wanner,' as we knew him. He was the ridicule of the whole school. Like I said, I can't exactly claim to have been incredibly bullied, not with old Flee-Bag about.

Man, that poor kid. We were all so mean to him. Now, even as long ago as that, I remember that I hated to see people unhappy. I talked to him once; I tried to be friendly because I could see he'd been crying. Unfortunately people saw me and I got picked on for the rest of the day because of it. Got picked on until to prove that we weren't friends, and to make people leave me alone, I ran up to him and tripped him over in front of everyone. Stupid really. You know I wasn't that old at the time but I still remember feeling like a right royal little shit for doing it.

Anyway, what was I saying? I told you I always do it, always off on tangents, tangents, tangents!

Oh, the grey shirt.

Anyway, so I turned up at school wearing a grey shirt along with Flee-Bag Wanner. Of course this instantly meant that he and I were best friends because we both had the same colour shirt on. So at lunchtime, all the other kids chased Nicky (that was his real name) and I into the woods at the bottom of the playing field. They then proceeded to beat us up. I remember one kid grabbed me in a headlock and kept smacking me around the head while the others ripped at my grey shirt. Stupid thing to remember really, but I recall feeling so ashamed because I was crying as well. The teachers weren't impressed. Teachers are normally pretty switched on, but Nicky and I knew it was in our best interest to just tell people that we'd, 'fallen over.'

You know what? I could take the name-calling; take the beating even, but the one thing that really hurt me more than anything, that really got to my heart, was my mother. I couldn't tell her what happened. She'd just approach the school, the kids would get in trouble, and it would all spell out for more disaster in the foreseeable future for me. So I just went along with the whole, 'I fell over' story.

She was so mad. So disappointed, because we couldn't exactly afford to buy me new shirts all the time. I didn't know what to do. I was in such turmoil. She was bound to go and replace the shirt somehow, but blatantly with another grey one.

Still, I swear mothers must be intuitive; it's really freaky sometimes. I never knew why but at some point she must have figured something out, because she came back from the shop with a brand new white shirt.

Ever since then, I'd tried to look exactly like all the models in the high store fashion displays. Ever since then, if I passed any kind of reflective surface, say a shop window, or a parked car, I'd have a quick check to ensure that I didn't have any hairs out of place, or anything else like that. You see, kids can be cruel enough to even mock you for having something as small and trivial as having a few hairs out of place. If you looked alright, you armed the bullies with less ammunition to shoot you down with.

So, yeah, I guess M.J fascinated me immediately. This guy knew people would stop and stare, but the bloke blatantly didn't give a tiny rat's arse! That must take some strength.

As I lay there, jacked into my tape player, every time a song ended I could hear snippets of my companions conversation drift in. My intrigue was further fuelled, and so as quietly as I could, I gently pushed the stop button, cutting off poor old Vivaldi mid concerto, and with my headphones still on, I secretly turned my attention to their conversation.

The girls didn't seem to be saying much, they were both merely gazing intently, and rather lustfully I seemed to remember thinking, at M.J as he preached. Sat there cross-legged, his eyes glazed over, he spoke softly as if half to his audience, and half to himself.

'It was a flash of inspiration that I was expecting,' he whispered, 'but what I actually got was a slow realisation, as of one slowly becoming used to the darkness of a room after they'd been stood in the light.

The truth of it has dawned on me whilst I've been here. Others find happiness in just jumping from one lovers bed to another, sleeping their way around the country, never giving anyone a real chance to know them, and never really allowing anything constant to settle. Personally, I can't see any point to this. Personally, I seek a woman, a soul mate, a star-crossed lover if you will. As I can truly say that love, not lust will complete me.

When I was in the temples of Japan, an old wise sage told me something I'll never forget. That there may be half a dozen right people in this life for us, but that there's only one right time and place. So I continue my search, never truly content, until I find her. Only then may I live my life to the full.

Others are imbeciles. They have this, they have the one they love, but the inner monologue is ultimately self destructive by nature, and they throw it all away, believing the grass ever to be greener on the other side. It never is. They have love, but they don't know the meaning of it all. It's literally staring them in the face. Just fill your heart with love for everything, especially your partner, because you are simply here to die.

Alas, we are nothing more than mere maggots in the gut of a corpse, trapped in by a wall of flesh, completely unaware that the only thing certain in this life, is our inevitable and unavoidable doom. So grab something during the journey for yourself. No one will remember us when we die. Whatever you accumulate materialistically in life is irrelevant. All that matters is love.'

'Oh, some say that life is really a quest for knowledge,' he continued. 'True. Yet open your eyes. The true clarity of the knowledge you gain you pass on to others. In these people it can live and breathe. It can blossom, before finally helping to guide them through the obstacles of the haphazard maze of life. This is the true purpose of knowledge. And in a way, it's the only way to continue to exist in this mortal realm once we're gone.'

At this point, one of the girls slipped her hand into M.J's, and it became apparent to me that the women were actually falling for the crap he was spraying. A laugh almost escaped my lips at the realisation that they were really falling hook line and sinker for these cheesy chat up lines.

Still, one of the Dutch girls drooled rather sickeningly, 'oh that's so true. We're so glad we met you. Promise me you'll move on with us tomorrow? Please.'

I waited to see how this little show would pan out. I waited with a slightly amused intrigue for M.J's response.

'Ah, I'm sorry ladies, but I must continue my travels alone, never knowing what is around the next corner, yet always hoping that it may be my true love.'

Smiling at them, catching their gaze in turn, he continued, 'it's okay. For friends come and go, but the true ones you hold on to, as they were appointed to you, your 'soul-mates.' They guide you in life. They also exist to share happiness with; as on our own we aren't always really capable of registering different heights of happiness, quite often we just need someone to be there to share an experience with. Its only when we communicate with each other that we can really fully comprehend something.

Look at us. We've shared so many wonderful experiences together already, but I'm afraid I must keep searching for the last piece of the puzzle, whoever she is, without you. I have to find her. If not just to prove that this wasn't just the mere ranting and raving of a mad man.'

With that, M.J looked down, visually vulnerable and upset, was he crying? Before I really knew, Yeldow leant forward and gently pressed her lips against his. As she pulled away from him, she slowly but purposefully ran her hand up the inside of his leg, along the side of his body, and held his cheek in the palm of her hand. Leaning forward, they kissed again, far more passionately this time. With that done, Jetske gently pulled Yeldow aside, before she to leaned forward and kissed M.J.

Right. Interesting. Just what the fuck was that all about?!

Anyway, I figured I should probably leave them to it, and as quietly as I could I made my escape. To be honest I don't think anyone would've noticed or cared if I'd stayed, but still. The last image I caught as I vacated the room was the two girls kissing each other and removing their tops.

Lucky bastard.

I NEED YOU MORE THAN WANT YOU, AND I WANT YOU FOR ALL TIME

WELL, as you can imagine I was pretty damned pissed off. Not only had I been kicked out of my room, but I was also feeling horny as hell, and Beth was a thousand bloody miles away to add insult to injury.

Ah, Beth.

I hadn't particularly followed everything M.J was saying, I kinda figured you had to be stoned. Oh, and that most of it had just been an act for the girls anyway, but I guess what he'd said about the whole, 'love,' 'star crossed lovers' thing had struck somewhat of a chord. I mean, Beth and I had been together since high school, and been engaged for 3 years. She was well, just amazing.

I still remember the day I proposed. Pretty sad really, people normally laugh when they hear it. In my defence I do try! I go for these huge romantic gestures but most of the time I just end up completely missing the mark!

Basically we'd already seen a ring, but as we were both at university Beth knew that I didn't have two penny pieces to rub together. The ring wasn't particularly fancy; Beth just wasn't that kind of girl. It was like her, no frills were needed, it was simply beautiful as itself. Literally it was just a thin gold ring with a single diamond. She knew I couldn't afford it, but my parents have always been pretty damned cool, and in secret, lent me the money.

So I had a ring, but no romantic place to propose at. Someone mentioned a nearby National Trust Mansion, and in the gardens, was a small marble open-air temple.

On one hot summers day I cycled down labyrinthine country lanes to try and find the place. In the end I had to leave my bike at a stile and wander across a farmers cornfield to get to the damned place. You see, there was a main road and entrance, but I couldn't afford to pay the entrance fee just to run around and check this temple out. So I was on a mission to find a back entrance.

Hot and sweating, I eventually managed to find one. In my youth I was renowned for my tree climbing abilities, I swear I was like a little chimpanzee. Fortunately old habits die hard, and I was rather impressed with the way I managed to scale an old oak tree and drop down over the wall without managing to break my neck. I scuttled around like an ant going mechanically about its mission, and eventually found the place.

Apparently it's an identical replica of a temple in Naples designed by one of the old Grand Masters. Engraved around the top in gold it bears the Latin phrase and translation, 'Love Transcends Time and Place.'

Yeah, it seemed as good a place as any to pop the question.

On the appointed day Beth and I lay on a rug in the garden. I was on my back with my head resting on her stomach, reading Lord of the Flies, and she was busy fiddling around making daisy chains.

Apparently she was growing a little tired of this though, as she came up with a new game that was obviously far more fun. It basically consisted of shoving the daisies she'd picked into my ears and up my nostrils. Such a pleasant young child! Knowing her like I do, I knew this was also secret code for, 'stop being such a boring bastard, put your book away, and give me some attention!' So she taught me how to make daisy chains, (not particularly macho I agree, but love can make you do strange things!) and also, I made a daisy ring and put it on my finger.

Later that afternoon we drove out to the above mentioned mansion to look around the gardens. On the way the bloody daisy ring broke on me. I got really shitty. Beth couldn't understand why I was so bothered about a daisy ring. Anyway, I kicked up such a fuss that we ended up sitting in the grounds on arrival, in front of a truckload of strangers, making soddin' daisy rings!

Eventually we got to the temple and I found that my hands were clammy, my mouth was dry, and I was more nervous than the first time I had ever had sex. I had to keep checking that the real ring was still in my pocket. So we finally got there, and as she read the inscription I got down on one knee, removed the daisy ring from my finger, took her by the hand and went to place the ring on her wedding finger. However, as I did it, I applied a little too much pressure and it broke again.

Beth smiled and sadly said, 'oh, it broke.'

'Never mind,' I replied. 'I think I've got a spare one here somewhere,' and with that I pulled out the real ring. 'I love you, I always have, I always will, will you marry me?'

Time stood still.

Now, that phrase is bandied around willy-nilly these days, but I can safely say that this was the real deal. It seemed to me that an eternity passed by as I awaited her response. In reality it was merely a few milliseconds, as Beth overcame the shock to answer, but in my head my brain stepped into overtime. Every possible negative thought went through my head. 'Maybe I'd gotten it all so, so wrong. What if she didn't actually want to marry me at all?'

Obviously she said yes though, else I probably wouldn't be telling you this story, and would be drowning in a bowl of Coco Pops somewhere right now!

Anyway, ah, my favourite word, normally a sure fire sign that once again I've gone off somewhere, rambling on like some headless chicken.

Hmmm, interesting, why would a headless chicken ramble? Surely it would just have a little lie down if it didn't have a head and hope one might grow back, or maybe look around for a new one if it was a cartoon chicken. I mean come on; you don't get very far in this world without having a head do you? Yeah, that's pretty weird.

What was I talking about?

Love. Beth. That was it.

Yeah, she was amazing, the light of my life, I loved her so much it was unbelievable. I'm not even going to try and explain it. Words can never really explain any emotion, let alone in the English language. We have the word, 'love,' and that's about it. It's thrown around in a futile attempt to explain a feeling that actually has thousands of different subtleties.

Take the Gaelic language for example. It has roughly 21 different words for our word, 'cow'. Granted it's an agriculturally based language, but still, if they deem something as simple as the word, 'cow,' to require 21 variations, how can the English language get away with tying up so many different complexities into the one word, 'love?'

Ah, once again I digress. Back home I was to become a lawyer, and Beth was finishing her degree in medicine. I'd always wanted to see the world, whereas Beth had never been particularly bothered. So on completion of my law degree, I'd arranged for my start date at the solicitors firm I was to work at to be postponed for a few months. Beth was hard pressed with her final exams and didn't particularly need me bumming round the place, so I'd come over to Australia on my own to scratch my travelling itch.

So here I was, on the first eve of my big adventure, sat completely alone in the television room of the worst hostel in history. Well, I use the word 'television room' loosely. According to the sign on the door this was indeed, the 'television room,' but I thought by definition this room would in fact harbour a TV. Ok, so call me crazy, maybe I was expecting too much as always, but I was just a little disappointed. After the day I'd had I just wanted to switch my brain off with a bit of Simpsons, or even better, Friends.

Wonder what the gang are up to? Bet they aren't sat alone in some shit hole, unable to sleep because some blond haired preacher is banging away on two Dutch girls, probably in their own beds.

I stand corrected though. For indeed, in one corner of the room, the carpet did have slightly less layers of grime and crap on it than the rest of the floor. Even more impressively, the mark resembled a square similar in size to a TV set. Right, so somewhere along the depths of time this was indeed a 'television room', rather than a well, 'room room' I guess!

Now, one thing that has always astounded me, is the brain's capacity to lose itself in bizarre mysteries late at night, when alone, unable to sleep. In this case, I got rather lost in the mystery of the missing TV. Where had it gone? Had two masked men burst in late at night holding all in terror, with sawn-off shotguns, and yells of, 'your travel irons or your television sets!', Before proceeding to steal the poor unsuspecting TV.

On closer inspection though, I suspected not. For in that corner of the room, I realised a small pool of water filmed the floor. So the set had blown up, and lets face it, probably electrocuted someone in the process as they went to tune in.

Oh yippee.

It's always good to discover that on the exact spot one stands, someone has recently died.

I decided at this point that the love machine sharing my room must have finished by now and so I turned tail and fled. Well, fled is perhaps the wrong word to use. Not quite sure what the word to use is when one attempts to leave the room, but finds his feet sticking to the floor on his attempted exit. That's how dirty this place was.

Now at university my friends and I were given a ten hour community punishment order by the university campus courts. You know, clean up the grounds, that kind of thing. All simply due to the amount of times the university had to pay for hired cleaners to come in and sort out our digs.

The campus authorities came knocking one fateful morning with a photographer to collect evidence against us. I heard them coming, but was not on top form due to the bottle of vodka that someone had tricked me into drinking the night before. (Yeah right!)

I'd attempted to hide in my wardrobe to escape them, but apparently my co-ordination was not quite back up to scratch yet. So as my bedroom door opened and the authorities marched in, they were happily greeted with the sight of me falling out of my cupboard stark bollock naked!

For some reason they were neither amused nor impressed. A trait that continued once they'd photographed the magpies that had flown in through the open kitchen window, and happily gone about eating the rotten food that was stuck to the floor. Nor did the dead goldfish corpse in the bathtub impress them it seemed. (Just how picky and pedantic are these people?!)

Poor old Mick Hucknall the goldfish. In our defence we'd gone home for Christmas vacation and no one could look after good old Mick, so we'd filled the bath with water and toys for him to play with, all the time unaware that the bath plug had a slow leak. Poor old Mick. We really were rather sad when we'd discovered just what had happened.

I soon realised that I could only deal with living in such conditions for a few months, before begging to move in with Beth. We got our own little flat together off campus and did it up real nice in the end.

Who knows, maybe that was the other reason I was over here? Apart from the Mick Hucknall story nothing particularly crazy had ever happened to me. I really was rather straight laced, but little did I know, that soon M.J would change all that.

Anyway, compared to this hostel, our place at university was a fricking paradise!

By this point of the day, I was absolutely shattered to be brutally honest. I no longer cared about anything. I just wanted to close my eyes and sleep everything away. Ah, 'to sleep perchance to dream.' Yeah, that would be so nice. Alas, it wasn't to be.

As I wearily pushed the door open, I was confronted with one of the strangest sights I'd witnessed in all my youthful years. Three fat, wax dripped, virginal white candles sat in the centre of the floor casting an eerie glow upon the devilish scene before me. One of the girls lay face down, prostrate and naked upon M.J's bed. My first startling thought was that she was dead, but I realised I could gently distinguish the sound of one peacefully sleeping.

The candles formed a loose triangle and placed between them was M.J and the second Dutch girl. There was no denying they were having sex, but it was in no shape or form I had ever been aware of. He sat in the lotus position, each foot crazily placed upon the other leg. She sat on his lap, legs wrapped around his back. The strangest thing to me was the fact that neither of them moved a muscle. They both just sat there, eyes closed, fingers intertwined, breathing deeply away in meditation. It was also obvious that neither had moved from that position for quite some time.

Puzzled, I turned and walked away, too in shock to remember to feel annoyed.

I couldn't tell you why, or how I got there, but the sound of the sea must have drawn me inexplicably to its side. A small group of dunes rested by the shore. So at the end of a long eventful day, I found myself at 2 in the morning, lying on my back in a clump of long grass, in the navel of two of the sand dunes, contemplating.

One thing I realised is that never before had I really gazed up at the night sky. I mean really, really looked up and seen it the way I saw it that night. I don't know if it was down to sleep deprivation, the half empty bottle of duty free Jack Daniels that lay in my hand, or a little of both, but I swear as I gazed with fresh eyes upon the heavens, I saw God looking right back at me. The moon had shed her masked hood from behind the clouds, and was peering out inquisitively at our little world with her full face uncovered. The stars, well, I could try and settle for old clichés here, or try and explain it all, but it could never do it all justice. Let's just suffice to say, that away from the glare of the city lights, I couldn't believe so many stars could be seen at once, and the sheer raw beauty of it all, overwhelmed my poor unsuspecting heart.

Perhaps understandably so, I eventually found myself thinking of Beth. Thinking that I wish she could be with me, because I'd never be able to explain the beauty of that night sky to her. A brief smile played upon my lips as I realised what I was thinking, and I chuckled away to myself and gently shook my head.

You know what? It certainly seemed that some of the crap that came out of that crazy naked bastards mouth was right after all! What was it M.J had said? I wanted Beth to be there, 'to share happiness with, as on our own we aren't always really capable of registering different heights of happiness, quite often we just need someone to be there to share an experience with.'

Well, that and the fact that I just missed her because I loved her. This would be the longest period of time spent apart since we'd first met and it was going to be very strange waking up each morning without her there. It was going to be difficult but I wasn't worried. You see, we were destined to be together. We both knew it from the moment we'd met.

When I was at high school I'd always hung around with a group of mates a few years older than me. Well, my friend Kimberly's father was a Duke and lived in a mansion house on the outskirts of town. And I mean, mansion house. This place was fricking amazing dude. It had a whopping twenty-six bedrooms and the living room on the ground level was so huge you would not believe. On the wall hung the antlers of a prehistoric Irish Bog Elk. I swear these things must have spanned a good ten metres across or something crazy like that. Yet, the room was so large this monstrosity was lost on the wall; it was that small and insignificant in contrast to the size of its surroundings.

Anyway, one weekend we'd all gone down the pub for a quick drink and next thing we knew, the barman was ringing away on his little bell with the ferocity of a man possessed, screaming, 'time please you bastards', and much to our surprise, we discovered we'd accidentally, and of course through no fault of our own, gotten absolutely shit-faced drunk.

Now, Kimberly's parents were away fly-fishing with some Lord Whatshisname that weekend, so she suggested we continue with the general merriment back at her parents' house. So she arranged for her sister to come and pick us up.

Well, five minutes later I became aware that my mobile phone was ringing. I had no idea who it was mind you. You see the Caller ID hadn't worked properly ever since I thought that my cell phone was a German grenade whilst drunk one day, and decided that the only way to save my comrades was by lobbing it out of my bedroom window.

Anyway, running outside to the front of the pub, it seemed that I was destined not to discover just who was calling me. For I was fully embracing that rather futile and infuriating game that is known as, 'HELLO, HELLO, CAN YOU HEAR ME? WHAT? WHAT? I'VE NO SIGNAL!'

In drunken disgust I hung up, and began a mock imitation of that infamous last gasp drop goal that Johnny Wilkinson had pulled off against the Aussies. Only replacing the ball this time with my mobile phone. It was then and only then, that I realised I wasn't alone.

A 4x4 sat parked just to my left, and a rather beautiful blond was looking at me smiling, obviously highly amused by my drunken antics.

'Don't suppose you know Kimberly?' she asked.

'Yeah sheeesshhh out wifffffffffff us,' I managed to slur in way of a reply.

'Would you mind getting her? I'm here to pick you up.'

'Nottttaaattttttttallllllllll.' I smacked the side of my head with the palm of my fist, causing a worryingly depressing hollow thump to reverberate around the streets.

'Sorry, I'll try that again,' I managed. 'No, I wouldn't mind at all. My name's _____ by the way.'

'Mine's Beth,' she laughed, 'I very much enjoyed your little dance by the way.'

I didn't think it wise to correct her and point out that it was blatantly a rugby drop kick, and settled instead for, 'yeah, apparently I enjoy meeting beautiful strangers and impressing them by making a complete and utter fool of myself.'

'Well it made me smile anyway,' she said kindly.

'Well it bodes well for me that acting the fool can make you smile,' I laughed in turn, 'cause most men were blessed with good looks, lots of money, or a sharp and piercing intellect. I however, was obviously ordering a pint from the bar when God was handing things out. By the time I figured out what was going on the only thing left to take was Prize Fool!'

'You shouldn't be so hard on yourself Mr Fool. But would you mind getting my sister now?'

Pointing an imaginary gun at my temple and pulling the trigger, I turned around and running back into the bar, I threw the parting comment over my shoulder to Beth, 'I swear the words 'brain' and 'dangerous' spring to mind!'

Returning to my mates I swear I meant to tell them immediately that Beth was here, but Gez got to me first grabbing me as I sidled past the bar. Gez and I had an ongoing tequila slammer fling going on, and he'd gotten us four shots to neck at last orders. Somewhere between the salt and the lemon I lost my message. Especially when Gez introduced me to a couple of longhaired rockers at the bar.

You see, a few of the group, well, me in particular, were underage so we had to go to the bars that wouldn't I.D us. In this instance, it was an old underground bikers bar called the, 'Wolf Den.' Filled with smoke and dark corners due to the fact that it was a subterranean cellar bar it was frequented by those who didn't want to be seen by the prying eyes of the law.

We were discussing music and instruments (I think the debate in question was over the genius that is Led Zeppelin. Both parties were in firm agreement that they were indeed the greatest group of all time, but I disagreed with their choice of greatest album. I stood firm with my decision of Physical Graffiti. It's not as listened to as 1-4, but superior I believe. They went for, '4' as it has 'Stairway to Heaven' on. Of course there was only one place to go from here. Yep, the age-old debate over who's better, Page or Plant? Being a huge guitar fan I'd have to say Page, but anyway, shit, I seem to have gone off on a tangent again, lets see if I can get back to the intended story else we'll be here all day?!) when one of the old time rockers asked me if I could play any instrument? (Bloody hell, I managed to get back! Best push on before I lose it again!)

Well, being a complete drunkard I made them laugh by explaining that, 'yes gentleman, I certainly do play an instrument, I am particularly adept at playing air guitar.'

With that said, Gez and I proceeded to prance around shaking our heads back and forth and playing the greatest air guitar rendition ever heard since Bill and Ted stepped out on their Bogus Journey. It would obviously be rude not to finish with the required sinking to the floor on knees, head back, eyes closed, air guitar held aloft like Excalibur to Arthur, move. Unfortunately when I opened my eyes, Beth stood over me. Doh!

Okay, so maybe she didn't realise we were destined to be together the first time she saw me, but I did. Judging by my performance so far that night, it's a small miracle I'd be kissing her by the time the morning sun rose.

Eventually we all ended up back at Kimberly and Beth's place. Everyone just carried on throwing down the wine and soon toilet stops were required across the board. Upon reaching the first bathroom I was met with that most hated of words, 'Engaged.' 'Oh balls.'

The situation went down hill drastically after I raced across the house to discover the only other bathroom I was aware of, bore the same word. It blazed away laughing at me, mocking me, taunting me with its pure evil nature. Have you ever noticed how the word is displayed in red? That's because red is the sign for evil.

Still, I reasoned that a house that size must have multiple bathrooms; it just required the finding of one. Tearing around the house racing from pillar to post, I was startled at the conversation that reached my ears as I gained access to the fourth floor.

'Okay you're starting to scare me now. It's not funny,' sounded a fearful female's voice, obviously in some distress.

A deep, heavily inebriated tenor rumbled back, 'No. A dare is a dare, and I'm not letting you leave this room until I get a kiss.'

As I reached the entrance to one of the bedrooms I could see to whom the voices belonged. Beth was trying to dart around the drunken idiot that was Nathan (I never did like him, I'd always thought he was a bit of a dick) to the open doorway and escape. Before she reached the sanctity of the exit though, his fat meaty sweating hand reached out, and caught her by the arm. She struggled to pull away from him, but his grip on her wrist was too tight.

'I told you that you're not leaving until I get my kiss,' he reiterated, slurring away.

I wasn't particularly sober myself, but things like this do push the alcohol to one side for a few moments. I just walked up behind him securing his neck in a headlock, then with my arm wrapped around his throat I flexed my bicep cutting tightly into his windpipe, and pulled us both to the floor. The colour in his face was turning a particularly worrying colour but I wouldn't release my hold.

Looking up at Beth I simply said, 'Get out of here,'
and jumping over our prone bodies she ran out the door.

Only when she had gone did I give Nathan's throat one last squeeze, just to knock any drunken fight that may have been left out of him, before releasing the wanker.

He sat up and rubbed at his red raw neck, 'mate, you really hurt me. She knew I was just messing around.'

'I was just messing around as well,' I said bitingly, but in his state the tone of voice was rather lost on him.

He simply got up and lying on top of the bed, said in an even more hurt and shocked tone of voice, 'you really hurt me,' then passed out through alcohol, snoring away loudly. When I mentioned it the next day he couldn't even remember the nights events.

I knew from memory that Beth's bedroom was on the same corridor as Kimberley's, and that's immediately, without thinking or hesitation, where I headed for. The bedrooms were situated in a separate wing to the house. As the swing door creaked open allowing me access to that section of the building, I was met by Beth armed with a baseball bat.

Seeing me she lowered it and smiled wearily but happily, saying, ' sorry. I thought it might be Nathan again.'

'That's alright, I just wanted to check you were okay,' I answered softly with concern and warmth in my voice.

Well, we ended up talking till dawn and as the first rays of the morning stole through the curtains she leant forward and kissed me. I can't remember most of what we talked about during that night, but I do know I fell in love with her right there and then. So that's how we met. She was transferring to my college from boarding school anyway, so things just went from there.

So, yeah, as I lay there in those sand dunes, I missed Beth something chronic. Unable to return it seemed to my hostel room, and rather intoxicated from the whiskey I'd been downing, I decided to jot down a few words on a postcard to show Beth I was thinking of her.

'It always hurts,
 When I think of you,
'Cause when we're not together,
 My heart is blue.

The stars won't shine,
 And the air's too thin,
The sun won't rise,
 'Cause being apart's a sin.

My soul is empty,
 The beach is bare,
Because your spirit,
 Doesn't dance with me there.

All of life's colour,
 Has faded to grey.

Silly really, never was much of a poet. Guess I do it just because it makes me feel a little closer to someone for a while.

Anyway, it was a warm night, the sound of the waves brought a certain amount of tranquillity to my mind, and so I decided, 'why not.' Tucking my pad and pen back into my pocket, I tucked my arms under my head, and settled down for the night.

YOU REALLY CAN'T NAVIGATE THE UNKNOWN. JUST JUMP INTO YOUR VESSEL AND ENJOY THE RIDE

IT WAS early evening the next day when I met M.J again.

For some unknown reason I was filled with a strange sense of apprehension as I approached the door to my room.

Now I've heard tell that we only use something like 40% of our brains. (My Old Man reckoned it was only 10%, and he's the most intelligent guy I've ever met, so I should probably have gone with that stat, but anyway, whatever the correct proportion, I reckon you get the point). So by my reckoning, there is a hell of a lot of unexplored territory in the mind. We've been evolving as primates for thousands of years, and I believe we will continue to evolve. Though no more will it be a physical evolution, but a mental and spiritual revolution. We will start to discover, develop and harness those parts of the mind that are seemingly useless at present.

I guess the way I see it, the human body is unbelievably fascinating. I mean, just look at your hand. Now explain to me just how the hell it all came into being and how it all works in such a harmonious way! Right in front of my eyes I can see a miniature miracle. Everything from the chill I feel in the air by the hair, to the bone and marrow beneath it all is simply staggering. Don't even get me started on how on any earth the synaptic firings that make me move my fingers just by willing it came about?

Seriously, the human body and how it all works is something so amazing we completely forget in the hustle and bustle of everyday, modern life, to be thankful that it's a miracle that we even exist at all! No part of the body is a mistake. Everything has a function no matter how small. (Well, it seems that everything bar the appendix has a reason for being. Although I reckon some day we'll find out why it's there. My personal theory is that it creates the fluff I continually find in my belly button. I mean come on! The bloody stuff has to be coming from somewhere!) Therefore, we will eventually evolve enough to harness the powers of the left over, seemingly unused brain matter. Discover its secrets. One of these perhaps will be the ability to foresee the immediate future.

And so this was the case as I walked into my room, saw M.J, and started to move my lips to speak. The part of the mind that can look forward, forward into the void of our future as we will eventually come to realise, told me that this was going to be the real turning point in my life. Something momentous in my life was about to happen. Something told me that everything would change from here on in. If I didn't voice the words I was about to utter I could continue along the path already well walked, yet to speak those words, in an instant, would set wheels into motion that would irrevocably change my future forever.

Unfortunately, future premonitions still belong to the unused 60% of the mind. I hadn't yet evolved enough to use this talent. In fact I think I struggle to use the 40% humans are supposed to use as it is!

Still, everything was about to change so irrevocably, that my unused brain matter tried to voice itself in other ways. It tapped in unconsciously to my gut instincts. It began tugging away now at my entrails, trying to protect my sanity. Trying to warn me that I should turn around and return right there, right then, to the comfortable, safe existence I had plodded along with up until that point. To continue would be to open up a can of worms that would gnaw voraciously away at all I had known, and reshape everything I was and everything I knew. Every nerve ending in my body shouted, nay screamed and pleaded with everything I knew and held dear, for me not to go through with it.

For some bizarre reason still unbeknown to me though, I decided not to listen to that warning bell. I decided that we are by nature forever tentative creatures concerning change, and so I ignored that old, primeval, primitive gut feeling that has protected mankind for centuries. I decided to speak those fated words, and step off the charted map.

You know what though? I'm bloody glad I threw caution to the wind, and thought, 'fuck it, why not take a leap into the unknown.'

'Why did you think I was gay?' I asked the dreadlocked stoner in front of me sternly. The answer halted me mid barrage.

'I didn't,' M.J coolly replied, not even bothering to look up.

This response caught me completely by surprise. I guess perhaps I had been expecting further insults or, I don't know, just something, but not this. M.J must have picked up on my confusion as I stood there trying to process my thoughts.

'You've only just set out from home, haven't you?' he asked, but this time he was looking me straight in the eye, and throwing me a cheery warm smile to let me know that there was nothing to be fearful of.

'Yes.'

Once again he flashed me that mystical smile, and there was nothing offensive in his body language. He just sat there silently, coaxing me somehow to go ahead, to speak my mind.

'So how do you know I'm new to all this?' I eventually asked with puzzled eyes.

'And?'

'And what?'

'And what's the other question you want to ask?' He persisted.

'Okay,' I finally relented. 'And why when I introduced myself did you ignore my question and insult me, just to turn around now and say that you didn't for one moment think I was gay? It all seems a little unfair to me?'

'Nice one mate,' M.J beamed broadly, 'that wasn't so hard was it? Proud of you dude. You could have ignored me for the rest of your stay, just leaving your whole thoughts on the matter festering away inside, but you decided to try and get an answer instead. Come on, if you truly want to know,' he said jumping up all of a sudden and heading towards the door, 'I'll buy you a beer and explain it all.'

Without thinking I followed M.J out the open door and just like that, I'd stepped off the known road, and onto a completely new path.

A few minutes later we were sitting in a quiet little bar, sipping away on a couple of Victoria Bitters. I had remained quiet since the room at the hostel. This was all new ground to me, I felt that I had been more than accommodating, and now it was time for this strange tattooed man to cooperate.

'The reason I knew you were new to all this was because you asked me where I was from.'

He leant back and smiled, obviously believing he'd just unleashed some highly prophetic piece of wisdom. However, after I just looked on blatantly none the wiser as to just what the hell he was going on about, or why he had spoken the way he had, M.J leaned in closer and continued.

'Once you've been around a while you'll discover you become so unbelievably sick and tired of the same old, bull-shit conversations. Everyone in life has something to teach us, we just have to give them the chance. Now in the case of travelling one is constantly meeting new people. So very many people, and yet we talk briefly with them, without them really saying anything. So many conversations go down the same line.

"Hi my name's blah blah, so where are you from? Oh really? I have a friend whose great uncle stopped to use a rest room there ten years ago. Know him?"'

'I swear I got to the stage,' he continued, 'where I just couldn't stand it any longer. I couldn't stand all the pleasantries and socially acceptable questions, all refraining anyone from actually learning anything real from, or about the people who just wandered briefly into their lives. So, I started to devise my own questions.

As soon as you threatened to be the same as everyone else, threatened to adhere to the code of etiquette devised by some nutjob a millennia ago, I threw you a question about your sexuality. In asking you a question that according to society is frowned upon for being a taboo topic, I frightened you into revealing something real about yourself. Not just where you lived or whatever. In an instant I discovered that you were so in love you were willing to sacrifice your very life itself for someone. In that one question I learnt far more about you than hours of polite crap would've uncovered.'

Sitting back, M.J paused for breath, before continuing his lesson. 'I myself crave for love. To meet someone I want to grow old with. To be one of those old couples you hear about where one dies of old age, and the other passes away shortly afterwards. All because their very heart just refused to beat anymore.

I've never had that kind of love. You do, and I'd love to hear if some of my theories concerning what I think it is like are true or not. So I waited and was ready and open to learn, but you were too unsettled by it all. I invited you to join us, but the way you reacted in body language basically told me to fuck off. That's fine. I get it all the time. Perhaps understandably so! Yet I'm glad you decided not just to ignore it all in the end. So, may I propose we play a game?'

I didn't answer at first; I wanted to take a moment to assimilate all he had just disclosed to me. I think one of the reasons I liked M.J was that he wasn't easily angered. He'd asked me a question, yet didn't become cross when I didn't answer straight away. He remained patient, allowing me time to process what was going on. I guess he was pretty intuitive. He knew I'd answer but it would be in my own time, when I was ready, and that he really didn't need to push me.

What was strange was the fact that although it all rather seemed like madness, I fancied I could actually see sound method behind it all, which in itself was both unsettling, yet undeniably intriguing as well.

'What's the game?' I eventually asked.

'It doesn't have a name; it's just something I made up one day. It's simply an offshoot of what I've already said. I realised that I had no time and energy for all those polite conversations, so I decided if I met someone who I thought would be open-minded, I'd propose this game.

Basically, it's as straightforward as just asking someone a question you want to know the answer to. The difference being that it can be anything. There are no taboos. There are no socially acceptable questions preventing people from uncovering what they really want to know. What really makes a person tick. I will answer any question put to me truthfully as it helps create an air of trust, and hopefully the other person will feel thus, that they can be truthful in turn. I've discovered it means you can really, really get to know someone in a very short space of time. It can create friends for life in a night. All it needs is a bit of openness and trust.'

Once again it seemed a highly interesting concept, so once again I decided, 'why not? Let us leap into the unknown once more.' I don't know if there is life after death, a heaven or a hell to go to. I don't know if we are reincarnated, or simply turn to dust. One thing I've realised now though is that we should treat this life like it may be our only one. Experience everything there is. Lock your fear of the unknown into a tiny tin chest and throw away the key. There's nothing to lose. If we don't enjoy the ride, we can just get off, and not only can we say that at least we tried it, we'll probably discover things about ourselves that we never knew before. This in turn means we can make informed decisions as we continue along life's journey, which in theory can ultimately lead to a happier existence. M.J taught me this.

So the game began. For the first half hour or so pretty much all we covered were things like, 'favourite movie?' 'If you had a three c.d disk changer what would be in it at the moment?' 'If you could be any famous historical figure who would you be and why?'

M.J seemed happy enough with this at the start. I think he realised that I needed a bit of time to feel comfortable enough to really open up, (and more beer!) and didn't go straight for the heart.

However, as the night progressed, and the alcohol flowed freely, we started to cover other things, more dangerous topics. I guess M.J started to turn the screw with the simple question, 'how many times had I ever been in love?' From there we covered most aspects of that. On my part, I eventually got round to asking what I considered to be the rudest question to date, (and trust me, we had covered a lot of taboos so far that evening) something I'd never normally be nasty enough to say.

'Aren't you just a hypocrite?' I asked. 'You piped on last night to those girls that you weren't like the other travellers over here, just trying to get laid all the time, because you were after something more, you were after love. Yet you then readily slept with both of them and most probably waved them happily goodbye this morning. Why?'

M.J looked at me almost half impressed. I instantly went to apologise for such a rude statement, but he merely cut me off.

'Not bad. Not bad at all mate!' He smiled, somehow managing to not take offence, or become defensive.

'Hmmm, well let me see?' He took a pause before continuing.

'I guess at the end of the day, it's that I do believe in what I was saying, and that I don't generally end up sleeping with that many girls. Yet yes, I am somewhat of a hypocrite.

The way I try and justify it all is that it's human instinct. Civilization you see is unnatural, a mere whim of circumstance that we strive to create and adhere to. For barbarism, blood and lust, always flow beneath the surface. It flows under the skin and it needs constant attention to keep it in check, else it ultimately triumphs. Alas, I am nothing more than a weak mortal it seems. I have grand beliefs, but lack the strength at times to see them through. I don't mean to, but I am a hypocrite.

Us humans are born into inconsistency it seems. I'm like a vampire who can resist the lust for blood for a while, but eventually its massed genetic flaw of barbarism overcomes it. Sex is indeed a healthy part of a relationship, but when I'm not in one, I'm afraid I do become somewhat of a slut, having numerous one-night stands. It is love I want, it's just that when I don't have it, I do eventually result to just having animal sex, as the vampire eventually takes blood in the end. For vampires after all were created as a visual representation of all human nature.

I do have a connection with the girls I sleep with, but I can't help but feel bad for the fact that I seem to just use them for sex sometimes, though maybe it's the other way round, them using me as well! I don't know, I guess I just think life isn't about notches on bedposts, but true love and what is on offer beyond the bedroom. Thus I get annoyed when I seem to be doing the former, rather than getting closer to finding the latter.

Of course I could be wrong about the whole love thing. Maybe I'm just an old washed up Bohemian. Maybe the greatest thing in life is not just to love, and be loved in return. Maybe the greatest thing in life is just getting laid! But yeah, I am a hypocrite.'

He drew a long sigh, and shrugging his shoulders conceded, 'oh well, no body's perfect hey? So how many women have you ever slept with?'

Now I did have a few girlfriends when I was younger. No, I tell a lie, I didn't even kiss a girl until I was 16 years old. Up until that point, they had scared the living daylights out of me! It seemed every time a girl came up and talked to me I'd turn into a gibbering idiot.

Perhaps this was all epitomised by one incident in particular at the age of 15. I was at an under 18's disco that my friend had dragged me along to, promising me riches of girls galore, and yet within minutes I'd found myself standing completely and utterly alone. My so-called-friend had disappeared on entering the premises and could be seen making out with a girl from the year below on the dance floor.

Now, I really wasn't cut out for these things when I was younger. Not only was I perfectly aware of the fact that I couldn't dance for toffee, I was also highly self-conscious about the bloody train track braces some evil bastard had demanded to fit onto my teeth. He didn't seem to understand when I tried to explain that I was quite happy to sacrifice a perfect smile for the sake of not having two clumps of metal shining away in view for all to see and mock. Even now, sub-consciously when I smile I quite often poke my tongue over my top teeth. It was some strange habit I developed from those damn braces, trying to cover them up when I smiled.

Anyway, the worst potential thing happened to me right then at the club. A girl made eye contact with me!

Now this may not sound like much to the regular person, but as soon as it happened to me I knew I needed to curl up into a ball and die. I instantly started sweating profusely, and my brain recoiled in horror as she started to walk towards me.

In fact, my mind chose that moment in particular to bail out altogether. You could see it instantly put up a little white flag of surrender, climb down out of my ear and in a James Bond-esque swan dive, pitch out of the blatantly doomed vessel it had been piloting so badly up until recently, tugging away frantically on the cord of its parachute.

T minus four. She had picked up speed and with gritted teeth was ploughing full steam toward me.

Three. A large boy screamed as she threw him clear out of her path and he landed with a sickening crack on the floor.

Two. Walking over the dead boy's body his spectacles cracked into shards beneath her stiletto shoes.

One. Nothing would halt her from her mission.

Zero. Houston, we have a problem.

Okay, okay, so it may not have happened exactly like that, but I certainly felt like a rabbit caught in the headlights.

She just walked over and smiling said, 'hi, my name's Jessica, what's yours?'

A thousand responses reverberated round my empty head, but were merely met with silence. 'Do I just tell her my name? No, no, got to be charming. No, no, I read somewhere girls like a guy who can make them laugh. Right, quick, think of something funny. Something funny? Can I do a clever word play on my name? Nope, can't say that. Or that. Hmmm, that's not funny. Right, funny about her name? I feel like a rabbit in the headlights, her name's Jessica, Jessica Rabbit! No, no, that's no good. Not wise as she'll think I'm insulting her or something.'

Luckily, I didn't need a response. Apparently a glazed, vacant expression must have stolen over my eyes. I mean, I hadn't spoken for a good minute or so. Basically I had just been stood there, sweating, (I would imagine I was probably rocking back and forth by this point as well) and Jessica smiled kindly in sorrow at the obvious local village idiot, and turned and walked away.

Oh, I also had this idea that was viewed as rather crazy by my mates, that I wouldn't have sex until I was in love. This may sound like a rather bizarre concept for a 16-year-old lad to have, but celibacy was not particularly a choice, rather a lifestyle for the village idiot who couldn't even tell a girl what his name was!

No, I did have a few girlfriends before Beth, but I only came close to sleeping with one of them. This girl, well, she was stunning, funny, and intelligent, everything I could possibly want, but I decided to split up with her. Pray do explain that one to me? I still don't understand it even now!

Anyway my parents were out and we were fooling around when she simply asked, 'do you want to have sex?' Now for a teenage male virgin these words are perhaps the sweetest one can ever here. I think I just about refrained from saying something like, 'is the Pope a Catholic,' or, 'ye ha, bend me over and call me Spanky baby,' and just settled for a conservative, 'yes.'

'I've a condom in my purse downstairs,' she started, but before she could finish the sentence I was off and running like a world champion sprinter. Taking the stairs two at a time, I'm afraid I'm rather embarrassed to admit that I may have punched the air with joy once or twice. Okay, okay, like 9 or 10 times.

Anyway, grabbing the handbag I fumbled around with shaking fingers at the zip for priceless seconds before settling for the manly approach of using brute force. Tearing the thing open I tipped the entire contents over the floor.

Here I paused for the briefest of moments to raise a curious eyebrow and rest an inquisitive finger on my lip and wonder, 'have you ever noticed just how much crap a girl can fit in her handbag?' I mean, the people who designed the purse must be borrowing technology from Dr. Who's, 'Tardis' or something! Even worse though, is the fact that us men should never mock it, because I promise you, hand across heart, every item there will be required at some point in an emergency, and if we recognise this up front, without questioning or moaning, we can save ourselves from the oh so embarrassing, 'I told you so,' speech.

Shaking my head to force myself back to the far more important matter at hand, I grabbed the condom and held it aloft like a prospector sieving for gold. Then shooting out of the room I managed to trip over the bottom stair and fall flat on my face like a complete idiot, but nothing would deter me, I was officially a man on a mission!

A doomed mission it transpired.

Upon entering the bedroom, grinning like a Cheshire cat, the young lady in question spoke those immortal words, 'you'd better not make me pregnant.'

Up to that point I had been completely up for it, if you catch my drift, but with those words things instantly headed southwards shall we say. And that's the way it stayed as we split up later that month.

Needless to say, the answer to M.J's question was that Beth was the only girl I'd been with.

'Speaking of sex, what the hell were you and that Dutch girl doing when I walked in last night?' I asked.

'Ah, that my friend, is Tantric sex.' M.J grinned with an obvious glint in his eye.

Before I could ask the obvious question though the music stopped playing in the background. A large fat man in a Hawaiian shirt tapped on a microphone and asked for everyone's attention.

Apparently some bizarre musical game was about to kick off and he needed twelve partners on the dance floor to assist. Although by this point in the proceedings M.J and I were a little worse for wear, having not quite realised just how much alcohol we'd consumed, I was still in control enough to know that there wasn't a chicken's chance in Thailand that I was going to get up and do anything.

Or so I thought.

MOTHERS ALWAYS TELL US TO WEAR CLEAN UNDERWEAR. I'D LIKE TO CHANGE THAT. JUST ALWAYS WEAR UNDERWEAR

TWO young ladies came over to our table and asked if we'd be their partners for the game. M.J immediately jumped up and grabbed me, dragging me to my feet, before shouting out rather loudly, 'we'd love to.' What the bastard had obviously realised was that I had a whole different answer planned. So he had decided on a pre-emptive strike before I could object.

We weaved our way through the tables towards the dance floor, M.J out front leading Chloe (as I would later find out) by the hand, and Destiny as she introduced herself, leading me.

The general gist of the game was this; the guys rotated in a circle in a clockwise direction, whilst the girls formed a circle within this and rotated anti-clockwise. The DJ would kick some cheesy tune into action as we moved, then abruptly bring it all to a halt. We would immediately have to locate our partners whilst Old Fat Hairy Microphone Man gave one of three calls; 1) 'Knight,' the man must sweep the lady off her feet and hold her in his arms, 2) 'Mount,' falling onto hands and knees, Destiny would vault onto my back as I was obviously a horse, and spank my arse for some obscure reason, and 3) 'Cavalier,' I'd get on one knee and she'd sit on my thigh with her arms draped around my neck. The last couple to perform the move were disqualified. It was basically musical statues for adults.

Oh great. Just what I was after. I'd just found yet another way of making a fool of myself in public. (As if I needed any help with my track record!) It wasn't so much the game that bothered me, more the fact that I'd forgotten to put any boxer shorts on.

Come on, cut me some slack! I'd spent the night before sleeping on the beach thanks to some grinning baboon with dreadlocks. (Yep, it was official, for the second night running, I wanted to throttle the guy for ruining my day once again. Did he know I had no underwear on? Was this all part of some elaborate cosmic scheme? Is life really some sick joke that someone is forcing me to play a part in? Had he set all this up, the girls, the game, Fatty-Fatty UgUg and that Hawaiian shirt that was held on merely by sweat, as it allowed his matted, hairy stomach to hang out wild and free for all to see?)

It seemed like I'd awoken with half the sand on the beach down my pants this morning. I agree, it is a mystery as to just how much sand managed to find its way in there. I decided that through the night, as I soundly slept, a couple of rather jolly young fellows had probably hired a very tiny, but very effective JCB, to systematically plough the beach throughout the night into my shorts. Yes one guy would stand there holding the elasticised waist high above his head whilst signalling and calling to his friend, 'ach come on Jimmy, there's still room for a wee bit more.' (Yes I know I was in Australia, so why would these men have Scottish accents? But you've never heard my impressions; they never sound like they're supposed to!)

I had already spent much of the morning as I walked back to the hostel deliberating over the matter. An interesting thing to deliberate for sure, but it kept my mind away from the itch the sand was causing in my shorts. It had become somewhat of a problem once I'd realised that I was scaring young women, and attracting the lustful gaze of old grandmothers, whilst I wandered down the street. You see, I had my hands down my pants, and was tossing my fists back and forth vigorously in an attempt to shake all the sand out and rid me of the itch.

Ah yes, what a pleasant walk that had been. Especially when two overweight policeman had spotted what I was doing from their elevated perch on pink cushioned high stools at the window of a Dunkin' Donuts, and had immediately jumped to the wrong conclusion. As a trainee lawyer I was pretty sure I knew that in a court of law, when charged with the summons of debasing myself in public, the argument that I was simply trying to shake the sand from my pants would never stick.

As the policemen huffed and puffed out of the doorway after me, I had been forced to bolt over somebody's back garden gate, unfortunately falling face first into a child's paddling pool in the process. (Especially unlucky really, considering the fact that the child whose paddling pool it was, had at that present point in time decided to use it as a 'dunny.' Oh joy of joys.) Then I managed to get chased down the side of the house by his rather irate mother (for some reason irate at a stranger appearing on her premises, rather than the fact that her son was pissing all over that poor stranger's face). She had also, quite by good fortune, been sweeping the patio area at the time, and so readily took to beating me round the head with her broom. Great.

Anyway, what the hell was I talking about?

Oh yeah, why I wasn't wearing any underwear. (Hmmm, did I actually have a point to make? Hmmm, do I ever? Best not answer that for now.)

Yes, sand in the crotch is not the most comfortable thing in the world suffice to say. Now before you say it, yes I did take a shower thank you very much. I'd itched away in the shower till my little heart was content. Happy to be free from the view of perverted old women and blubbery old coppers, until I'd successfully removed all forms of sand from my being.

I'd wandered back to the luxurious settings of my room, whistling as I walked, blocking out the strange feeling underfoot and making a mental note that in a hostel like this, flip-flops should be worn at all times, and set about changing.

It was then, and only then, that I made my crucial discovery. It seemed that yes, I had packed such essential items as my ever faithful travel iron, a small tin whistle someone had given me to ward off bears, (not particularly sure if there are any wild bears in Australia? Perhaps more to the point, not entirely sure just how much notice a giant grizzly is going to take of little old me blowing away on my penny whistle as it charges toward me, hell bent on ripping my head clean off with the whistle still pursed between my lips.) but alas, I'd packed no underwear.

It was fine, not a problem, I'd just go without until I got to a clothes store and bought replacements. I mean, what's the likelihood of me having to get on all fours in the middle of a crowded pub and have my 'meat and two veg' fall free for all to see?

So, this was my small predicament. Welcome to my world!

Just as we left to form rank, Destiny pulled me close to her and whispered, 'sorry, Chloe dragged me up. We might as well give it a try though hey? Who knows, we might even enjoy it?' With that she flashed me a grin and winked before dispersing.

Once again, that complete and utter prick that is M.J was completely bloody right. Destiny and I did give it a try, and for the first time since I arrived I just laughed my arse off throughout the whole proceedings.

I guess it all got a little more serious when I realised that a whole host of drinks vouchers were up for grabs. I was suddenly a man with a calling! After a quick fiddle in the first round I discovered that by unbuttoning my shirt and taking the two separate folds, I could tie the two pieces together in a knot below my schlong. Not only did this stop anything from falling out for the duration of the game, but the extra bulge that it created in my shorts caused many a cheeky grin from the ladies sat watching the insane proceedings. With that taken care of, I had alcohol to win.

Due to the sheer amount of bodies, and sheer consumption of pre-party drinks, it was a fiasco. Men and women were hitting the floor hard everywhere I looked, and I was vaulting over prone people, or simply trampling on the crowds to get to Destiny.

Luckily I have a good memory, even when drunk. It stems from a test I used to have to pass whilst younger. It was called the, 'Have you been drinking young man,' exam. If my father ever was unsure he'd make me recite the following Salvador Dali phrase, 'the instantaneous reconstitution of a fraction of desires in a cycle of memories,' or something similar once he suspected it was becoming second nature to me. The slightest hesitation or slur would incur some small form of punishment. I barely ever failed to remember what was required of me whilst hammered.

Others were not so fortunate. On one call a particular young lady somehow ended up laid on her back with her legs in the air, (?!) whilst another time a girl stood holding the man aloft in her arms instead of the other way around, and so on so forth. M.J and Chloe faltered in the fifth round. The call had been 'Mount,' and when Chloe leapt onto his back she had clear disappeared off the other side!

So we found ourselves in the final. A face off commenced. Once again it was the mid-west, my rival and I stared into each other's souls, trying to root out the fear. Neither of us blinked, and I chewed my gum as if it were tobacco and I a cowboy. The music played, we circled slowly, matador and bull, which one was I? Everyone held their breaths, the whole placed looked on, transfixed at this final duel to end it all.

Then, silence.

'KKKNNNIIIIGGGHHHHTTTT,' roared the Fat Man With The Microphone, and I moved.

Charging forward with a huge sweep of my right arm I burst through our enemies' ranks and whisked Destiny off her feet into my arms. As I held her there in my arms she gazed up into my eyes and in that moment we shared the same look instantly, the same feeling, euphoric drunken victory!

Turning around I surveyed the battlefield, and that's when I saw my enemy lay strewn across the floor. Apparently as I flew towards Destiny, that sweep of my right arm had thrown the girl clear off her feet into the crowd. Ooppss, my bad!

Well, technically I still hold firm to my argument that she slipped but oh well, you win some you lose some. In this instance, we lost some. That Fat Fuck ruled us as disqualified! Oh 'the horror, the horror!' The sheer injustice of it all!

Still holding Destiny in my arms, (in all the excitement I'd plain forgotten to put her down) I carried her back to the table greeted with cheers from all around and pats on the back. As I sat down and gladly took the fresh beer M.J was offering me, I was grinning like a stupid kid.

In the end I had to admit out loud, 'that was fun!'

M.J looked at me as if to say, 'that's why I dragged you up', but in the end just settled for, 'cheers mate,' and the four newfound friends all raised their glasses to that.

The girls took a shot from their glasses before excusing themselves to use the restroom. Of course this meant that they both departed in tandem, quite why, I don't think I or any other man shall ever really know. It seems to be one of those unanswered mysteries.

As a man there has always been an unwritten code of conduct concerning my friends and I, that no matter how desperate our needs are, we can only remove ourselves to the urinals after our mate has returned. Heaven forbid if we should up and take leave at the same time! I think a great chasm will split the earth in two and swallow us all whole if this eventuality were ever to arise!

M.J seemed a prophetic and wise man. Thinking perhaps he could shed some light on this phenomenon I leant forward to comment. However, as I went to speak he merely placed a finger upon his lip and signalled for silence. I quickly became aware of why.

Two women were sat at the end of our table. One was hollering down her cell phone whilst the other sat hunched over, quietly pawing at the dregs of her beverage. A young gentleman was sidling nervously up to their position.

Beyond the point of no return; he made a small coughing noise to draw the attention of Dregs Lady.

'Hi my name's Bob, Bob Chang,' he muttered, extending his hand in welcome. (I should probably point out right here that this was most certainly not his real name. It's a name I use when I look for the correct fact in my memory banks and my memory responds with, 'come back tomorrow, I've got a hangover.' So, I figure Chang is the most common surname in the world, and Bob, well, it's just a funky name.)

The young lady looked up smiling and replied, 'hi, I'm Tinuviel.'

The two smiled nervously at each other for some time before Bob tried, 'so, where you from?'

'Seattle, America.'

'Oh that's cool,' he responded over zealously, 'I once went to Florida.' (Hmmm, right? The poor guy looked like he wanted to die there and then when he realised what he was saying. In European terms, it's basically like hearing someone's say, Irish, and you saying, 'oh wow, I once went to Romania! ??')

However, he needn't have worried, she tried to help him out.

'That's, cool? Where you from?'

'England,' he quickly replied a little too loudly, trying to mask his evident embarrassment.

'England, wow! I met a really cool guy from England. Now, what was his name? Sam Goozee, that was it. Do you know him?'

Grimacing in obvious pain when she realised the idiocy of what she was saying, (I mean, England's a pretty big place, with quite a few people, I think people forget that sometimes) I don't think she was too surprised when the answer came back.

'No, sorry.'

The two then continued to look at each other for a particularly long and awkward silence, before Bob stated, 'well it was nice to meet you,' and bowing his head, turned and walked away in shame.

It seemed like once again, interlaced within M.J's madness, there seemed evident glimpses of genius. I felt this even more so when the girls returned. Destiny and I had barely spoken a word throughout and yet were evidently enjoying each other's company. (Not in that way thank you! She was nothing compared with Beth! Although even I could recognize objectively, that she was indeed a particularly beautiful young lady.) One huge uncomfortable silence could have destroyed everything in seconds though.

As they took their seats, we all four looked at each other for a few seconds, smiling before Chloe launched in with, 'so, where you guys from?'

I found myself shocked to hear my internal thoughts shout aloud 'no!'

There was no need to fear though, for M.J simply responded with, 'first thing that comes to your head. Childhood memory that makes you smile and why?'

It seemed far less obviously offensive than his, 'are you gay' question at first, but I quickly realised that if anything, it was far more invading and personal an ask.

Suffice to say, I liked the girls straight away. Unlike myself, proud and hurt, they didn't become defensive. Destiny simply tilted her head, obviously musing upon it all for a second, before answering.

'Before Vietnam my father used to be a farmer. In the aging barn out back he kept an old bi-plane to spray his crops with. He used to love to fly, but after he returned from the fighting my mother told me that'd he'd been unable to settle down again. He just seemed to have lost interest in everything. I know I barely saw him throughout my childhood, because he had given up both his farming and fighting life to become a long distance semi-truck driver of all things. I couldn't understand why he would want to spend so long away from home. It always seemed such a lonely existence to me, especially with a wife and child back at the farm. I suppose war changes a lot of things I guess.

'Anyway,' (hey that's my catchphrase you cheeky so 'n so!) she continued, ' I remember dusk was settling one hot summer's day, and I was sat in my daddy's old plane, pretending to be flying up in the clouds. I used to do that a lot, reckon I might have been a bit of a tomboy at heart!

So there I was, pretending to be flying over the world with the birds and angels for company, when Dad popped his head round the old rotten barn door. I hadn't seen him for so long, but without saying a word, without even a smile, he just started up the plane, gently kissed me on the forehead, and sat me on his lap.

As the plane left the ground I remembered I was so excited, but so scared. I just hugged my daddy's chest, squeezing as hard as I could, so hard I could hear his heart beating away at a hundred times a minute. He never seemed to smile, but at that moment I just knew he was happy. We soared so high I thought I could reach out and touch the very stars themselves. I even tried. I stretched out as far as I could, but they always seemed to be just out of my grasp.

Silly really. Still, that memory always makes me smile. My father was cool. So why d'you ask?'

M.J immediately explained about his theory on meeting people, and the girls instantly agreed to it all, I think they saw it as a breath of fresh air. Personally, I simply gazed in awe at Destiny. She'd been so open. Wasn't she scared that these strangers would hurt her for displaying her heart so much? Why? These people amazed me to be honest. They seemed to belong to a world so different from that I knew. Was I simply afraid to be that open? If so, what was there to be afraid of? I realised only Beth really knew me, and it had taken us months to trust each other enough to let down all our boundaries, all our walls. Was I simply afraid to just be myself? Should we always wear our hearts upon our sleeves? Is there not something fundamentally and melancholically lonely about that? If we never really open up to people, how shall we ever really know each other?

Anyway, so it was that the four of us all found ourselves playing the, 'ask what you really want to know game,' until the bar finally closed. I suspect the only reason they decided to finally close was because we'd devoured their complete stock of alcohol between us. That and the fact that I was breaking continually into a rendition of Queens, 'Bohemian Rhapsody,' which much to my surprise and entertainment, the whole of the bar followed me in singing raucously.

Upon exiting the pub I eventually found myself on the sandy beaches of Bondi again. What was it with the lure of the sea? Is civilisation really just a whim of circumstance created to control our barbarism? Is it just the flip side of the same evil coin? Is it possible that there may be a different solution? Can the coin land on its edge? I mean, now that I had broken free from the myopic life of society, I was becoming at one with the natural world, a world I had forgotten we actually belonged to after all. It certainly seemed that the tide washing in and out echoed the rhythm of the 'lubs' and the 'dubs' of my beating heart. Was I finally in tune with things? Or was I just steaming drunk?!

Either way, the four of us found ourselves gathering firewood in the same sand dune as my previous nights rest. So it was, around that great and wonderfully warming campfire, I passed out. However, just before unconsciousness came upon me, I could have sworn that I saw two strangely Scottish sounding Australian men, driving in my general direction, upon a very small, but very effective JCB.

OH YEAH, APART FROM THE UNDERWEAR THING, ALWAYS CARRY A BOTTLE OF VINEGAR AS WELL. APPARENTLY

I WOKE very slowly. I did not feel good.

I became slowly aware that someone was kicking me in the side, shouting, 'move your sorry arse! Its morning sleeping beauty!'

After forcing a bloodshot eye open, (In itself not an easy task. For some reason whenever I awake after a heavy nights drinking session it seems like my eyes have been glued shut with some strange gooey paste substance. I don't know where it comes from, but you discover you're picking it continually out of the corner of your eye for the rest of the day!) I had to concede that technically M.J was indeed correct. It was morning, just not in any form I had ever known. There was an eerie grey light that seemed to be casting a profound peace over everything. Seeming to be quietly reflecting the coming of the new day with the sun due to rise soon.

I pulled myself to my feet and squinting through heavy eyelids that were about as convinced that I should be getting up as the rest of my body, I realised the others were watching me, grinning mischievously. It seemed that I was the sleeping beauty after all. For the others were not only wide-awake, but seemed to have magically produced surf boards from somewhere.

'I just woke up early and thought it would be a good idea,' M.J stated matter of factly.

It seemed we differed slightly in our definition of, 'good idea.' Mine being that it was a far better idea to go back to sleep and remove the tiny man with the jackhammer from inside my head.

I thought better of mentioning this and settled instead for, 'where on earth did you get surf boards at this hour?'

'They're ours, and the others we borrowed from the hostel,' Destiny chipped in.

It's funny how your mind works at stupid-o'-clock in the morning, but I found myself concentrating on the fact that their hostel was so good that they even had boards for hire, (Granted I bet her place didn't have such points of natural interest as a large range of flora and fauna growing from the carpet, and local insect wildlife to gaze upon as one showered!) rather than the more obvious problem at hand.

'Lets rock,' M.J said quietly, and throwing me a long board (and to my great relief, a spare pair of swim shorts!), he sprinted away towards the water's edge.

The girls went to follow in hot pursuit, and it was only then that I suddenly remembered the more pressing point at hand, and shouted out, 'hang on, I don't know how to bloody surf!'

Destiny ran back alone, 'that's why we got you the long board silly.'

I was extremely impressed as I picked up my surfboard. It seemed from what Destiny was saying, that apparently it contained some sort of mystical surfing powers, which would instantly turn me into Kelly Slater or something. Muchos impressio!

'Come on then, I'll give you a crash course now,' Destiny said smiling, apparently seeing the doubt on my face. 'Honestly though, as long as you have some balance (Well that ruled me out then! All the alcohol in my system made me feel like a one-legged donkey, stood on a boat at sea, trying to keep his balance whilst biting his toenail!) you'll be standing in minutes with a long board.'

Once again my features must have betrayed my doubt because Destiny grabbed my hands. Interlocking her fingers with mine, raising our hands to my chest, she leant in closer to me, and looking into my eyes, softly spoke.

'Please. Just trust me,' she smiled.

So it was, as the sun finally broke over the horizon, I found myself sat in the water aboard my, well, board. Destiny had shown me what to do on the dry land, and now I was supposed to put my moves into practice.

For the mean time though, I was content to just sit there, floating peacefully, watching the others. It was all so very tranquil, so beautiful. The sun sat low in the sky, and its rays were reflecting upon the waves, twinkling away. There was still a refreshing chill in the early morning breeze. The hairs stood to attention on goose bumps, but I didn't notice. I was just completely and utterly zoned, for want of a better word. The sound of the tide breaking and washing upon the shore just seemed to calm my very soul. I just closed my eyes and let it all wash over me. There was no sound of vehicles. No sound of people screaming irately down mobile phones. No sound of any of the manic hustle and bustle of everyday life. It seemed I'd somehow managed to escape society itself. Somehow removed myself from it all, and perhaps the strangest thing of all was that I felt it was only now that I was actually seeing things clearly.

Is it only once we take a step outside the circle, and gaze inwards, that we can see things in their entirety?

Hearing splashing nearby, I opened an eye, and saw Destiny paddling over.

I flashed her a smile, 'hey.'

'Hey you,' she grinned back, and parked her board up next to mine.

We both sat there in a long comfortable silence, just taking it all in, just enjoying being a part of it all. I don't know how long we sat there, but when Destiny eventually spoke, the sun had shaken itself rid of its early morning yawns, and gotten on with the task of climbing high in that beautiful deep blue sky.

'So, you gonna give this surfing thing a go? Or you just gonna sit there being a big girly wimp?' She mocked.

I turned my face slowly to her, trying to look particularly stern and offended. Destiny just laughed away, having obviously amused herself.

'Oh, look at Mrs Funny over here!' I joked, before pushing her off her board into the sea.

She surfaced still grinning. Crossing her arms on her board, resting her head on her hands; she winked up with the sun shining in her eyes.

'I would kick your arse, but I figured I'd see you surf first,' she smirked.

Then spotting movement over my shoulder, she suddenly ordered, 'Go on! That waves perfect! Move, move, move!'

I dropped to my stomach and paddled my little arse off, somehow managing to catch the wave. Reaching the point of no return I just decided to go for it. I quickly raised myself onto hands and knees to give myself a platform to jump up from, and then in one swift motion threw myself to my feet.

Much to my surprise, I didn't fall off immediately, as I'd seen happen in my minds eye. Even more to my surprise, I realised I was actually surfing! I could hear Destiny whistling and whooping in the background whilst I just concentrated on keeping my balance.

As I finished riding the wave into the shore, I let myself fall into the sea as my ride died. Diving downwards I swam along the seabed before turning over, and looking up at the blurry sun above me. I felt truly exhilarated, euphoric, and so I just stayed there, at the bottom of the ocean, looking up at the haze of colours filtering down through the water before me. Feeling at one with everything, just knowing pure and simple happiness.

As my breath began to give out, I kicked up towards the shape that had appeared on the surface. Destiny was sat smiling away as broadly and insanely as myself. Clambering onto her board I gave her the biggest hug ever. And I mean a proper hug, not one of those annoyingly non-personal ones people often do. One where you actually hold each other and commit emotionally to it all, allowing part of yourselves to flow into each other.

'Thanks,' is all I could manage to say at first. Then as I sat there next to her, reflecting on it all, I actually spoke my heart. 'I'm so glad you woke me this morning. I haven't felt this alive for a long, long time.'

'The lesson I can take credit for,' Destiny said, 'but it was all M.J's idea.'

Looking out over the water, I watched him race across the open sea, flying on a wave, with blond dreads flowing wildly behind him.

'That bastard certainly is one crazy hip-cat,' I laughed.

The rest of the day flew by. When we weren't surfing we were sitting on the beach soaking up the sun, chattering and laughing away, not a care in the world. M.J cooked up a brilliant bit of tucker on the barbie for lunch, and I washed it all down with cold beer.

However, it appeared the craziness of the day was far from over.

I was quite some distance from shore, just treading water next to my board, when out of nowhere I heard myself screaming out in intense and excruciating agony. Looking down, a Blue Bottle jellyfish had washed up against my stomach, wrapped its stingers around my chest, shoulders and back, and injected massive amounts of poison on impact. As I ripped it away from me, its tentacles lashed up round my neck just for good measure.

Let's just say it stung a wee bit!

M.J had seen me thrashing around, and as I swam towards shore he intercepted me. I guess I was in a bit of a panic.

'Where you going mate?' he casually asked, like jellyfish attacks on his friends were a commonplace occurrence.

I very calmly and quietly explained that rather unfortunately it would appear that I had a large amount of poison in my body, and that I thought I might perhaps seek out the assistance of a medical professional. You know, before that little slight inconvenience known as, 'death,' came upon me.

'Not worth the bother mate. Just a Blue Bottle sting. Only really causes fatalities in small children and the elderly. (Oh that's fine then. Ha, ha, ha, silly of me to worry! I'm such a hypochondriac really. Only kills the young and elderly, its basically harmless!) Not really anything a doctor would do to be honest. Not when it comes to a young healthy chappie like yourself. Your immune system will sort you out. Although if you're in a spot of pain, best thing for it is a bit of vinegar. Sorts it out right good and proper. Takes the edge off the sting.'

Vinegar, right.

I'm halfway out to sea, the beach is a good mile from any fish and chip shop, but it's alright, because, ah yes, that's right, I never surf without a trusty bottle of vinegar strapped to my ankle!

I'm guessing M.J must have caught the look on my face because he quickly went on, 'the way I see it mate, you may as well just carry on surfing. I mean, there's nothing to be done about it, so why let it ruin your day?

It's the same as life bro. Shit happens, and it's our actions, its what we do when the storm hits, that define us as men. So face the pain, and yell at it to do its worst. You can let it control you, or you can overcome it.

Most of the real pain comes in the unexpectedness of it all anyway. Once you know its here to stay, then take a grip, and try and block it out mentally. Fight it. You're stronger than it. I'd just carry on surfing and tell it to go fuck itself.'

'Well, that's just what I think anyway,' he finished, before turning his board around, and heading out to sea.

I didn't move. I just sat motionless, bobbing gently up and down on the ebb of the tide, thinking. A few seconds passed as I sat there deliberating, then I just gritted my teeth.

'Fuck it.'

Then I turned and headed out after M.J.

I was later told that the pain from Blue Bottle stings last for hours normally. Within twenty minutes mine had subsided. Perhaps the sea salt just washed it all clean, or perhaps once more that bloody little know-it-all had been right.

As the day drew to a close, we found ourselves toasting marshmallows over our campfire. By this point everyone was extremely tired from too much sun and the exploits of the day, but happy. Especially as once again we'd all consumed copious amounts of alcohol!

Don't even ask me how, but somewhere along the way the words 'skinny-dipping,' came into the conversation. (No prizes for guessing which filthy old pervert suggested that one!) Far more to my consternation, was the fact that the girls all agreed that it was a great idea!

In the short period of time I'd been here, I was more than aware of the fact that I had changed considerably. Yet, old habits die hard. I most certainly was not about to strip off exposing my penis to a load of strangers. I don't really know why. Embarrassment, confidence, grey school shirts, who knows? It's just that down the years streaking had never been a serious pastime to me.

It seemed that this was not the case for the others.

Instantly someone took up the shout of, 'we're going streaking. Come on everybody, we're going streaking through the quads to the gymnasium.'

A particularly strange chant I felt at the time, but the others were laughing and singing along, so I just pretended I knew what the hell they were talking about and joined in. (I now know its based on the catchphrase for the character, 'Frank the Tank,' in the movie, 'Old School.' Man, that guy cracks me up every time! Oh crap, forgotten what the hell I was talking about now. Ah that was it. Now pay close attention, if you're lucky you might just spot some intended script come up in a minute!)

M.J and Chloe were already off and running and Destiny grabbed my hand and pulled me up after her, literally dragging me toward the sea. (There you go, did you spot it?!) The other two were already laughing and splashing around in the sea when we got to the waters edge. Giggling, Destiny without a second's thought, pulled her top up over her head, and revealed a rather tanned and firm pair of breasts. I was trying to look anywhere else but I must confess that I did try and steal a sneaky glimpse out of the corner of my eye. Especially when she squeezed out of her tight little shorts as well.

I felt guilty as hell actually. If Beth were there she would've killed me!

Then again, there was no denying that Destiny was stunning, but as she stood there in front of me, completely naked, plucking strands of long wet blond hair out from in front of her emerald green eyes, and tucking them behind her ear, it was actually Beth who I was longing for. (For all the men out there screaming, 'you idiot! How gay are you?' In my defence, in Beth I had found someone I wanted to be with for all eternity. As I'd told M.J on that very first day I met him, I'd die for her. I have no qualms in admitting that if she stood in the way of an oncoming car, I would not hesitate to throw her to safety and take the impact myself. She was more important to me than life itself, and if she were taken away from me, I could find no reason for living anymore. So I wasn't about to jeopardise all that).

So there stood Destiny, naked in the moonlight, and grabbing my hand she called, 'come on!'

This time I resisted, my feet stayed rooted to the spot. She turned back and her smile of happiness changed to a look of concern.

'You okay?'

'Yeah, fine, it's just, well, I guess I just don't want to.........I suppose it's...,'

Here she cut me off,

'Ah no worries, you don't need to explain silly, it's not a problem, just swim in your jeans instead.'

'Well, they're my only pair of CK's, and they might get ruined.'

I instantly regretted saying this. I instantly realised how stupid it must sound. At that moment I was happy that the moon had briefly hidden its face (probably in embarrassment) behind the clouds, and that I didn't have to see the look I imagined must have appeared on Destiny's face. M.J and Chloe were laughing and swimming away, both of them free, and I was about to refuse myself an enjoyable and never forgettable experience, and why? Because I was so abashed I was ashamed of what others may think of my body. Or worst than that. I was so materialistic I didn't want to ruin some piece of clothing with somebody else's name on. In that place, in that instant, I realised something fundamental.

I smiled such a broad cheeky grin in my moment of clarity that I think I scared poor Destiny. She must have thought I was a complete nutcase!

In an instant I whipped off all my clothes, tied the legs of my jeans around my forehead in an imitation of Rambo, and sprinted naked as the day I was born into the surf, shouting back over my shoulder,

'what the hell are you waiting for, d'you wanna live for ever?!'

After multiple naked piggyback fights, Destiny and I had to eventually admit defeat when Chloe lashed out and caught me a glancing low blow. Man, trust me when I say I went down quicker than a five-dollar hooker!

Mentally the day had brought me many a revelation, physically however, it wasn't such a happy love story. I'd now been injected with poison by a jellyfish and kicked in the testicles but oh well; without the lows how can we judge the highs, hey?!

I think everyone rather ached from all the physical exertion of the day, because I saw M.J rubbing his aching shoulders. Turning to face us, he spoke those words that were starting to haunt my dreams with mixed emotions of excitement and panic.

'Hang on. I've got an idea?'

Before I knew it we were sitting in the shallow of the sea in a massage chain, passing a hip flask of whisky between us. I seemed to have drawn the short straw. My back was still a mess from Monsieur Blue Bottle and pressure on it was the last thing I needed. So I sat at the rear, Destiny in-between my legs, M.J before her, and Chloe at the front of the group. All of us laughing and massaging away under the hazy light of the starry night sky. I remember thinking what a strange sight we must be, four naked strangers, sat relaxing in the sea.

As we curled up around the camp fire, the embers of the fire burning low, the stars stretching as far as the eye could see, and the hypnotic sound of the waves singing us a lullaby, Destiny came and climbed underneath my blankets.

'Hey you,' she said softly as she pushed her body into mine, pulling my arms around her. 'Mind if we spoon?'

I pulled my arms away and told her rather abruptly it seemed in hindsight, 'don't. You know I'm in love with Beth.'

Her reaction was particularly strange I thought. She just giggled aloud and spun over to face me.

'You don't know what spooning is do you?' She asked teasing.

'No, but...I ....well it's.....you know........but,' apparently it seemed I was having trouble with my words again.

'Don't look so worried, it's nothing sexual,' she laughed.

'Oh.' I was suddenly aware my face had gone as red as a baboon's bottom. 'Sorry.'

'Its basically like hugging, but lying down,' she finally explained to put me out of my misery. 'Two people just lying intertwined, like two spoons tessellating, enjoying feeling close to someone they feel comfortable with.'

Once again she spun over and pulled my arms around her. I was still a little apprehensive at first, before I realised there really was nothing sexual about it at all, and so I snuggled into her back and finally relaxed. Closing my eyes I felt truly at peace, at one with everything, and that night I slept like a baby.

PART TWO

I REMEMBER PHOTOGRAPHS, MEMORIES OF THE PAST, BUT THEY DON'T REMEMBER ME

IT'S ALL A BIT RANDOM REALLY

DAYS and memories melted into one, and so it was that I found myself sat on a grassy knoll on a sheep station, wondering just how in hell I'd gotten there.

Destiny and Chloe had long gone unfortunately, having to return to their studies in New Zealand. Alas, the inescapable misery of the traveller, to always have to say goodbye. Still, Destiny and I had swapped e-mail addresses and been pinging short essays back and forth over cyber space ever since. I liked talking to her, and rather strangely found that I missed her presence more than many of my mates from back home.

Anyway, M.J and I had eventually found ourselves on a bus heading into the outback, a long, long way from those opening adventures in Bondi. We'd hitched as far as a roadside café in the middle of nowhere, before a coach load of tourists pulled up into the parking lot.

As they eventually filed back on board no one had noticed the two stowaways tagging onto the back of the line. It took us as far as this sheep station, and whilst they're all off watching how one sheers a sheep and such things, I'm sat in the lush long grass, puffing away on a cigarette, (oh yeah, apparently I smoke now, shit, Beth will kill me when she finds out!) musing over events to date.

M.J had disappeared as soon as we'd arrived. He'd been strangely quiet on our slow approach, gazing off down old cattle roads and long forgotten trails that wound away into the distance.

My last sight of him that day was in the steaming hazy heat of the early afternoon sun. We'd wandered around awhile exploring the old nooks and crannies of this 19th century sheep station. Finding thousands of tiny rusted treasures wherever we dared to look.

We'd reached one of the more abandoned corrugated iron sheds when M.J suddenly perked up, obviously finding a new toy to fuel that crazy hip-cat mind of his.

I'd been stood off on the track, gazing toward the ground at nothing in particular, chatting away in my own absent minded kinda way. Kicking away at a few loose stones, I noticed M.J pulling a crate up below one of the windows. Climbing on top of it, he removed layers of age old grime and dust from the window with the back of his sleeve, before pressing his nose right up against the transparent spot he'd created, to gaze inside.

With a turn of speed that rather startled me he'd vaulted to the ground like a pouncing cat, and torn the iron door aside with a great groan. Disappearing inside I'd remained at the threshold, peering inside, trying to ascertain anything in the darkness, as my eyes struggled to become accustomed to the change from the harsh sunlight of the world outside.

An eerie moan broke the silence away to my right and I'll hold my hands up, right here, right now, and admit that yes, it did make me jump like a frightened little five year old. Mummy, can I have a fresh pair of underwear please?

As I composed myself a cobweb covered monster appeared out of the gloom, grinning away victoriously, bearing his trophy below him. It seemed that M.J had managed to commandeer by far the oldest looking bicycle in history.

I didn't know it at the time, but my guess was strangely accurate for once. You see, it was actually a Penny-Farthing, one of the oldest bicycles after all from history. The front wheel was huge, yet above this monstrosity perched M.J. Even more to my amazement was the fact that as he set his legs in motion, the contraption actually creaked and groaned into life, and somehow still moved!

Laughing manically he did a number of loops around my puzzled frame before setting off towards the horizon.

'Where you going now Numbnuts?!' I yelled after him, grinning, and yet shaking my head still in disbelief.

I mean, its not everyday you find yourself on a sheep station in the middle of nowhere, watching your crazy friend pedalling at dangerous speeds away from you on a Penny Farthing, the bicycle wobbling dangerously as it crashes over the rock strewn dirt track. The idiot's blond dreadlocks stream like the tail of a kite behind him, as he concentrates more on punching the air with one hand whilst whooping to nobody in particular, than trying to keep control of the thing.

Just before M.J disappeared from view behind a clump of trees, I could have sworn I caught his reply on the wind.

'I've got an idea!'

Lying on my back, staring up to the sky, watching the stars settle, the end of my cigarette glowed away. I did try briefly once more to try and backtrack, to piece together the events and ascertain just how I'd ended up here, but I soon gave up this game. If there's one thing I'd realised by now, it's that it's often best to just go with the flow. We're just tumbleweed blowing in the wind my friend. The best-laid plans can so easily come crashing down around us.

I seem to recall sitting in on a friend's philosophy lecture in my first year at university. I'd actually spent most of the time sending Beth dirty text messages. (Hmm, I forget why I admit that right now? Yes, scratch that, forget everything I just said, I shall now play a short song on my little Tin-bear-scaring-penny-whistle and you shall forget my previous statement. 'dedededadafahlalaly, skippitydadodahde.')

I'd actually spent most of the time in the lecture deliberating over Descartes' profound statement of, 'I think therefore I am,' before another particularly interesting idea caught my attention.

Apparently some well wise dude spent like, a gigilion hours formulating the following concept. (I should point out here that gigilion may in fact be a word I made up, and for those who are unfamiliar with it, the number, 'gigilion,' is actually only, 'two.')

Anyway, so yeah, he'd spent like, a gigilion hours working out that if our lives could convert into a percentage, we are only humanly capable of controlling a mere 5% of our lives.

As for the other 95%? Well, everything happens for a reason, and quite often it's far better for us to simply go with the flow. We do not know what is in store for us, or what the grander scheme of everything is, so why try and fight something that might actually be carrying us to where we actually want to go?

Still, that doesn't mean you can just lie back and wait for things to happen. For some reason it doesn't work like that unfortunately. For some reason it's imperative that we ensure we do take control of the 5% of things we can. Our decisions still count for more than we realise, if not just to get us to our destination quicker.

Anyway, I'd like to add as a footnote here that I am well aware that the wise man who worked out the percentage thing did in fact take much more than two (or a gigilion to us strange people) hours to create his theory. So before the copyright people come bursting in, guns blazing, exclaiming that I'm badmouthing his genius, really, I'm not at all. It's merely for comic effect.

Oh shit, they're here! Cue windows crashing, masked men rolling into my room as we speak. Not sure what the guys in the straight jackets are after? (Stop laughing and pointing at me!)
Barely............time............to............react.........Must....get.....pennywhistle....
Must..... rewind....time....again.....
'skippitydadodah, skabbetydadodeh,'

Just before M.J disappeared from view behind a clump of trees I could have sworn I caught his reply on the wind.
'I've got an idea!'

Returning to the main building with the rest of the group later that night, I ate like a king. The chefs cooked up an absolutely wonderful stew out of fresh meat and vegetables they had grown themselves in their gardens. A small bar was also open in the main dining hall.

So it was, with a full stomach, and a cold beer in my hand, that I leaned back and smiled contentedly. However the smile was short lived, as it was then, and only then, that I realised just what was going on.

Large men were removing tied back ropes from the corners of the room. A large number of mattresses were being brought in from the rear doors, and stacked in the middle of the floor. As the last rope was released a large empty barrel swung down to take pride of place in the centre of the building.

Strapped to its back was a leather saddle, and someone had gone to the trouble of gluing on horns, and painting a cow's face on the front. Four people would pull up and down on the ropes it was suspended from, and the crate would buck back and forth accordingly. It was apparent that this was their very own home made, 'Bucking Bronco.'

What was not so apparent, was why large wicker baskets were being thrown open all around us to reveal stores of women's clothing. As a buck toothed local man tossed me a dress, grinning, I was suddenly aware that all was not well.

I needn't have worried though. Well, not for my sexuality anyway. Apparently the sheep station's famous drag parties were all part of the entertainment in these parts.

However I must confess as to still not being completely comfortable with the situation. Sometimes the age-old adage, 'when in Rome,' is not always applicable I now feel. Especially when one is forced into wearing a dress!

Far worse though, was the fact that as I held that long blue satin ball gown in my hands, I couldn't help but notice how lovely and soft the fabric felt between my fingers! Surely we were all being bewitched!

No, seriously now, everyone just got completely trashed and figured, 'why not?' It was rather amusing actually! I have one particularly terrible mental picture of me sat on that bucking bull, in a long flowing gown, holding on for dear life to try and win free beer! (Haha, always means to the madness hey?)

I managed like, 34 seconds or something, the best by far, until some bloke came along with a false pair of boobs and a bunny suit, and dashed all my hopes with 1 minute 13. Damn it!

EVERYONE'S SEARCHING FOR THAT LITTLE BIT OF PEACE

WANDERING around the fields in the early morning sun two days later, I heard the creak of peddles in the distance. Looking up, I saw what could only be M.J appearing, trundling over the horizon. A newly acquired Stetson cowboy hat took pride of place on those golden locks of his. Just where the hat had appeared from I had no idea, although I feared I was about to find out.

As he reached me, in a particularly brave and daring, no wait, just plain stupid feat of showboating, M.J attempted to pull a skid on his Penny Farthing. Of course this merely resulted in the bike crashing to the floor and M.J being pitched over my head into the bush behind me.

'Oh well,' he smirked as he removed himself from the foliage, 'worked in my head!'

Sweeping his hat from the floor, he took a pre-rolled, though now rather dented, joint from his pocket, straightened it out, and lit up. I knew he was just toying with me, happily toking away on his joint, just waiting for me to ask. In the end I thought it far easier to merely relent.

'Okay, so where on earth have you been? And where the hell did you find that hat?'

'Well mate, I've found us a job if you're interested?'

Raising an inquisitive eyebrow I ventured, 'dare I ask?'

'Nah, probably best off if you don't mate! Trust me, you'll like it. It's a surprise. Grab your pack and we'll get trekking now.'

Before I knew it I was jogging off after him down the road, pulling my pack onto my shoulders, and trying to puzzle out just what was going on. I knew getting information out of him was like getting blood out of a stone sometimes, so once again, I figured 'fuck it.' He'd given me no reason not to trust him to date, and to be honest; I think I was starting to grow quite fond of not always knowing just how my life was about to pan out.

We trekked for the duration of the day, crossing brooks and fields, following old dirt trails, seemingly in a haphazard fashion. It was only after I stooped to investigate the shed skin of some form of snake that I spotted it. The faint tell tale signs of a bicycle wheel track, more specifically, a Penny Farthing track. It seemed we were in fact, much to my surprise, following some pre-determined trail after all.

As the heat of the day started to wane, and the sun grew heavy in the sky, tired at its hard days work, we finally found ourselves in particularly lush pastures. A sturdy wooden fence dissected the meadows. Pulling up parallel to it, we began to trace a line in our walking beside the fence panels, obviously following it to wherever it may lead.

In the field beyond, four horses stood grazing. A mustang, two tanned, and one magnificent black beauty that blatantly seemed to be watching over the group. Upon seeing us, this beautiful beast broke away and raced toward us to investigate, placing himself between what he saw as his family, and us the potential enemy.

M.J pulled a raw carrot from his pack and although the creature was a little hesitant at first, M.J eventually coaxed it into coming a little closer. Reaching out, he gently stroked the horse's mane, and extended his other open palm forwards, with fresh carrot on offer.

The proud animal relented, and accepted the gift. As if a silent signal had been sounded, the other horses trotted over to investigate as well.

Eventually we pushed on, waving our newfound friends goodbye, and continued on our journey. So it was, with yet another clear night sky trailing away above us, we happened upon a great stone farmhouse. Climbing the steps on to the veranda, I noted an old black Labrador sleeping peacefully in a wicker rocking chair, and the delicious waft of someone's dinner assailing my nostrils. After a long days walk, boy did that smell good!

Once more I figured it best not to ask, and was content just to follow M.J, trusting him implicitly. As he pulled back the wire mesh fly stopper screen and raised his fist to rap on the wooden door beyond, I heard the sound of a deep resonating voice singing the cowboy blues, come to a halt. A pretty young girl, no older than 8 or 9, with ribbons in her hair pulled the door open.

'Hallo M.J, please come on in. And this must be the friend you told us about? Well don't just stand there sillies, you're letting the night in!'

From the depths of the house that same deep voice bellowed,

'I hope you're being nice to the young men Isabelle?'

'Ah, they know I'm just kidding with them Papa.'

As we walked into the entrance hall, a man appeared from what must have been the kitchen, wiping his hands in the apron that hung from his neck.

I guessed he must have been in his mid-fifties. I wouldn't have called him particularly plump, but there was no denying that his waistline had definitely seen better years! His face was as tanned as leather from years of working out in the sun, and he bore the most extravagant grey moustache I think I'd ever seen. Below bushy grey brows, two blue eyes twinkled away. I found genuine kindness in those eyes. Though I was sad to see that they also bore a great pain as well behind it all. He extended a huge clammy hand and introduced himself.

'Hey, how's it going? Pleasure to meet you. I'm Gus and I think you've already met my little Bella? You must be _____. M.J here has told us all about you and I see you're just in time. Come in, come in!'

As we wandered through to the kitchen I found the thing we were, 'just in time' for, was that which my belly was dreaming of. A huge pine farmhouse table took pride of place, groaning under the feast before us! There lay fresh racks of lamb, honey glazed ham, and everywhere you looked you'd see a bowl overflowing with some steaming vegetable or another.

Salivating heavily, I was ushered into a softly cushioned chair, before a glass of red wine was thrust into my hands, and I was told to just, 'sit back, relax, and dine.'

Sweet Dude!

I didn't talk much through dinner, content to listen and learn. Well, that and the fact that I was being a complete and utter pig, far too busy cramming food down my throat to converse!

M.J spoke for both of us really. Especially as I noted that Isabella seemed to bear a little crush on my friend and wouldn't relent in her endless questions to him! During that king's feast, and brandy and cigars by the fire after that, I determined just what the hell I was doing there!

It seemed the lady of the house (my poor host seemed so upset by it all that I never asked her name) had passed away some time before, leaving Gus to raise the children. The two eldest sons were both off studying at university and so the ranch had become somewhat dilapidated as of late. It seemed into all this M.J had arrived on his Penny Farthing, inquiring as to the possibility of work.

Around twenty miles away, one particular piece of land had gone untouched for some time now. Gus had promised us provisions and our choice of horse if we would be so kind as to clear the land for him, so the cattle could once again graze there. He had taken his old Ute out there that very day, leaving chainsaws, petrol, oil, ploughs, and every other tool under the sun that we may need. He'd also left roll mats, blankets, and an almighty family tent for M.J and I to live in as well.

It seemed the old man was quite taken with M.J. I wondered if he saw something in those wild eyes that reminded him of his youth? Whatever it was, as M.J had departed to find me, Gus had planted his most trusty Stetson on M.J's head, telling him to watch after it for a while.

As midnight struck we all found ourselves yawning, and more than just a little tipsy. Before Gus showed us to our beds he staggered off in the direction of the storeroom, signalling for us to follow. Pulling the cord lamp switch, he rummaged through a number of old boxes that lay on the floor.

'Ah, I knew they were here somewhere,' he muttered to himself. 'Well boys, we can't have you riding off into the wilderness without being suitably dressed can we!'

So it was that M.J was offered a great Bowie knife and ornate leather cowboy boots to go along with his Stetson. For my part, I became the proud owner of a fantastical pair of snakeskin boots that happened to be so comfortable that I still wear them to this day.

After a hearty breakfast, came the great moment of choice. It was no surprise that M.J opted for the loan of the great black stallion he'd befriended the day before. 'Thor,' was his name, and I was besotted with the Mustang, 'Troy.'

Tamed by Gus back in the States, the half-wild horse drew me to his side in the same way that M.J had. Although an accomplished rider, I still wondered if I would come to master the beast, or whether, like M.J, he may lead me to my eventual destruction!

We soon found ourselves tracking through woodland as Gus led the way on his own steed. As we passed under the dense foliage I couldn't help but lean back on Troy and notice the beauty of it all. Every shade of green could be seen. I watched a small white feather dance and swirl in the ray of sunlight that had broken lazily through the leaves above, and in everything there was peace.

This was the same for the plot of land we were to work upon. A number of scrub trees had broken free from the woodland beyond, and fallen branches from the winter before had clogged up estuaries of the river that irrigated the land. It was our job to clear them, and it was a task we set about doing happily.

For three weeks solid we worked the land. Waking early, we'd cook up a staunch breakfast to work the morning away on. Breaking for a long lunch and siesta so as to bypass the hottest rays of midday, we'd then work straight through till dusk.

Gus regularly brought out fresh food for our mounts and us to enjoy, and when he wasn't there, we kept meats, and beer (no beer tastes as good as a cold one after a hard days toil in the field) in ice coolers we'd set in the cold stream. Other foods we hung from ropes in trees to keep the wilder animals away, and there was forever a fresh supply of gorgeous cool water available (with a little help from purification tablets).

Our trusty steeds would take us wherever our hearts intended, and we could often be seen meandering over the mountains at last light, having successfully fixed some fence post or another in the wilderness.

The sunset glowed behind us, casting long shadows over the ground as our mounts picked a sure and steady path down through the rocky hills. We'd just ride on, glued to our saddles, lightly holding the reins, a cigarette hanging from our bottom lips, and not a care in the world.

We lived like free men. We lived like heroes. And there were no need we couldn't cater for. Especially as M.J had enough forward thinking to bring a copious amount of cannabis along for the trip!

So it was, that one particular morn, as M.J sucked on a joint, I reached out and plucking it from his lips, stole a drag for myself.

AM I NOTHING MORE THAN A PLAYER ON A STAGE?

THIS was my first experiment with drugs, and at first I felt no different.

I took a couple more tokes, holding the smoke in for longer and longer each time.

Still nothing.

So I raised it to my lips once more. This time however, M.J interceded.

'Wo, wo, man! Don't take too much else you'll whitey (not a good thing apparently). That's plenty. Just let it do its work.'

That it did. That it did.

Very soon I discovered a small green angel floating above my head, with two thin wires held in each hand. Somehow these wires had become connected to the corners of my mouth. As the fairy floated above me, she pulled away on those strings, forcing me to smile and giggle insanely, as if I were just a marionette, and she the puppeteer. I laughed uncontrollably, incapable of failing to smile at every thought I had, and every word that was spoken.

At the time we were dining on jacket potato and beans. Please don't ask me why, but I seemed to believe that the greatest idea in the world right then, was to see if M.J and I could gain entry into the Guinness Book of Records by eating a mile of baked beans!

This would obviously present problems in itself. Would one of us lead the way heating the beans up as we went to make it easier? Would the challenge still be legitimate if we strategically placed Barbecue Beans into the equation at certain points when we felt we could stomach no more? Perhaps it would be best if we attempted a mile of raw potatoes instead?

Believing this to be the best way forward, I took the challenge on right there and then, grabbing our bag of spuds, and taking a raw dripping bite out of one.

Unfortunately this was as far as I got. For I then peeled over in fits of laughter, lay down on my back and kicked my legs crazily in the air, just because it seemed like a fun thing to do!

Thus the 'beached whale' was born. This would become notorious around the coast of Australia in the future for signalling that I was more than a little stoned again.

I really don't know why, but M.J decided that the mewing noise I was making as I lay there on my side, arms and legs flailing in the air, blatantly resembled a beached whale.

Later on in time, we were to frequent a picnic table outside a small café named 'Whalers.' Whenever I was particularly baked the whole group would chant, 'beached whale, beached whale,' and I'd rise from my seat, lay on top of the table, and imitate the beached whale impression from that first day. I'd only stop once a true friend offered me a hand up, and then I'd smoke a bowl to celebrate. So the 'beached whale,' was created.

Anyway, I soon found I'd enjoy a carefree smoke with M.J after a hard days toil in the field. I wouldn't always crack up in fits of laughter at the most bizarre things though. At times in fact, I'd wander off for long periods to be alone with my thoughts.

In those moments of contemplation I'd regularly find myself thinking of Beth. The day we'd left Gus' I'd entrusted him with a quick note to send to her, letting her know where to reach me, and that all was just fine and dandy.

At times I found the cannabis would send me reeling deep inside myself, thinking of her, or just clutching at thoughts and ideas I'd never even comprehended before. It seemed that whilst with M.J, we'd laugh hysterically, yet when alone, I'd dive within my sub-conscious to ponder questions I never even knew existed.

So it was I found myself sat below a tree, M.J's Stetson pulled down low over my head, scribbling away furiously on a notepad. It had rained everyday for the last week, and progress in the field had become hard and slow. I had taken to smoking joints to fill the time and explore the newfound avenues of my mind.

Sat against the trunk of a eucalyptus tree, poncho pulled tightly around me, rain dripping from the brow of my hat, I found myself writing to Beth.

Troy stood off to my left, chewing away unperturbed on the grass, mane drenched with rain, matted to his side. In that moment of clarity, I was as oblivious to the weather as he was.

I felt with my drug induced higher state of consciousness, that I was finally seeing things clearly. I finally understood the things I felt, and I just wanted to make Beth see, how she had come to be, everything to me. I just wanted to make her see how very much I loved her. Show her how she'd saved me, even if she never really knew she'd done so.

So, as I sat there, my imagination and the drugs ran away with me, and I penned a fictional short story to Beth. A story of philosophy and love, of being lost and found, a story of being saved when all hope is gone.

I doubt most of it even makes sense now. I mean, for some strange reason I'd become a character called William, and Beth had become an angel! Hmm, interesting? No idea why, but I just wanted to try and show her, well, everything I guess. Oh, by the way, did I mention just how stoned I was? Surreal is an understatement but anyhow, this is the story I wrote.

'He had changed.

In a fast and hectic lifestyle, society had once again whipped him off his feet, and catapulted him towards the eye of the storm without even a backwards glance.

From there, long periods had passed, where one had been so blinkered by the haze of images continually flashing in front of ones eyes, that you failed to recognize that you were even trapped at all.

It was almost like a carousel.

Here he was, stood in the very centre of the swirling melee, constantly forced to retreat by the same things, not even realising at times that they were indeed that. Nothing more than the same shit, just a different day, as someone so aptly put it. Perhaps, 'day,' wasn't quite the word though. Same shit, different moment in time would perhaps have hit closer to the mark.

That's all it was. He had become sub-merged in the everyday, and the same things were forcing his head continuously back under.

For times it was possible to jump onto horseback and join the ride, but it always ended up costing you and eventually the outcome was always the same. You would be tossed back into the middle where you would be forced to stand in solitude once more, debating whether to stand there, caught up and trapped, to pay for another ride, or maybe, just sometimes, to take that brave step outside and look in on the ride. To look in and realise what was really going on.

So here he was, stood briefly on the outside, hoping to stop himself from being drawn back inside again.

But hey, everyone else is going round, trying to ride that porcelain horse, unaware that it will eventually be dashed to pieces, taking them with it if they hold on too tightly. Yet, if everyone else is there, isn't it right? Shouldn't you allow the mob to drag you back into that vicious circle of unawareness? Is ignorance really bliss?

No. For a while he sat there, and he realized that whilst he'd been stuck on the ride he had changed. It had been gradual, as of one slowly becoming used to the darkness of a room, and darkness indeed it was. He had changed.

William Bankes raised his chin from his chest, and deeply exhaled. Perhaps it was the melancholic sigh of a young man forced to feel far too old by an unrelenting society. Forced to rush rapidly through life at such a terrific pace that it seemed impossible to try and stop, for the thing you were sub-consciously aware of, was chasing you and might catch up. Might place a clammy hand on your shoulder and turning you around, force you to face your fears. So you keep on running.

William had barely seen a score of spring times pass, but he already felt that everything had made him run so fast, summer and autumn had passed him by in the blinking of an eye, and he was deeply rooted in the winter of his discontent.

As with the carousel, people needed the constant movement. They cared not that it was only ever going round and round, a small fraction of a cycle of memories, repeating themselves like a slide show projector on autopilot.

When it all draws briefly to a halt, if you look closely you can see the restless fear in all the participants' eyes.

What if it never starts up again?

What then?

The seconds seem to draw out; beads of sweat start to draw themselves to those mopped brows, ready to freely cascade downwards, joined by a torrent of tears if the thing doesn't move. Each person is silently willing the horse to pick up its hooves and pull the rider into the same old, safe but circular movement.

And so, like everyone else, William had rushed quickly through his time. Rushed on, with his head down and his teeth gritted. He dared not risk that clammy hand that somebody somewhere had imprinted not only into his sub-conscious, but everybody else's' as well. No, he had pulled up his collar, dug his hands into his pockets, and forced himself onwards.

Or perhaps he was just aware of his exhaling now he had brought himself out of his reverie. That was the problem. Nothing seemed particularly clear anymore. Nothing had the blissfully euphoric black and whiteness that a child's eyes hold firm to.

"I've changed," William muttered to himself as his eyes came to rest upon a younger version of himself.

He was chasing a ball in a field. It seemed a lifetime ago.

Using his arms he raised himself out of the chair, and strode slowly but purposefully over to the dresser where a number of pictures stood proudly.

Drawing the photo closer, William tried to recognise himself in those young, blond haired, blue eyed boy's eyes. Those eyes held the innocence of childhood.

He was chasing a ball. It was one of those brightly coloured plastic balls that every child had. This one was blue with yellow hoops and large pink spots dotting it like a funny case of chicken pox. All those eyes cared about were the ball; nothing else mattered at that moment in time, just happiness.

A solemn smile briefly played on William's lips, but then he caught sight of his thumbprint as he lovingly placed the photo back onto its mantle. The thumbprint was caught momentarily on the glass where he'd held it so tightly. It was a perfect replica, tracing every contour of that which was unique to him alone. But now it started to fade.

It was becoming patchy as some parts disappeared faster than others. The lines were forced to follow suit, and now William realised that that once whole negative had become almost unrecognisable. It slipped away under his very gaze, slipping away into nothingness, leaving no notable mark that it had ever been there at all. Almost as of one casting a pebble into a still mill pond, watching the ripples play momentarily on the surface, before the pond swallowed both ripple and stone whole. Nothing left, bar whispers of what had been.

William turned his back from the picture and eyed the crystal decanter beckoning him from its dominating position in the centre of the old oak dining table. The table had become warped and eroded but the decanter shone on as if it had stood there since the dawn of modern civilisation.

William sipped at his bittersweet tonic, following the exploits of a robin on the other side of the large bay windows. It hopped around briefly in the virgin white snow, before disappearing from view, burying itself in the old hedge that his mother had planted years before.

Yes, it had been many years ago now he pondered upon it. When he was still that small, blond haired, blue-eyed boy.

He could remember standing by in wonderment as his mother knelt on the freshly tilled ground, carefully planting this plant and that with a loving tenderness only a mother could really know. He had stood there in his big red Wellington boots staring as hard as he could, trying to catch the precise moment when the plant grew. Back then everything had a fresh new mysterious haze about it.

His mother could remember his questions, such questions, unrelenting in the small boys thirst for knowledge. Everything was so amazing back then, and now Mr. Bankes lamented at his seeming inability to ever find that fresh young vivacity in anything anymore. All there was, was that same old carousel. With those porcelain horses that never changed, save perhaps becoming brighter and brighter, shining on like the decanter in his hand.

The image beyond the window disappeared. Large flakes of snow began to fall, and the small delicate footprints of the robin were covered over and washed away. The sky grew dark and heavy. In the fading light William could make out the reflection of a second photograph within his glass.

It was William's 18th birthday and the people he had grown up with surrounded him. He was smiling as broadly as the rest of them, but the eyes are the portals to the mind, and those eyes were screaming out with unhappiness. If you really stared closely you could almost see the ghosts of those horses being ridden by each and every member of the picture, but William stood completely alone in the centre of it all.

Everything about that young man was yelling out for help, was silently saying, "I'm so lost." Yet all around were holding on to the reins far too tightly to notice, and in fact, didn't really care if the truth be told.

The blond haired, blue-eyed boy with the football was barely recognisable. All that remained was a shell, the hint of a shadow, and William knew he had changed.

The man had donned a mask and taken the role of a player on the stage, but that role had slowly eaten away at his vitals, creating a fear so strong that this role may have to be acted out for all eternity.

The mask was that of those around him. The name brand clothes, the items that yelled, "hey, all that matters are materialistic things." The very notion was that money makes the world go around, and that they were more than happy to be led by the reins like that.

And so they were, but William could not, would not. He was trying so hard to, it had stolen that look he had held so very long ago, stolen it from his eyes like a thief in the night.

He had changed, and everything had become a vicious circle with him standing completely alone, trapped at its very core. Knowing that if he carried on down that road, his eyes would die completely, leaving nothing more that a bottomless chasm.

Yet this was all there was. His choices were painfully simple. Don the mask, jump onto horseback and follow the others, never being happy but at least not being alone. Being melancholically aware that this was not life, but what other option was there? To stand alone, watching everyone else destroy themselves.

He could not help any of them. He had tried before but they did not want to listen. They were happy being in a never ending stage performance and if that was the case, who was he to drag them from horseback? He was not God; in fact he was just alone, in solitude, wondering why he had been made aware of what was really happening. Wondering why he couldn't just switch it all off, like a light switch, and re-insert himself back into society.

He must be true to himself, and alone, or become another masked rider. Either way was to be unhappy.

A single tear broke free from William's eye, and slowly cascaded toward the picture. It traced the contours of a face that had been creased and scarred by society far sooner than it should have been. It stopped at his jaw, holding firmly, but with more pressure building up, acting on it, eventually it had to fall and explode on the picture frame below.

William knocked back the remaining contents of his glass when a loud rap at the front door echoed so suddenly throughout the empty house that the photo slipped from his grasp.

It shattered into a thousand fragments upon the floor, broken forever.

William had become so used to his solitary confinement that a visitor at this hour in his life was completely unexpected.

A new wave of apprehension he hadn't felt for years pulsed through his veins.

Picking up his feet he marched like a general to the call of battle into the hallway. It was then that he realised that the front door lay wide open. He had been sure that it had been firmly barred and locked from the inside, preventing anyone from getting past his walls of defence, but there it was, lying fully back on its hinges, with the snow falling upon the floorboards.

Everything suddenly became so very surreal. For there in the doorway stood the most beautiful vision his now cold eyes had ever borne witness to. William had to blink several times as for a moment, perhaps it was due to the reflective qualities of the crisp white snow, it seemed like this woman was surrounded by a faint, glowing aura. Indeed, although it was blowing a blizzard outside not a single flake had settled upon her perfectly angelic features. For that is what she reminded him of, the description by Joseph of Arimathea concerning the angel who had visited him and changed his life forever.

He could never forget that first real time he saw her. He felt sure afterwards that she had always been there, but this was the first time he'd ever really opened his eyes and perceived her. He tried many times afterwards to put her image to paper, but nothing ever did such beauty justice. To use words would be to place her into the realms we know, but it would be an ultimate injustice to pull her down from that greater plateau she'd transcended to. She belonged with the stars. All William could remember thinking at that moment was, "please, please don't disappear. You are the most beautiful entity I have ever dreamt of."

Without saying a word she grabbed him by the hand and rescued him. She saved him in a way she could never fully comprehend. Together they turned their backs on the carousel and hand in hand, walked away from the park.

And now?

Now if he catches himself looking at his reflection, that young boy stares right back at him. Sure the ball had been replaced, but the look is the same. It is the look of pure and simple happiness.

But he never looks for too long, because his is not the only reflection in the mirror.

She is there in his arms.

His head rests on her shoulder, and his arms wrap around her waist, where she gently caresses his hands.

He is looking up into the mirror.

Her hair tickles the side of his face but he doesn't mind, because there's nowhere else they'd rather be than in each other's arms. They could stay there forever, and gaze into each others eyes for all eternity, without ever regretting a single moment shared.'

Okay, okay, I agree, what the hell was that all about hey?! Guess it was nothing more than the words of a big fat stoner! I'd so wanted to be romantic just like the old great lovers, like Romeo, or umm, Patrick Swayze (?!), that the weed had once again played havoc with my mind, and all of a sudden I'd found myself lost in a different world, trying to write something that would really mean something to her.

I just wanted to let Beth know how lost I was until I found her. I hadn't seen her for a considerable amount of time now, and so I just wanted to reach out from half the world away and say, 'look, still thinking of you. Still loving you.' Yeah, I'm officially embarrassed now. Think I'll shut up!

Days soon passed into weeks, and still the torrential rain showed no sign of letting up. We had all but finished our work by this point. The stumps had been felled, the fences been fixed, and the waterways cleared. So much so in fact, that the river and its inlets flowed so fast that they threatened to climb their banks and wash us all away!

Yet still M.J and I remained. I guess we had all the heart to stay and none of the will to go. Such was the case until that fateful day.

M.J and I had been out all day checking that our newly erected fence line was holding good in the weather. As we neared camp late that afternoon, we found that Gus had left fresh supplies.

Along with all this, sat a letter. Although the rain had flashed in through the flapping doors of our open tent smearing the handwriting, I instantly noticed the postmark from home. Beth!

It had been so long I couldn't wait to hear from her again. Despite all my adventures, all I had newly discovered, I missed her so, so much.

I tore the letter open with the enthusiasm of a child discovering his presents on Christmas morning.

As I read her letter, everything changed.

NOBODY HOME

A TEAR broke in an instant from the corner of my eye, and slowly traced a contour down the lines of a torn and broken mans face. Breaking free, it burst onto the writing on the page, and then my sanity tore itself free as well.

I crushed the letter before me within my fist, as once the paper is crumpled, it can never be perfect again. And so it fell upon the ground, to rot away, to be eaten by the worms, to turn to dust and die along with everything I knew and loved.

I turned and burst from the tent, tearing into the howling storm outside.

Wrapped up in my own passion, my own pain and hate, M.J's words were lost to me. 'Where the hell are you going, what's wrong? For God's sake come back inside!'

But no, I am lost to the world now. There is no going back, there is no shelter, there is only the lashing rain upon my face, stinging me into action. There is only insanity, and the flash of lightning across the haunted night sky joined in battle by the war cry of his brother thunder, echoing my internal screams of madness.

I burst into a run, fleeing into the night. Sprinting through the trees in darkness, the shards of branches break against me like the waves on a jagged rock, and cut me all over, tearing strips out of my flesh and clothes, but I can't feel a thing. If anything the blood drives me on.

Bursting from cover I fall upon our terrified and startled steeds. As another flash of lightning illuminates the scene, a madman can be witnessed in the full height of his rage, can be seen uprooting the very fence pole that his horse stands tied to, in a super human show of strength.

Tossing the stump to one side as if it were mere plywood, he vaults into his horse's saddle.

I no longer exist within myself. A small part of me floats outside the insane soul that has been lost to the devil, watching my actions from outside my very body, as if a bystander.

I dig the heels of my boots so strongly into my poor steeds flanks that blood immediately flashes steaming into the cold night, and from the torn and jagged gash, red rain falls into the murky puddles we leave behind.

The horse whinnies in a scream of pain and horror, but once again all other noises seem drowned out to me, as if I am submerged beneath water. The only thing I can hear is my maniacal cry and the roaring of thunder.

We bolt into the night, moving at incredible speeds. The wind lashes against my face, blinding me, whilst the rain drenches me along with my tears. I bleed from my cuts as freely as the horse below me, but still I drive us both on. Still I throw my heels into its open and raw flanks. Still I force us on at incapable speeds.

We fly on as if on wings, until we reach the shores of the swollen river.

I do not stop.

I can't stop.

I am no longer in control.

I am merely on autopilot.

There is no one at home.

I can't stop.

I can't stop.

I just drive us on.

My horse goes to throw me. It can see where I am driving us, can see the intention that not even I am aware of. That even if I wanted to stop, I couldn't. It tried to throw me in its desperation and terror, but it was a slave to my hellish and insane soul, bound to me.

So we burst into the river. The swift flowing water hits us like a freight train, engulfing us, sucking us beneath the surface, dragging us down to our bed of hell. Our battered bodies are turned over and over, crushed between boulders, cracked against rocks, and my screams are drowned out.

I must have lost consciousness, as when I came to, the first rays of light were upon me. I laid in an inch of mud, my body broken and bleeding, half-drowned.

I'm so, so sorry, for I must report that my poor horse was lost forever from this world. That horse I loved so dearly. It should have been me. It deserved to be me. If I could change just one thing that has happened in my life, it would not be anything to do with my happiness, it would be to have saved my loyal and trusty steed.

At the time, I did not see it that way, I should have died, why hadn't I?

'Damn you all, I should be dead!' The internal scream reverberated around my skull.

Pulling my hand free from the sodden mud, I pulled myself forwards. I forced myself to crawl on through the mud, blood and filth of the ground and of my mind. I was plastered from head to foot in grime, and there was only one way out.

To my right lay the broken strap of a rein that had come loose on impact when we hit the water at full charge. Clambering to my knees, I tilted my head back to the sky, and scowled up at the beautiful happy sun with bloodshot eyes. With a renewed burst of energy I pulled myself upright and grabbing the rein, headed for the nearest tree.

Just above its base the two main forks of the trunk branched out in opposite directions. Standing upon this I threw the reins up over the branch above me. Then without a second thought, I placed my head through the noose, and stepped off my perch into oblivion.

It's funny, but nothing hurt anymore. There was no more pain. I didn't fight it. I just looked up into the early morning sunrise, and saw the true beauty of it all.

The sky was a multitude of colours. Directly above me the last few stars could still be seen stamped on blackness. As I hung there, gently swaying back and forth in the morning breeze, I traced the colours down towards the horizon.

The black slowly turned into dark shades of deep purple, lightening in shade until the whole sky became blues and whites. Around the sun the clouds danced with reds and yellows and pinks and just over the mountains in the distance, it must have been raining, because where the light broke through the clouds there, you could see a heavenly waterfall sparkle down upon the earth in every colour of the rainbow.

I smiled, and gently brought my lashes down in rest. The light behind my eyes slowly faded to black, and then closed inwards, until all I was aware of was a single white circle in front of me.

Out of this stepped Beth. She walked barefooted through the early morning dew. She was dressed in white again, like an angel, and as she walked she gently ran her hands over the tops of the grass, letting the watery crystals tingle and cascade upon the ground.

She stopped just before me, and flashing me a smile plucked a large white daisy, and tucked it behind her ear. A few strands of golden blond hair fell over her eyes as she reached me, and gazed inside me.

The eyes are the portals to the mind and in that instant we could see the eternal love of each other's souls. As she glanced up into my eyes, she smiled softly, and I traced the contours of her face with my fingertips.

As they stroked down past her cheek she nestled her nose into the cup of my hand, and pressed her lips ever so gently against my palm. Bringing her hands up our fingers interlinked, and standing there, at the very end of it all, holding hands, she leant forwards and kissed me one last time.

Kissed me one last heavenly sublime time, before with the faintest of smiles playing upon my lips, and my ravished heart filling one last time with love, I heard the beat of angels' wings as they lifted me up on high. I heard the heavenly choir sing sweetly by my side, as my loving heart gave out one last resounding beat, and then I died.

PART THREE

GET BUSY LIVING, OR GET BUSY DYING.
WITHOUT THE LOWS HOW CAN WE JUDGE THE HIGHS?

OFF THE MAP

SO I'm afraid you'll just have to trust on M.J 's words for now. As, well let's face it; I'm off with the fairies as always!

Anyway, (still my favourite word it seems!) M.J watched me blaze a trail into the fiery night. Calling after me to come back he snatched up the shreds of the discarded letter from where they lay upon the floor. It only took him seconds to read the last few lines of what Beth had written to me, before he knew without hesitation he must go after me.

Unbeknown to me in my wild dash towards the end of all things, the moon had once again broken free from her shroud to watch the insanity of the world unfurl below. With its aid, M.J had managed to just about track me to the point I had hit the water. There he faced his biggest decision.

The turmoil of it all was the fact that he could either follow the river in the dark, and miss me in the shadows of the night, or wait until first light, by which time it might have all been too late. He'd decided on the latter and returned crestfallen to camp, to spend time alone with his own personal horrors, all of which I can but only imagine and apologise for in that long fateful night.

Without sleep he and Thor had pushed back out to the river before dawn broke. There he moved as quickly as he could without the risk of missing anything. Unfortunately as the first rays of light fell over the mountains he'd discovered the broken and battered body of my poor horse, lying drowned in an inlet. Poor Troy. I'll never forgive myself.

As M.J 's steed mounted a rocky peek he saw me off in the distance. I was just clambering towards my tree, with my back toward him. The downward path was steep and treacherous and both rider and mount almost fell on the descent. As M.J hit the bottom he spurred Thor on with all his will. As he leapt from the last broken rock, his footing as sure and true as ever before, he accelerated onto the open plain with a dazzling turn of speed.

Thor moved over the grass with the grace of an angel, and as the wind whipped up around them as they tore over the turf, even M.J 's beloved Stetson was torn from his head. He saw me fall from afar, but still rider and steed pressed on, refusing to relent.

As Beth walked slowly towards me from in front, M.J was bursting onto the scene from behind. As the horse pulled up at last, with all breath finally gone from its lungs, incapable of carrying on, I was doing the same.

M.J hit the floor rolling and in one swift motion exploded upwards onto his feet supporting my weight with his left arm, whilst tearing his Bowie knife from the sheath in his boot and slicing through the strap with his other.

In the end, it had not been the beating of angels' wings I'd heard, but the falling hooves of Thor. And it was not the singing angels who had lifted me on high, but my friends voice screaming at me to come back to the light as he carried me aloft. So you see, I did die, but only for a few seconds, for M.J somehow brought me back.

The next few days were lost to fever and madness. All I have are snapshots, M.J's memories and my mad scribbled notes in a torn and dirtied pad of paper.

M.J had carted me back to camp strewn over that wonderful creature Thor, to whom I owe my life for bearing M.J so far, so fast. I must have briefly regained consciousness as somewhere in my memory banks I retain the thought that I must be in some kind of limbo. For as I opened my eyes I remembered thinking, 'what kind of strange purgatory is this? That all should be upside down, that the sky should be below me and the very birds themselves fly the wrong way up? I am floating through the afterlife, and all is madness, look how even the grass itself falls like stalactites from heaven.'

M.J, upon hearing me mumbling away madly to myself, threw a glance over his shoulder as he rode, to see me hanging there upside down upon the back of Thor, dragging my hands, seemingly trying to reach out and pluck away the grass as we passed over it.

This was merely a taste of things to come, for the time being, I was lost inside my mind, unaware of what was dream and what reality. M.J had to indulge many a strange convulsive outburst of insanity apparently as the fever of both body and soul took a tighter grip.

That night he'd made a huge fire, and placed me wrapped in many blankets as close to its heat as he dared. For my part I firmly believed that I was in hell.

I had been carried through the after world and was now sweating away before the very fires of Hades itself. The fires filled all my vision and I must be bound in chains, as I couldn't move. In fear and horror I'd screamed away my sanity. Screamed for God to come and rescue me. Oh how the fire burnt. Burnt so brightly, the flames danced and glistened in my very eyes, and my whole body smouldered and smoked. I could feel the flesh peeling away from my very bones. Although I couldn't move my head, I could see in my minds eye all that was going on. The flesh would be glowing beautifully in colour, gently changing from yellows and reds before leaving the colours of the rainbow to simply burn pure white, as the heat reached its most intense, then char to black. Slowly cracks would rent and flash glimpses at the bones below, before it all stripped away.

Oh how the stench of burning flesh assaulted my nostrils, the knowledge that it was my very own matter that cooked forced me to scream out one last, lung breaking cry of horror.

How I cried until the very oxygen ignited in my throat, stopping me abruptly and flowing on peacefully inside, as if a shooting star flashing through the night sky. It washed its way into my lungs to merely turn them to ash and smoke. Every internal organ felt like it had been doused in petrol and the Devil himself had sparked that match and set about watching me burn for all eternity. He was there, watching me, enjoying my torture and pain.

He was there. I knew it. I couldn't see him but I could feel him, feel him sat there right at the edge of my vision.

M.J sat near by, watching over me all night. I had spent a long time almost drowned in the mud and water the night before, and so the worst of the fever from this had taken its grip on my body. M.J knew those next few hours would determine whether I was to live or die, and so he'd watched on as I burned away. He'd watched me wriggle and squirm away attempting to break away from the blankets he'd wrapped around me.

'Just what delusions is he lost within,' M.J had wondered. Yet still he remained vigilant in his night watch, fearing I'd break loose and run into the very fire itself, or simply just give up the fight, close my eyes and peacefully slip away.

The trickle of a raindrop gently flowed down M.J's rescued Stetson and hung briefly upon its rim. As another drop hit home it automatically took up the trail its brother had just created. Like a toboggan taking up the bob sleigh track, it raced along the path before slamming into the previous raindrop that was hanging so precariously upon the precipice. The force caused both to break out over the edge, where they fell together until brothers alike exploded upon M.J's hand, waking him. The downpour had drowned the fire, and I was sleeping, having seemingly managed to finally find rest after my long nights battle.

And so I continued to sleep, I slept on for two days straight as my body attempted to recuperate. For the time being though, although the fever of my body was diminishing, the fight for my mind continued to rage. The next time I awoke, it just didn't register that I was floating down the swollen rapids of the river.

You see, when those first drops of rain had awoken M.J he'd realised a decision had to be made. We were in the middle of nowhere and although I really shouldn't be moved in my present state, the underlying fact remained, that I had murdered a man's horse. M.J knew not what the resulting repercussions would be, but he felt sure that the time had come for us to take our leave. Thus he set about his business for the day.

Felling young pliable trees from the woodland, by the shores of the river he trussed his cuttings together to form a raft. He then removed part of our extensive tent with his bowie knife and secured a large sheltered area that took up the majority of our raft. Only the front was left uncovered, so that one man could steer the bulk of the vessel downstream with the aid of a smaller woodcutting, as if a gondolier on the waterways of Venice.

M.J never told me much about those dark days, but he alluded to the fact that he deposited a large amount of money in the trunk of a tree to try and aid Gus a little in replacing the beloved horse that was lost. I also know it must have been a sad moment indeed when he had to say farewell to Thor, before pitching us into the river and away from that place we'd loved.

Over rock and rapid M.J steered us, never knowing as to where we'd end up, but figuring we would eventually be washed up once more upon the shores of civilisation. I however, remained oblivious to all this.

I was waking, eating, sleeping, but the whole vessel, was merely on autopilot. There simply was no one home. M.J would just listen to me chattering away to myself.

As the rain washed down we both allowed the river to take us where it would as we perched inside our shelter. M.J would peer out, wondering when the sun would appear again from the continuous storm, before turning to gaze upon me, and wonder when the ravishing of fever would relent. He'd watch me as I'd sat cross-legged aboard our little raft, blanket wrapped round me, gently rocking back and forth, often scribbling away furiously.

For my part, I have no real recollection of that period of my life. Prolonged exposure to the harsh elements on the fateful day I'd received Beth's letter had caused me much sickness. I was delirious for many hours, all the time fighting a battle I was not even aware of. Mother nature had seen it befitting to place upon my tortured body and mind a sickness that not only demanded my physical, but mental health as well, whilst beneath it all, my very soul struggled to regain control of the otherwise doomed vessel.

The only recollection I have of where I was, are from the piecing together of crazy rants I found in my notepad. From what I can ascertain, after the initial struggle to survive the hellish torment of that first night in fever, my brain short-circuited, and as I drifted down river alongside M.J, I was oblivious to reality. That psychotic scribbling suggested some internal struggle to make sense of things, but they were dark days, and at times it is not always wise for the sane to glimpse insanity.

I only truly recall one thing clearly. I don't know where it's from, but the quote, 'get busy living, or get busy dying,' resounded throughout.

And so, with that idea still reverberating around my head, my eyes finally flipped open, and I was actually back. My soul had proved the eventual victor in the battle for my body and mind. I was back in reality, I was cold and hungry, and I was also wondering why a half naked Aborigine was perched grinning insanely right before my face.

THERE'S NOTHING LIKE THE FEELING OF
WHEN THE TRAIN FINALLY REACHES THE STATION

'WELCOME back to the land of the living,' the stranger said, and offering me his painted hand, helped pulled me up into a sitting position.

The Aborigine was scantily clad, with a mere animals pelt wrapped around his waist to hide his pride. Thick black matted hair parted his dark skinned face, and deep brown eyes gazed out at me betraying obvious intellect. Painted tattoos adorned his body. Small white spots traced lines from his hands, trekking up his arms, across his shoulder, before finally dancing upon his cheeks. They followed some mysterious trail that I did not understand. As for what the paint consisted of, I could only hazard a guess at what wild plant had been carefully picked and crushed to create those colours. For everywhere along its strange path the virginal white was interjected with brilliantly crimson reds, and golden yellows. It seemed to me that a multitude of rainbow coloured candles had been passed over this man, allowing the wax to drip and harden along his features. His very body had been used as a magnificent canvas to create a very real and breathing work of art.

In his hand he held a small wooden pestle and mortar, full of a thick black paste that gave off a rather pungent smell. It reminded me instantly of black magic, or what I'd imagine an ancient apothecary's work board to smell of.

As I sat there slowly awakening back to the world, I ran a cold and clammy hand over my wearied and weathered brow. As my fingers came to rest upon my temple my nails caught under some strange secretion hardened upon my skin. As I peeled the layer slowly away I noted it to be of the same origin as the mixture in the Aborigine's bowl.

My eyes must have slanted with perplexity as the man explained, 'don't worry; it's just a little natural medicine. A little concoction I can make when the right plants are in season to remedy the throws of fever. Do you feel much better?'

'Yes, yes I do,' I returned, smiling for what felt like the first time in weeks. 'Thank you,' and I gazed into his eyes as I spoke those words, so that he could glimpse into my heart and see the real and sincere gratitude that I harboured there.

Reaching out to shake his hand I asked, 'what's your name?'

'James,' he replied.

Once again my features must have betrayed my ignorance and confusion.

'I do not know my real name, James is the name the White man gave me,' he smiled solemnly. 'When I was a boy it was the law of the land to remove my people from our home and family to live in modern society, all in an attempt to integrate us with the White community. We were placed in camps under the pretence that we were being given the chance at equal schooling, but really it was so that we could marry into White families, and gradually the colour of our skin would be bleached away down through the generations.'

'I'm sorry,' I said sadly.

'Not to worry,' he flashed a brilliant smile full of knowledge back at me. 'People can take away your name, but they can never take away what's inside, however much they try. They can never take away your spirit. My history made me the man I am now, and so my name is James. I took the best parts of my life, the best parts of what I learnt, of what appealed to the man I am, and then I set out along a path of discovery,' he said, tracing the trail of paint that wound along his body.

'I set out on a quest of knowledge, learning all there was, what the white man could teach me, what the other religions could preach, and what the ways of my true roots were. I took the great truths I learnt from all things, and in doing so, I became a separate entity, unique from all else, I became the man who stands in front of you now. I do not have to adopt different roles upon the great stage of life, I do not have to hide away behind different masks, I can merely be myself. Besides, as your Shakespeare would say, 'what's in a name?''

As he released a deep hearty laugh I heard a call break out from the trees away to my right.

'Coooooooooooooooeeeeeeeeeeeeeeee!' (It seemed that whilst I'd been lying at deaths door M.J had been quizzing James about the life of a man gone 'walkabout,' in the great outdoors. Cheers mate. I'm lying there, ready to snuff it at any time, and you're off gallivanting around the undergrowth searching for giant grubs to eat, or trying to wrestle a crocodile and kill it armed with just a toothpick or something similar. Cheers buddy! Anyway, oh yeah that was it, the reason M.J was calling, 'Cooeee,' is because James had told him that if you're ever lost in the outback, it's best to call 'cooee,' instead of, 'help,' because the sound travels further along the airwaves, increasing the chance of one being heard and rescued. M.J wasn't lost though it transpired, just delusional. Tearing around the bush, beating his chest and yelling aloud as if he was bloody Tarzan or something!)

The woodland around the call burst into life in a cacophony of noise. The beating of wings filled the air and every shade of the spectrum filled my view as scores of birds took to the sky in the darkening dusk. Into the clearing appeared a dreadlocked apparition and approaching us it set the firewood it had collected upon the ground.

'Glad to see you decided to join us at last,' M.J laughed, 'so you actually gonna get up and make yourself useful, or have I still got to do everything around here?'

I can't exactly recall my response but I'm pretty sure I told him to rearrange the following words into a well known sentence, 'my kiss please arse.' Like I said though, I can't recall exactly, but it seemed like my sense of humour had somewhat returned at least!

That night we ignited a huge bonfire beneath the stars and cooked up a great feast courtesy of James' ability with a hunting spear, and the herbs the ground was happy to yield. I was ravenous, and ate long and full. After I'd gorged myself to bursting, I laid back, with my head on my pack, and listened to James' calming voice tell tales of the Dreamtime.

'The Dreamtime,' he explained, 'is the stories and beliefs of my native people. In the beginning my ancestors walked this earth in the guise of humans and all manner of other birds and beasts. It was back in this dawn of time that they created the world as we know it today.'

As he looked around through the ghostly veil of moonlit night he explained, 'you see, even now our ancestors are still with us, visible for all to see, we're forever connected to our past.'

In the background the dark shadows of the local hill range overlooked our camp. As James' eyes settled upon them he continued, 'the hills for example, were all created by a great dispute over food can you believe! The buck kangaroo, Urdlu, was too mean to tell his starving friend, Mandya the euro, where his food hole was, and when Mandya did find it, he was too greedy to see the furious Urdlu approach. The two friends became entangled in such a titanic battle that Mandya's wounds would create the hills, and his blood would stain the ground crimson in the red plains they now call Mandya Arti, or 'Mandya's Blood.' And so the hills were formed.'

'In the ranges near where I was born, lies a great mountain that can be seen standing proud and tall. In its rock face the great hero Butcha, of the Ugarapuls tribe, lies entombed staring out over all time. Before my days, a terrifying tyrant of the Baluchi tribe was carving carnage like a whirlwind of death through the Ugarapuls. No one could face his wrath and live, no one that is, until the young Butcha confronted him face to face in the heat of battle. Butcha was wounded many times, and yet still he fought on unperturbed and undaunted. At the end, spotting the opening he'd been waiting for, he pounced, bringing down his waddy with all the strength left in him. He brought it down and smote his enemy, crushing the butcher of Baluchi's head with a strike that would have rent the very ground itself in two. He had saved his tribe, but as his people rushed forth to congratulate him, so his spirit finally gave up the struggle, and his body moved no more. Butcha had achieved the impossible through strength of mind and will alone. His soul animating him long after his body had given up the fight. So you see, it is all in our mind. We can overcome all boundaries, all obstacles, all walls, if we simply believe with all our heart and mind, because at the end of the day, life is simply a matter of keeping the faith.'

And so we listened to him talk on through the night. Under that mystical moon, with that bewitching voice that seemed to echo that of many voices speaking out down through the ages, he told us of the Dreamtime.

He told us of how the red ochre clay used to paint his body was formed from the corpse of an evil witch's red hound. Of how the Three Sisters rock formation M.J and I had visited in the Blue Mountains, was in fact the bodies of the three beautiful sisters, Meehni, Wimlah, and Gunnedoo of the Katoomba tribe. They had been set in stone by their witch doctor to protect them, only for him to fall in battle, therefore entrapping them to remain frozen in rock for all time, and many more tales of wonder.

So he spoke, until a large owl settled down upon the turf in front of him, startling me from my dreams of ancient times. The owl simply cocked his head and, well, made an owl noise. (Apart from twit-twit-twoo I'm not entirely sure how to write an owl noise. If it's any consolation I am imitating the sound out loud right now as I puzzle over how to spell it, and the people around me are casting me strange looks. Why do I feel like the men in white with the straight jackets shall soon be on their way again?!) Both man and bird simply stared into each other's eyes. Then, as suddenly as the owl arrived, it burst into flight off into the night, and James immediately rose as well.

'Well, I'm sorry my friends, but it appears that I must leave you now,' he said forlornly.

Moving first to M.J and then myself, he embraced us both, before taking his leave and disappearing out of sight, into the dark beyond the campfire's light.

M.J and I merely stood there, too stunned to say anything, or even move for that matter. I never even said thank you properly.

Years later I heard tell that an Aborigine has a spirit guide, a creature appointed to him in life, an animal that comes to him in times of need and trouble, letting him know that his presence is desperately needed someplace else. This is as close to an answer as I've managed concerning James' sudden upshot and disappearance. All I can say is, I hope if you ever catch wind of all this James, that things weren't too bad, and that everything worked out all right in the end. Oh, and by the way, thanks.

RISKING ROCKS AND RAPIDS IN LIFE,
IS NEVER AS FUN IN FULL SAFETY GEAR

AS DAWN broke a gentle drizzle fell. Collecting up our possessions in the damp morning air, M.J and I once again took to our trusty raft and pitched out into the current.

I guess it was just yet another regular day, you know, floating downstream on a raft built by a dreadlocked Buddha, not knowing where you're going, where you are, or indeed until recently, just who the hell you are! However, things were about to take a turn for the surreal.

About an hour out from camp I started to notice some particularly strange activity going on along the shores of the bank. Through the thicket of scrubs and undergrowth I could make out bright shining red globes bobbing up and down, almost out of view. However much I strained though, I just couldn't quite make out what on earth they were. It all seemed rather bizarre, especially when I could make out patches of luminous pink as well. Still, as we continued swiftly downstream, the foliage once again closed to swallow up its strange secret for the time being.

Swallowed up its strange secret that is, until our small vessel stole around a bend in the river.

I guess we heard what was going on before we saw it. For as we broke around that bend the crescendo of gallons of tumbling water engulfed our eardrums. Down below us the river broke into swift flowing rapids, interjected along the way by bone breaking rocks. The cacophony of rushing water almost deafened us.

Rather fortuitously we were floating upon the calm before the storm, obviously at the start of this lovely little rapids run. Just below us however, a number of large inflatable dinghies were casting off from land into the white waters. We could distinguish around ten people per craft, all armed with oars in hand and dressed in the little solution to my previous problem. For they were each adorned with luminous pink life jackets and scarlet red safety helmets. The outbreak of reds and pinks I could barely make out further upstream was now obviously apparent!

M.J and I steered our little wooden raft into the riverbank to gather our thoughts and watch the remaining rafters prepare themselves on the opposite side of the shore.

As we hit dry land M.J immediately leapt like a gazelle away from the raft into the trees, Bowie knife drawn in hand, leaving me to stand alone.

There I remained for some time until a small cry of 'cooeee,' sounded close to my ear. The bouncing blond dreadlocks bobbed back into view, carrying two sturdy freshly cut wooden poles.

'Figured this is gonna need both of us to steer, and that one looks a little worse for wear now,' he said matter of factly, and tossed me one of the gondoliers cabers.

Catching it in my spare hand my first thought was that he was certainly right, the new steering pole was certainly of far better quality than the other piece of crap I was also holding, so I let it go. My second and perhaps more important thought of the two was, 'oh shit.'

Personally, I had thought the plan would be to somehow trek around the waterfall by land. You see, I'd almost drowned once that year already, and call me old-fashioned and boring, but I just didn't quite fancy giving it another try just yet. I'd manage to pull myself through some pretty fucked up shit and you know what? I just kind of fancied giving life another chance at that point in time.

'Right mate, you undo the bindings for the shelter, 'cause I reckon the best plan is for one to steer from the front, and one from the back,' M.J said.

Well stupid me, of course! What an idiot! There was obviously a plan of action for all this. Yes, that's it; the idiots in their dinghies can keep their safety helmets and life jackets, because we had no need for them. Ha ha ha. No need at all! I mean we had a fool proof, carefully thought out plan of action for this dangerous, life threatening experience. Yes, I see now. One of us would stand and steer with his pole from the front of the hastily constructed wooden raft that was secured by nothing more than a few knots in an old rope, and the other would stand and steer from the back. Brilliant! Fool proof plan! There wasn't a chicken's chance in Thailand that anything could possibly go wrong.

'You know,' I stated, 'whilst I agree that is a very good plan and a very valid point, may I just interject with an idea of my own at this juncture in time? How about, NO jackass!'

M.J just smiled in response, 'come on man, don't even pretend like you're not gonna do this. What is it they say, 'we take these risks not to escape life, but to prevent life from escaping us,' and besides, its gonna be fun!'

'I swear you're gonna be the bloody death of me,' I muttered.

'Hang on, you're the one who tried to string himself up in a tree,' the cheeky bastard replied!

You know, I don't even know why, I mean it was some pretty serious shit that I had been through, but all of a sudden, the seriousness and burden of it all just left me, and I laughed long and hard.

'Yeah, I guess you've got a good point there dick head!' It seemed my demons had finally been released. And also you know what? It did look like a lot of fun. Life is just a picture book of stories to look back on and tell, and this would certainly make an interesting one. So I just asked, 'who's gonna stand up front and who's up back?'

So it was that M.J and I found ourselves pitching down the rapids alongside the befuddled gaze of the dinghy drivers around us. They in their heavily kitted inflatable crafts, with top of the range paddles and safety measures, dressed to the nines in wet weather gear and protective, but rather fashion challenged (I mean, luminous pink and red really does clash badly lads, and doesn't exactly scream of masculinity) clothing, and then there was us, on a home made raft. M.J stood up front yelling orders over his shoulder like a general in battle, dressed only in his wrap around sarong, dreads and torso soaked from the spray of the river, and me stood up back, risking the odd rock to raise a hand and wave as we passed the other vessels by, chirping, 'good morning.'

When I look back on it, the mental image in my mind's eye that makes me most laugh, is of just before we pitched over a small four-foot drop. A line had been set up immediately above its fall with a photo camera attached to it. You know the kind of thing; take a photo of the tourists so they can buy it at the end to remember their day out.

Well someone out there (and I'd love a copy if you're reading this) must have a photo of a dinghy full of horror stricken and panicked people screaming in melodramatic fear as they reach the point of no return and look down over the tiny fall, and there in the background, is a crudely fashioned wooden raft just pulling alongside them to plummet together. Two men stand aboard it, one half naked and whistling away to himself, not a care in the world, and the other stood behind, pole in hand, waving and smiling to the camera.

Like I said, if anyone knows where that picture is you'd make me a happy man if you could send me a copy.

PART FOUR

WE ARE JUST A 3-D JIGSAW PUZZLE,
LOOKING FOR THE RIGHT PIECES TO FIT TOGETHER

APPARENTLY, BEING SO DRUNK YOU WANDER AROUND COLD, NAKED AND BLEEDING, INCAPABLE OF SPEECH, DOES NOT IMPRESS THE LADIES

ONCE again I found that days and weeks blurred into one.

You see the thing with travelling, is that you soon find that you start to exist outside the realms of time, and how truly liberating it is. There is no need for a watch or a calendar to keep record of the days. When you are exempt from the pressures of needing to clock in for work, or pay your monthly bills, then time no longer rules your life. You are no longer a slave to old man time, ticking down your living hours with that chattering laughter of his ticking and tocking, mocking you. You are free of his clutches, and suddenly life takes on a whole different perspective. So many pressures are lifted from your shoulders, so many responsibilities, no longer do you yell the cries of, 'there just aren't enough hours in the day,' or, 'is that really the time already? I really must go, how ever much I don't want to.' You are free to live in the moment until it draws to a natural conclusion, rather than let the grandfather clock cut it off prematurely.

I must confess as to looking back upon those days with a hint of remorse. When I'm sat here now in the local pub with my friends, discussing life, liberty, laughing at the memories of things gone by, before catching sight of the time, and having to leave it all behind.

Now, I wake at 7.26, literally the last moment possible if I want to make work on time. Shower, brush teeth, style hair, move downstairs, sift through the bills that arrive through the door as I eat breakfast. 8.12 get in car and crawl through bumper-to-bumper traffic to arrive at work for 9. Cup of coffee, 11.15 go outside for cigarette break. 1pm take lunch. 3.10 afternoon cigarette. 5pm clock out. 6.30 take dinner, relax, ensure back in bed by 11 so I'm not dead on my feet in the morning. Wake up and repeat process.

Yes, how liberating it was to eat when I felt like eating, not when the clock in work determined, to go to sleep when I wanted, to wake up when I wanted, to not be a slave to work, money, and thus forth the time and calendar.

Perhaps the greatest thing it all destroys is the ability to be spontaneous. How much fun it is to be free to wake and decide, today I think I'll fly to Spain for the week. Or, 'you know what? Lets take a picnic and saunter through the newly blossomed Bluebells that bedeck the local woodlands, and make love in the afternoon sunshine.' All without having to go through the whole bullshit and rigmarole of having to phone someone and pretend to be dying of some newly created disease. Ah, the great guilt and role-play that is pulling a 'sickie' day off work.

'Yes sir, (cough, cough, snivel) I just woke up and my throat was a bit sore and had funny lumps on it. What? Oh yes I know Jenkins came into work when he was showing similar symptoms. Though what I have is slightly different. You see I was brushing my teeth ready to come to work still, despite my sore throat, because I love my job so much, when unfortunately my arm fell off onto the bathroom floor, made a terrible mess I can tell you. Of course I fetched a darning needle and thread so I could still drive to work, but I'm afraid I had to admit defeat after accidentally sewing it on back to front. You see it's rather hard trying to sew with just one hand. What? Oh, no, there's no need for that, I'm sure I'll be back in work tomorrow, it's bound to grow back overnight.'

Yes, it's rather hard to keep track of the realisation that we work to live, rather than live to work!

Anyway? Ah, that was it.

Weeks, perhaps months later, M.J and I found ourselves at Hervey Bay sharing a room in a far classier establishment than the hostel from our first days. I mean, the cockroaches here wandered around in Armani sunglasses and always greeted you with a friendly, 'Good Afternoon sirs. Let me get the door for you.'

That morning we were due to set off to Fraser Island with Benny Boy and Dan, or Dan Gin-Beer as he appears in my address book. The reason for this being that he co-founded the genius that is Gin-Beer along with yours truly.

You see M.J, Benny Boy, Dan and I were all sat in this sauna. Hang on, hang on, I seem to be getting ahead of myself. Let's just rewind that a second, 'anuas siht ni tas lla erew I dna, naD, yoB ynneB, J.M ees ouY,' and start at the beginning.

M.J and I were a little down on our luck, and were once again stood at the side of one of those concrete highways that dissect every country like some pulmonary artery or vein in a body, whisking the blood from one organ to another.

The rain was pelting down, we were drenched from head to toe, and resembled some kind of swamp monster after one truck driver deemed it incredibly amusing to steer his semi at incredible speeds through a mud puddle that lay right next to us. (Yeah mate, you really are funny, haha, I'm bloody wetting myself. There's nothing more amusing than splashing two lonely old souls down on their luck, with a tonne of mud and water as they stand hitchhiking by the side of the road. Ha ha. Oh by the way, you're a complete dick.)

As to how we'd ended up there? Well, we'd stumbled upon an old cotton farm in the middle of nowhere a few days before and the half-blind but kindly farmer had sold us a couple of 50cc postmen's motorbikes at a very reasonable price.

So there we were, scooting along the tracks of the outback, looking like a couple of crazed madmen on the road to nowhere in particular. I guess we made a strange sight to those we passed along the way. As we sped through small towns, (well, I say, 'sped,' but that's not entirely possible on 50cc bikes. Perhaps 'trundled along on our chicken chasers,' is a little more accurate and closer to the mark) old men smoking long pipes on their verandas, would raise an eyebrow in curiosity at our passing by, as the rain dripped in big old drops from the holey, dilapidated roofs around them. Plump grandmothers with hairy upper lips would wipe their hands in dirty, once white aprons, before smiling and waving from their kitchen windows, whilst small children garbed from head to toe in wet weather gear and galoshes, would take a rest from splashing in their puddles to race after us down the street.

Up front raced that crazy hip-cat M.J half-naked as always with his cowboy hat pulled down low, a pair of world war two pilots goggles he'd found in some old charity shop strapped tightly to his face, and a long woollen scarf flowing behind him dancing in the wind. For my own part, I was draped in a dark green, 1950's, waterproof trench coat that my grandfather had given me before I had set off travelling. (What a great man he is, as are all my elders. No man could ask for greater, or wiser guides than I have been lucky enough to have known, during this crazy journey we call life). My pack was tied to my back, covered in polythene bags to keep out the rain, and a pair of circular swimming goggles pulled tight over my eyes After much searching, it was the best thing I could find!

So, there we were, looking like a couple of alien outlaws, making slow but steady progress, until we hit lesser distinguished tracks.

Now the wheels on these things were no thicker than those of a baby's pram, so as you can imagine, keeping the thing upright in the muddy conditions was not an easy task. We took it in turns to slip and slide around corners, often ending up with the thing on its side and us pitched into some mud bank or roadside hedge.

Our final demise came at the point at which the road rounded a corner to run parallel with the irrigation trenches of an outback farmstead.

M.J was a little ahead and he disappeared from view around the blind bend in the road. As I sped on in his tracks, I realised far too late just how tight the corner was. In a futile struggle I wrenched at the handlebars to turn my machine in time, but the only thing I got in response was for the bike to slide out from underneath me as the grip went and the mud and slime took hold.

Trapped beneath the bike we flew across the open ground, both lying on our sides, slipping away towards the ten-foot drop of the trench wall. As we reached its edge I looked down and realised in a brief moment of panic just how far the drop was, 'oh shit!' And so as the bike pitched downwards I turned and caught hold of the banks' edge to save myself from falling with it.

I don't think I would have particularly hurt myself to be honest. I mean, being an irrigation ditch, it was merely full of mud and water, but I guess your instincts take over and you just grab for anything to stop yourself falling.

So, there I was, hanging from the side of the road, legs dangling over the edge of a ditch when I realised I wasn't alone. Looking down at my ragged and broken motorbike buried beyond repair at the bottom of the trench, I caught sight of its brother a little way off. As my eyes traced the contours of the ditch I caught sight of someone smiling away insanely at me. His instincts must have taken over at the height of the precipice just as mine had, for just off to my right, also hanging from the side of the road, legs dangling away stupidly, was M.J.

'Alright mate? How's life these days?' He casually asked as he hung there, joint drooping from bottom lip. (Just don't ask me how in hell he'd managed to spark up!)

'Oh you know how it is,' I laughed in response, 'same shit different day.'

So the bikes were a right off, and we'd found ourselves walking and hitching by the side of the road again. We'd been stood there with our thumbs out for about 3 hours, when the rain finally relented, and the sun decided to poke its sorry head out from behind the dark and desolate clouds at last. I was looking up, head tilting towards its warm embrace as the flowers do, when an orange VW campervan coughed and spluttered over the horizon.

M.J raced clear into the middle of the road and waved both hands, thumbs up, frantically above his head. The van swerved and screeched to a halt on the far side of the road. I couldn't see through the side window as it was blacked out by a huge Canadian Maple Leaf flag, but as the side door started to open I was pretty sure the angry inhabitants were about to burst out with fists flying in rage.

I was wrong.

As the door opened a cloud of cannabis smoke billowed out, and through it stepped a clean shaven giant of a man, dressed in just a pair of shorts and flip flops, holding a bong in hand.

'Need a ride?'

So this was how we met Benny Boy and Dan. Ben was the 6 foot 5 giant built like a brick shit house, and Dan was his Canadian cannabis smoking compadre behind the wheel.

I guess they were as different in looks as M.J and I. One, the huge American football playing jock, the other, a short bearded man with the craziest black curly Afro I'd ever seen. I swear this thing must have been a foot tall in itself, and the same in width! Despite their physical differences though, both shared the same kind of personality, as in they were both completely and utterly nuts!

I mean, at the first town we stopped at for munchies, Benny Boy walked into a very classy jewellery establishment and tried to sell them the miniscule amount of gold he'd found whilst sieving upstream. Suffice to say he was asked to leave.

Whereas Dan found a huge palm branch along the side of the street and was running up to tourists asking if they'd hire him to fan them. Trust me, after smoking copious amounts of cannabis in the back of the VW, I found this all to be particularly amusing!

I know you probably think they sound like complete jackasses, but actually they were both extremely intelligent guys. They weren't actually causing anyone any harm. They just like to mess with the, 'man,' as they liked to call society. (I can still hear their favourite whooping cry echoing down the years, 'Don't let the Man get you down!') They just liked to see the panic and horror on people's faces when they did something a bit different.

'Watch their faces,' Dan said when we were in the middle of a supermarket and he and Ben decided to sit down on the floor and instruct, 'the philosopher Nietzsche stated, "that which does not kill us, only makes us stronger." Discuss.'

People would stop and stare, whisper under their breaths, turn their noses up and just generally think, 'you can't act like that in public.'

The guys' response would simply be, 'why not?' Why do we instantly have to stop being ourselves once we step outside our front doors? If we laugh too loud why do people stare? I mean, fair enough if you do it in a cinema or something, that's just being pig ignorant and showing a complete lack of respect to those who are trying to enjoy the movie. Yet why do we all become these ashen-faced zombies that march around with stiff upper lips and stern looks plaguing our faces when we step out into the world? It seems we all become so frightened of what people might think, what they might say about us if we act slightly differently.

One of my favourite memories, is of us being sat there in the middle of the main street one day discussing life after death, as the world, society, and the 'Man,' rushed about us in a crazed panic to the dance of old man time.

As we sat there a Monk who had been handing out fliers, preaching the words of Sri Krsna, came and asked to join us. Sitting there, he explained that he believed that it was possible to transcend and travel to a planet where time barely exists. A mere moment on that planet would equate to centuries on our own mortal Earth.

Perhaps the most interesting concept I took on board as we sat there was the following. Basic science teaches us that energy cannot be destroyed; it merely changes state, 'potential,' to, 'kinetic,' and so forth. Thus, when we die the energy that makes up our souls must continue to exist, we must go somewhere, or become something else, for energy cannot be destroyed.

As we sat there discussing all this an aged professor with the stereotypical elbow patches sown onto his suede jacket (why do they insist on this?) from the local university, came and sat down next to the Monk and ourselves. He argued that there was no life after death, because life after death required a God. Whereas God was merely a concept we had created hundreds of years ago as a safety blanket. We had created Him (or Her) to merely make us feel a little less alone in the universe. We had created Him to make ourselves believe that we actually all mean something, that we're not merely another grain of sand on the beach of time, that we have some importance, some kind of significance, rather than recognize the fact that we simply, 'are,' and nothing more. God is simply a great illusion that Man had created to pull the wool over everyone's eyes, and fulfil that great longing need to feel connected with something, the need to feel that we all have a purpose. Therefore, there was no life after death.

A Priest had obviously been listening in on this little speech oblivious to us all. As he slowly walked over and pulled up a pew, so to speak, he smiled at the Professor and simply stated, 'it's alright to show your fear and doubt my son. I see that you do not believe in God, but it will be alright, for he shall always believe in you.'

So there we were, M.J, Dan, Ben and I, a Krsna Monk, Baptist Priest, and University Lecturer, all sat cross legged upon the floor in the middle of the street, discussing life as the rest of the world bustled by.

Yep, I think I can safely say that although we didn't whole heartily agree with all the crazy things Benny Boy and Dan Gin-Beer did, M.J and I definitely liked them from the start.

As to how Dan became Dan Gin-Beer? Well, that first night we'd met, we'd all checked into a three star hotel to celebrate our newfound friendship. Trust me, after weeks travelling on the road this place felt like a five star paradise to me. A power shower was like heaven! There was even an ironing board provided in the room if my travel iron needed it!

So it was, in these infamous lodgings, that Dan and I discovered the genius that is Gin-Beer.

Basically the fridge contained multiple bottles of gin, and the lads always carried vast amounts of beer in their Campervan. So we decided to mix half a pint of gin together with half a pint of beer, thus creating Gin-Beer. (Clever title eh?! Some bright spark must have used their brain when they came up with that name! However did I manage it?!) Within minutes you could feel it sneaking up behind your eyes, and in a very, very short period of time, you discover you're pissed as a fart.

We even came up with a slogan for our drink. 'If you can't remember it, it didn't happen. Gin-Beer, it fucks you up!'

Eventually we'd found ourselves in the sauna on site drinking late at night. Ben pointed out that if you dripped a wet cloth over the thermometer then it can't really register just how hot the room is, so everything becomes a little crazy as the sauna pumps out more heat to compensate! Crazy, because the heat draws the water out from you in sweat, so the alcohol can hit you even harder.

I can't really remember where we met them, but we all ended up back at our room with two girls now accompanying us.

Dan was vomiting in the toilet and I went to check on him only to lose my balance as I leant up against the wall, and slipped into the empty bath. One of the girls and M.J appeared and decided to hose me down in the bath with the shower. Soaked to the bone I just decided to strip off all my clothes and wander around stark bollock naked in front of our newfound friends. I don't think the girls were particularly impressed to be honest, but in my defence, I was wet and naked, and it was a particularly cold night!

Although perhaps it was actually the point where I couldn't find an ashtray, and decided to put my cigarettes out on my chest, that they were particularly appalled at! Can't blame them really! Although to be fair I barely remember it, and if, 'you can't remember it, it didn't happen!'

My last real memory is when I tripped over for the umpteenth time and fell arse first onto a wine glass, shattering it. Somehow we'd left the door open in all the commotion and into this weird scene the manager walked in to complain about the noise. The sight of me laid out naked on the floor confronted him. I was bleeding from the gash in my bum cheek caused by the broken glass, and I was gibbering like an idiot. He was trying to talk to me but all I seemed able to manage was, 'shmmmmmiglh, a summa ma.' It seemed I'd created my own language! Though he didn't deem it as impressive as I did for some strange reason.

Suffice to say, we were all kicked out of the hotel that night. Can't think why?

I LIKE ANTS. THEY'RE COOL. AND AIR GUITAR. I RULE

SO IT was early morning in Hervey Bay and Dan, Ben, M.J and I were off to Fraser Island.

Fraser Island is the largest natural sand island in the world so they tell me, with its grains so pure that NASA refuse to make their windows with sand from anywhere else. All very interesting to know I hear you cry, but why were we off there?

Well, truth be told, we heard tell that they have some of the wildest parties around out there!

It seemed that since Beth split up with me, I was rather hitting the self-destruct button on regular occasions. The Gin-Beer incident being a prime example! I don't know. I just felt at that period of my life (M.J would tell me it's nothing more than one of the many stages of the healing process when trying to get over losing someone you love) all I wanted was, 'a little time out of my mind,' as Bob Dylan would say.

(You know, lyrically the guy's a genius. He always struck me as a poet rather than a singer. Did you know his real name is Robert Zimmerman? Apparently he was a huge fan of the poetry of Dylan Thomas, so that's where the Dylan came from.

Now his son on the other hand, Jacob, well, it must be hard living under the shadows of someone so famous, but he actually has a kick arse voice I think. Seriously, his band, the 'Wallflowers,' really is sweet dude.

Hmm, for all you out there who don't really use the phrase, 'Wallflower,' it's basically the people who stand alone at the side of the room at a school disco. They just stand there, waiting for someone to ask them to dance, but no one ever does, so they just lean against the wall, growing roots as they watch all the others dance around them.

I guess they don't realise that all flowers are beautiful in their own right. They forget that beauty is in the eye of the beholder. Everything in this world is unique, and they forget that nothing that is unique can ever be ugly.

Hell, I remember my first school disco. The bloody teachers made us have one. We were only 12 at the time and it basically consisted of all the guys standing against the wall on one side of the room, whilst all the girls stood on the other side!

I was leaning there laughing with my friends, pretending to be all laid back and cool, but you could tell we were all secretly thinking the same thing, 'please, someone ask us to dance.' See we were all too chicken shit to actually go and ask anyone.

Personally I had fancied this girl called Ruth for the last four years of school. Basically since I'd met her. She was the only girl who I was actually friends with, and we'd hang out, chat and laugh forever, and she was heaven. Unfortunately she was far too divine to ever think I could be her boyfriend. Or so I decided. You see, can you believe that in those four years before she disappeared off to private school, I never ever told her I liked her!

So, I just stood there, trying to catch her eye and will her to come and ask me, but she never did. My friends and I just stood there like wallflowers, pretending we didn't care, watching the popular confident boys go and dance with the girls, whilst secretly wishing we could all go and ask our prospective Ruth's' to dance with us. Ah, the beautiful fear that is rejection, how it turns the best of us into wilting shadows!)

Anyho, think I got completely sidetracked there, ummm, Wallflowers, Bob Dylan, ah that was it, 'time out of my mind.'

I guess for the time being, I was drinking copious amounts of alcohol, putting cigarettes out on my chest, spending most of my waking hours completely stoned, and all in all just pressing self-destruct somewhat. I basically figured I'd either wake up on the other side of it all lying dying in a ditch, or with my soul returned in full from its holiday.

For now, part of my soul was still officially on vacation whilst I struggled to overcome the last of the fever that was heartbreak. I had waved it off at the station with bags packed, a straw hat to stave off the sun, and a pocketful of condoms, whilst I got on with the task of destroying my body through alcohol and drugs. You see, after heartache, you basically return from the worst of it after a few weeks, but it takes months before most of the parts slot back into place properly.

Anyway, that morning we set off for Fraser Island. We'd booked it through some tour company and so we turned up at 9 am to get our briefing. As we sat there stoned out of our little tree, with the worst case of pink eye ever, ('a wake and bake,' as the boys called it. Roll out of bed and skin up straight away, such a tough life!) we tried desperately to assimilate all the information being discussed.

Personally I found processing it all a bit too much at that present point in time, and opted instead for jigging about in my seat, playing the drums on my thighs in tune to the radio playing in my head, and humming along under my breath. I think it was, 'Sweet Home Alabama,' by Lynyrd Skynyrd. Yeah, that's right, because I was just kicking into the air guitar solo when I became aware that a short Japanese man was standing in front of me smiling away politely.

I quickly put my leg back down on the floor, suddenly aware that it wasn't actually my guitar actually, and I wasn't playing a live gig in Pittsburgh, and I sat back very slowly, putting my hands in my lap. The Japanese man and I then proceeded to stare at each other, obviously waiting for some unknown signal, both with fixed smiles on our face.

After some considerable amount of time had passed by in this little venture, I broke eye contact at last to see the guys all sat around me in the same enterprise. All with crazy glazed eyes on the Japanese man, and forced smiles on their lips.

I gently leant over to my right and out of the corner of my mouth whispered to M.J, 'what do you think he wants?'

Without removing eye contact from the man, he leant back and whispered, 'no idea mate.'

I then became aware that Dan was trying to get my attention. So very slowly, still without taking my eyes off the Japanese dude; I leant back over to my left to hear what Dan wanted to say.

'Bro, there was this food on the floor, and this cool line of ants started taking it away. So Ben and I did an experiment by dropping parts of sandwich on the floor and recording the ants' response time to gather it. Ants are wicked mate. Did you know that they can carry like, fourteen times there own body weight? Or is it forty, or maybe fifty, or is it seven? Anyway, they're well bloody strong! They seem to prefer the pickle to the salami, which is weird, cause I thought it would be the other way round. Though I told Ben they'd like my doughnut most, cause it has got the most amount of sugar in see. I said to him, 'like dude, you're talking crazy, it's bound to be the doughnut they like most man, cause its got the most amount of sugar in.....'

'Did you actually have a point you big fat stoner,' I cut him off with.

'Oh yeah, sorry. Right, so we completely forgot to listen to what's going on, and when I'm following the path of ants carrying the cheddar cheese, this Japanese guy's big old feet go and bloody well stand on the poor little buggers! Now he's just stood there smiling at us, so what's going on? What do you think he wants?'

'Sorry mate, no idea' I replied honestly. I was Lynyrd Skynyrd playing live to 100,000 people in Pittsburgh before he turned up!'

'That's cool. I once dreamt I was playing a gig in my dining room in front of Hitler, James Dean, Princess Di and the entire cast of Phantom of the Opera. That guys mask is scary as hell man I can tell you. Anyway, then I turned into a snake, and a mongoose leapt out from the concert piano to get me, but luckily a large bald headed eagle swooped down and picked me up in its talons...'

Luckily at this point one of the ladies from the tour booking company wandered over, saving me from this rather surreal situation with some answers.

'Right then, now you've had a little time to get acquainted, here's your itinerary, and the keys to your 4x4.'

Due to the fact that Fraser Island is merely made of sand, it's impossible to get around without the use of a 4x4 jeep. The tour company kitted us out with the jeep, tent, cooking appliances and a map. What we hadn't realised, was that they require a minimum of five people per vehicle, and so this is where the Japanese guy fitted in. He was teamed up with us to make up the numbers.

Unfortunately he didn't speak a word of English, and we, not a word of Japanese. We tried to do the whole name thing, but even this proved beyond our grasp. So, in the end he became known as, 'Chief,' 'Japan,' 'Matt,' and, 'Headbanger,' after he gave us a heavy metal CD to play as we drove, and preceded to rock out like a crazed man.

For my part, it looked like fun in my stoned state of mind, so I rocked out with him, which seemed to cause him much amusement!

The only problem with the guy was that apart from his head banging antics, he was so bloody quiet. We almost left the poor bloke behind on numerous occasions! Oooppppsss! In our defence though, we were all so bloody baked we couldn't even remember ourselves half the time!

We eventually reached the ferry jetty after numerous wrong turns just after mid-day. We were actually feeling rather pleased with ourselves actually. You see, we'd managed to stop at the supermarket to stock up with food for the trip, fill the car with gas, and eventually get to where we were meant to be, all without crashing once!

Well, I did somehow manage to run a red light, but driving has never particularly been my forte. I mean, I managed to fail my driving test twice and that was when I was sober! The first one was for speeding, oooppss, and the second, well, I inadvertently kind of knocked off a parked cars wing mirror (stop laughing!). I thought there was enough room to get through the gap, but apparently not. The examiner had realised far too late what I was about to attempt to do, and had dived for his dual control brakes. Unfortunately he missed and almost head butted the windscreen.

It was one of my more memorable moments to date having to park up in my driving exam, and stick the damaged car's wing mirror back into place. I can't believe the cheeky fuck failed me! I mean, it's not as if I hit a person right?!

Driving around the island was a huge laugh. The tracks were just sand dunes, and some of them were stupidly bumpy. By bumpy by the way, I mean you drive fully down into a crevasse and then stick the thing in first and hill climb mode, pray the thing doesn't stall, and attempt to climb up the other side of the hill without becoming stuck.

Oh, the drop offs to the side of the so-called, 'roads,' were rather fun as well. Hit the accelerator too hard and you'd pitch up off the bumps, off the tiny thin track, and plummet into the woods situated about twenty feet below you!

Like I said, I loved it!

The best part is when you meet an oncoming vehicle, there's no room whatsoever to fit two jeeps abreast, so you end up having to do it all in reverse till you find a passing place!

So the five of us wound our way through the forest on sand tracks barely wider than the 4x4, aiming for our first destination, 'Lake McKenzie.'

It was here I confirmed the thought that this was one of the most beautiful islands I've ever been to in my life, and I've been to a few. The waters were literally a thousand shades of blues, greens and turquoises. The sun was hot, the water warm, and everything just made sense there.

We spent most of the afternoon just lazing around, feeling like kings, blissfully and euphorically oblivious to all problems in our lives and the surrounding world. We had officially stepped off the metaphorical map into uncharted waters, and no one could find us.

We smoked pipes on the beach, tried to make inroads into the huge amount of munchies we'd bought for the expedition, (I truly believe we thought we were feeding the five thousand!) napped in the glorious sunshine until we became too hot, and then wandered down to the waters edge to swim and float around without a care or thought in the world.

We were just at one with everything. The beauty of the time and place put everything into perspective, and we were simply free to let the peaceful tranquillity of our surroundings wash over our hearts and souls.

Later that afternoon we set off reluctantly for a short drive to Lake Wabby, only to happily find a place equal in beauty to Lake Mckenzie.

The foliage meant that we had to leave our vehicle at the top of the hill, forcing us to trek on foot down through the trees.

The group gradually became broken up, as we allowed ourselves to wander off into our own reveries. I was exploring a spider's web when I realised I wasn't alone.

This spider's web was absolutely enormous. It traversed the tops of the trees like a giant net waiting to catch the unsuspecting victim. The Golden Orb Weaver spider in the middle of it all (easily the size of my fist! They really are one big mofo! Australia doesn't seem to do things in halves. Everything is massive, including its creatures. I mean, you'll be walking past a high street shoe store, only to look in and find a centipede gazing into a mirror admiring himself in his scores of size 15 Dock Martin boots!

Oh, a word to the wise by the way. If you're in Australia, it's not always wise to wander off the beaten track to investigate its inhabitants. The Orb Weaver isn't a killer, sure it can give you a nasty bite, but Oz does officially have more creatures that can kill you within its borders, than any other country.

Although funnily enough, did you know it's actually the Daddy Long Legs, that silly looking flying thing that continually bumps head first into your windows until you let it out, that poor creature that all kids pull the legs off at an early age, that is one of the most potent killers around! It carries more poison in its blood than many of the other creepy crawlies, but luckily for us it has no way of penetrating the human skin!) had fixed me with its many beady eyes.

If I eventually grow the ability of reading minds, I'm pretty sure that great spider was thinking, 'yes, come up here my boy, come closer into my web, you'll fit well inside my belly,' when a voice behind me asked, 'what are you looking at?'

Turning around, I'm afraid to say that my jaw literally hit the ground. Oh dear, not cool at all.

This girl now stood before me was absolutely gorgeous! She had long dark hair falling over perfect features. A beauty spot was dotted just to the right of those thinned pursed lips. With olive skin and a body to absolutely die for, barely hidden away in a small pink bikini, my jaw remained on the floor!

Since Beth's letter I think I'd forgotten the fact that I am actually a man at the end of the day, and this girl brought that fact startlingly back into view. Perhaps illustrated best by my response.

'Fucking hell, you're stunning!' (Yeah nice one mate, well done, way to be cool!)

I went as pink in colour as her bikini, as did she, before I grabbed a spade and attempted to dig my way out of the situation.

'Oh crap. I kinda hope I didn't say that out load? You know one day I'll master the whole think before you speak concept. Bloody brain, always letting me down!'

Luckily for me she laughed out loud, and moving swiftly on in a futile attempt to pretend that nothing had happened, I pointed up towards the Weaver's web.

'Oh, the sun glistening on the spiders web up there caught my eye,' I said, pointing away towards the top of the tree line. ' I just stopped to take a closer look. It really is beautiful.'

She moved in closer and asked where I was looking. Apparently she suddenly saw it all, including the giant spider sat in the middle of its web, because she grabbed my arm and pushed her body slightly into mine in shock.

'That spider is huge! Is it dangerous?'

All of a sudden I became David Attenborough and launched into a small spiel about the wildlife and local flora and fauna of that island. Truth be told, I didn't have a fucking clue what I was talking about. I just didn't seem capable of shutting up though, a particular problem I have when I'm nervous.

Luckily for me she actually seemed relatively interested in what I was saying, a whole new concept to me! That or she wasn't actually pressing into my back in interest, rather that she'd realised the fact that if the spider was about to pounce and eat us alive, she could use me as a human shield!

We eventually moved on, and as we wandered lackadaisically down to Lake Wabby, we shared a conversation and a joint in the warm afternoon sun.

It turned out that she was from California, but was over here studying. I prayed that after my little lecture on wildlife, which mainly consisted of bullshit that she wasn't about to turn around and tell me that she was studying zoology or something similar, therefore knowing that I was completely full of crap! After my opening embarrassment that would have capped things off just nicely!

So it was that we ended up talking about everything, seemingly incapable of silence due to the cannabis, chatting on and on as we traversed fallen trees in our path. Pushing on through the undergrowth the trees eventually fell away and to our surprise, we suddenly found ourselves stood atop a vast and open sand dune.

At the bottom of the dune there lay a lake just as beautiful as Lake Mckenzie. The waters of Lake Wabby were so inviting I immediately ran forward and pitched into a roly-poly. Turning head over heals in circles down the steep slope, I kicked up sand in my wake, as the lady with the pink bikini stood atop the crest of the hill and just watched and laughed.

I eventually tumbled into its shallow waters as the sun began its final descent of the day, and swum around in those picturesque surroundings. The sheer pleasure of the place overloaded my heart, and I must confess as to being incapable of feeling anything bar happiness.

We spent the last of the daylight swimming around, play fighting with the others who had finally come to join us.

Once again the sunset stole my heart away as so often had happened during my travels. When I close my eyes, I can still see the glorious pink early evening sky and those amazingly azure waters even now. I can see me floating on my back, with a joint pressed between my lips, and the sound of laughter filling my ears.

Man, I wish I could show you my memories. I wish I could show you that time and place, instead of trying to explain it all. Alas, once again the sheer incapacity to explain a vision through the medium of words plays heavy on me, but such is life. I guess it's only in experiencing something that things finally make sense, and we can finally understand what someone was trying to tell us.

Before the light gave out completely, we had to leave that wonderful place behind. Trekking through the undergrowth attempting to find Lake Wabby had been a lot of fun, but no one, not even that crazy madman M.J fancied the challenge of trying to find our vehicle in the darkness of night.

Pink Bikini (for some reason neither of us had felt it necessary to reveal our names, strange thing I guess) and I continued to talk as we wound back up the trail and it turned out that she was sharing a jeep with 4 other girls. She invited us to join them for the evening at a campsite, (Fraser Island is a protected area of natural beauty, and camping is strictly prohibited bar in designated places) and in answer to this invitation, I for once kept my tongue in check and didn't whelp aloud, 'is the Pope a Catholic? ' Or as my friend Sam would say these days, 'Does a bear shit in the woods?!' Settling instead for a simple, 'yeah, that sounds good.'

As you can imagine, the other three single guys who shared my vehicle (well, 'Headbanger' may have been single as well, but I'd been unable to even find out his name before, so bailed completely on the task of trying to determine his sexual status, or even sexual preference for that matter!) seemed more than happy at the prospect of sharing the night with a number of young ladies.

It somehow got decided that the girls would follow us as we set off to find a spot to set up camp for the night. It was about this point in the proceedings that things went down hill drastically.

You see, this whole decision was based around Benny Boy insisting that despite being rather stoned and drunk, he was still the, 'greatest map reader' in the northern hemisphere. I blame myself for not noticing that a) we weren't actually in the northern hemisphere and b) that he was actually holding the map the wrong way up.

So it was that we set off on our rather doomed voyage, with Dan struggling to peer through his cannabis smoke filled cock-pit at the road ahead, and Ben sat beside him believing he knew exactly where he was directing us, despite his upside-down road map.

It wasn't far into our journey that we became aware that the girls 4x4 a little way off behind us, had come to a standstill. They had come to a halt, and were flashing their lights like crazy to try and get our attention.

'Better stop,' M.J shouted from the back, 'may have broken down.'

'Na mate, see they're turning round,' Ben called back.

Now I'm yet to determine who spoke the next lines, but when I do, skulls shall be cracked. Later when I confronted them, Dan insists it was Ben, and Ben insists it was, 'Headbanger,' I am still yet to be convinced, but never the less, those words definitely reached my ears.

'They're going the wrong way man, come on, we haven't got time to mess around, they'll catch up.'

Surprisingly enough they never did catch up, and I never did see Pink Bikini again. I was set for a heavily drunken night of partying with beautiful women, but the night I had in comparison, was far more amazing. Oh yes indeed, I landed on my feet for once. I traded in my night of sex, drugs and rock and roll, for a lovely evening driving around the island with 4 men.

Wow, how lucky am I?

Yes, that's right, the girls had cleverly spotted that we were going in completely the wrong direction, and had turned around trying to signal for us to follow. But no, we drove on, thanks to some numbnuts. Yep, we drove on, for an hour and a half to be exact, before through the darkness we spotted a rotten signpost through the mist of the headlights.

'CAMPSITE – 2 HOURS DRIVE.'

And what direction do you think it was pointing? Yes that's right, exactly back down the route we had come. 'Oh balls.'

So it was that we spent our first crazy night of partying on Fraser Island, hungry and alone. By the time we'd eventually found a campsite, it had become completely pitch black and there was not another soul in sight. It had been enough of a struggle to pitch the tent under the fading beam of Dan's torchlight, that the notion of cooking was completely abandoned. We all hit the sack, cold, hungry and grumpy, and as I eventually passed away into the land of slumber, M.J swore he heard me mutter, 'Pink Bikini.'

DAY TRIPPIN'

WAKING late the next day, my mood was not lifted. It was completely pissing down outside my tent and all I felt like doing was rolling over and going back to sleep.

Alas, my rumbling stomach finally got me up and moving. Well, that along with M.J mentioning the fact that we may run into Pink Bikini again.

We didn't.

In fact, we failed to see another living soul all day! Seeing the weather closing in, all the sane people had decided to head home. Not surprisingly this did not include us. Nope, not us, we were busy putting our heads together to make 2 + 2 = 73 gigilion as always.

Somewhere along the line it got decided that the blatant party place on the island to be, would be somewhere called, 'Indian Point.' After spending four hours driving down the beach, racing the surf, we discovered Indian Point to be deserted. Doing some quick math to see if we could get back to the ferry and thus civilisation, before sunset we faced our fate and set up camp on the beach.

The only good thing was that the rain finally relented in the early evening, and the sky cleared beautifully, all in an instant. It could be like that over here. Though in essence it did little to relinquish our misery, and so we decided to make the best of a bad situation and drink as much alcohol as humanly possible. Always a wise plan I feel.

Unfortunately, our supplies ran out just after sunset, (I bloody said we should have bought the whole lot down from the jeep!) and it was quite a trek back up to the vehicle. No one could be particularly arsed to attempt the walk back, and the truth be told, no one was in any particularly fit state of mind to attempt it either!

Our mood once again plummeted. Not only were we out of alcohol, but the weed was all gone as well! Oh horror of horrors! So we were sat in the middle of nowhere, a little drunk and stoned, with absolutely nothing to do. Someone suggested we turn in for the night, but it was even too early for that!

'Well, I have got these,' M.J eventually piped up hesitantly at the point when we'd all lost the very will to live.

As we all huddled around to look, M.J pulled a small metal tin from his bag. Carefully removing the lid, we all struggled to make out exactly what its contents were.

'Mexican Magic Mushrooms,' he explained, 'the offer is there if you want some. Though it's up to each individual to make up his own mind.'

No one bar M.J had done anything bar Cannabis before. I knew it wasn't particularly dangerous, not even slightly in the same league as the big chemicals like Ecstasy, Cocaine and Heroin, just another Natural like Cannabis, but at the end of the day I was well aware that it was going to do some pretty weird things to me. I mean, the way it works is because it is a plant that poisons you on ingestion!

The overlying point though, was the fact that I still hadn't finished my self-destructive phase created from my breaking up with Beth yet.

'Count me in.'

Taking the handful of dried mushrooms from M.J's hand, I went to throw them all into my mouth at once.

However, gently laying a hand on my shoulder he explained, 'take a third every hour. Respect the drug man, and it will respect you, everything in moderation. Have fun with it, and if you feel you need more take the next third and so on.'

Following his advice, I carefully and methodically, with perhaps a hint of apprehension at the unknown, split the pile into three. Placing the first lot onto the back of my tongue, not particularly interested in finding out how they tasted, (I never even liked the regular mushrooms you take with your bacon and egg fry up, and these most definitely did not fit the bill of regular mushrooms) I swallowed the lot in one gulp. Before the stuff had a chance to stick in my throat, making me gag, I threw a little cold water down the hatch as well, washing away the brief earthy flavour that had settled in my mouth.

Everyone in the group followed my lead, including to my slight consternation, 'Headbanger.' M.J had only given him a little, so he wouldn't feel too left out, (and in the most extravagant game of charades you will ever see in which we tried to explain just what the Mushrooms were, what they did, and would he fancy some? He had nodded along enthusiastically in acceptance and eventually reached out for a portion!) but I really couldn't help but wonder if this little fellow from Japan, who couldn't speak a word of English, really knew what he was getting himself into.

We all lay back, and gazing at the fire, waited to see what would happen.

We were all sharing anxious conversation at first, but as time elapsed, the group gradually became silent, allowing the psychedelic trance music (rather fittingly, M.J had put his 'Infected Mushroom,' CD on) to fill the void and carry us away.

I became aware that my feet were twitching convulsively to the fast step beat of the drum and bass, my heart seemed to have quickened in pace, and I noticed the lights in my peripheral vision had slowly begun to dance along with the beat of my heart and the music.

As I concentrated my gaze on the fire, I experimented with the focus of my eyes. Crossing them ever so slightly, intentionally allowing everything to move in and out of focus, I discovered a brand new spectrum of colours that I never even knew existed. I was suddenly aware that I was looking through a kaleidoscope it seemed. The crimsons and tangerines of the warm rainbow of the fire danced in the middle of my eyesight, surrounded by ultramarine blues and lilacs, before disappearing at the edge of my now tunnel-vision, into the purples and blacks of the night. The colours all formed similar patterns and shapes to the snowflakes I used to cut out from paper at primary school. They circled, spinning clockwise, then anti-clockwise, pulsing in size, shape and movement to the soundtrack filtering in through my ears.

As I gazed on, I felt almost as if I had stepped through the peephole of the kaleidoscope, into the mechanism itself, and there my silhouette spun back and forth in front of the lights, as some greater being rotated the cylinder back and forth.

I can't remember thinking anything, processing any thought patterns. For the time being the analytical and logical side of my mind seemed to have temporarily disengaged. I just explored the vision, the rainbow that danced before me.

During my travels I once met a Dutch guy called Merlin. We'd shared a late night joint together on a hammock by the river's edge. He'd told me about his drug experiences, and one in particular seemed to catch my attention.

Don't quote me on this, but I think the drug was called DNT. Merlin told me that the only time our body releases X amount of chemicals (I forget the exact amount to be honest) into our bloodstream, is when we're born, and when we die. DNT however, could trick the body into releasing the same amount of chemicals separately. It was basically a way of experiencing death.

During his experience of 'death,' he'd found it strange that when his mind left his mortal vessel, it was not the mind that he had floated away with, rather that he'd remained within his actual body. He told me that all of a sudden, he thought he was in a clearing in a forest. A deer burst from the bushes to his right and sprung away into the sunlit glen beyond, and he'd wept tears of pure joy at the beauty of the sight. Yet his tears of joy instantly turned into those of sorrow when he saw a butterfly lying dead on the crest of a sunflower.

You see, without a mind to process what he was seeing, he was incapable of registering and analysing what he perceived. He was merely capable of experiencing the emotion. What he saw was linked instantly to his heart, and I found myself remembering this story as I looked upon that fire, gazed up into the sky, or looked out to sea. I was seeing everything with fresh virginal eyes, as if I'd never really seen any of it before, and I realised just how beautiful this world we live in is.

As instantly as I'd explored this thought and memory, my mind had shot back inside itself. I flowed back into my past memories, and relived old conversations with M.J, and past events from university I'd never even realised I'd retained. Someone had grabbed the slide projector of memories in my head, and spun it round fast and hard, like a Wheel of Fortune.

Rather fittingly, the topic I seemed to be exploring now was, 'Drugs.' You see, I'd sworn to only ever try the Naturals when it came to drugs, on M.J's advise. He'd sampled a variety of different class A specimens, 'everything bar heroin,' he'd explained, 'even I won't go there, it's just a slippery slope my friend, a battle you'll never win,' and it was from this he'd drawn the conclusion to stick with the Naturals.

'The problem with your class A Chemicals,' he'd regularly preach to those who were tempted, 'is that you never quite know what you're getting, just how dirty and dangerous the things are. More to the point, I've pretty much sampled a little of everything, and you know what? None of them compare with the Naturals. You can take your Ecstasy and your Cocaine; I'd choose Magic Mushrooms every time. Stick with what grows out of the ground, the things that you can pick yourself. Far safer, and far more fun!'

So it was, I'd only ever smoke cannabis, or try a few mushrooms once in a blue moon, but that was it. I was just too scared of the other stuff.

M.J would tell me stories of how he'd seen people throw down Ecstasy tablets like they were candy sweets. Taking dozens in a night, often for a number of nights on the trot.

'The thing was,' he'd tell me, 'is that they'd become nothing more than mere shadows, ghosts of their former selves. When you're happy, your brain releases Serotonin. Ecstasy triggers a massive chemical burning of these happy fibres, but the problem with the drug, is that they never grow back. So the more you take Ecstasy, the less pleasure normal life holds for you. You literally become more and more physically incapable of experiencing pleasure, as your body wont create it. The other problem, is that it's too nice, too much pleasure at once. Suddenly nothing in the natural world seems to be able to give you the same rush you foolishly believe, so you take more and more, and just watch how pale a portrait of yourself you become. Take a look into those giant pupils of yours next time you're rushing, and you'll realise no one is at home anymore. I've lost track of the number of friends who have now become dependant on anti-depressants because of it all,' M.J explained.

'I for one, only tried them a couple of times, and trust me when I say; I wish I had never succumbed to temptation. I wish I'd never even taken just one. I used to believe only a fool can discuss something he's never experienced, but as I've grown older, you know what I've realised? Sometimes ignorance really is bliss. My life has forever become just a little tainted and duller ever since I tried hard drugs, and so I'll forever regret it. I wish I could go back to my naïve life before it, I could reach levels of happiness back then that I'll never reach again now. Stick with the naturals, with them you are free to explore your mind, rather than fuck it up.'

For some reason, although in reality M.J sat by the fire next to me, enjoying his own mushroom trip, it seemed to me that the memory was in fact reality. It was as real a hallucinogenic experience as I'd had, for all intents and purposes, I would have sworn we were actually sat on the bed of a youth hostel back in Nimbin discussing drugs.

Personally, perhaps the experience that scared me off hard drugs forever was in my time at uni. A guy I knew had taken a few pills and then double-dropped. I got on well with his girlfriend Sarah, and she'd asked me to keep an eye on him. By the time I'd cottoned on to what he was up to though, I'd realised he was missing.

Wandering outside the club, onto the metal gratings of the fire escape on the first floor, I'd discovered him with his arm around a metal pipe. He was mumbling to it, stroking it, and even kissing it much to my consternation.

Approaching him, I grabbed his shoulder, shaking him and shouting in his ear, 'MATE, ARE YOU OK?'

After what felt like forever, he eventually seemed to recognise me. 'What? Where's Sarah gone?' he asked.

'She's at home mate. Remember? She didn't come out with us,' I tried to explain.

'But she was here just this second ago, we was chatting about....well, I can't remember what about, but she was definitely here,' he tried to argue, now staring vacantly at the pipe he was still holding more than a little perplexed, with his head gently lolling from side to side.

'No mate, look, it's a pipe. You were talking to a pipe. Trust me, Sarah's at home.'

I remember thinking that I never ever wanted to voluntarily be in that state of mind. M.J told me that with the Naturals, if you didn't like the ride, you could get off at any time. You can force your true inner self to take control if you ever really need it to, but with the harder shit, you ride it till it bucks you, and trust me, it can buck you pretty far.

Two friends at uni were watching the sunrise, sat out on their terrace roof, after a night on Coke and E. One guy went for a piss, only to be interrupted by a knock at the front door. Upon opening it, a young scruffy looking kid out doing his early morning paper round, pointed to a bloodstained mess sprawled out on the concrete pavement by the side of the road. Our friend who'd been left behind on top of the veranda, had decided that he could fly, and fallen headfirst off the second storey of the building. He'd been hurt pretty badly. Actually scrub that, he was left a complete fucking mess.

No, M.J was right, with the Naturals you can release your mind to go walkabout for a short time, leaving the shackles of your physical form to explore whatever you want it to, but you could call your soul back at any time you wanted.

Just like that, that's what I did. I came back. I guess I kinda figured I'd check in on what the others were up to, after my little exploration into the colours of the spectrum, and the freaky pipe fetishes of my friends! It was all pretty damn funky actually.

The most relieving thing though to be honest, because I was a little scared at first, was that despite it all, I never felt the anxious underlying emotion that I wasn't in control. A little time out of my mind was one thing, kissing pipes in the false pretence that it was my girlfriend was a whole different kettle of fish, and not one I was particularly interested in experiencing.

As I gazed around the glowing form of the campfire, our own little miniature Ra the sun god, I took in the image of my friends.

To my right, half naked as ever, lay M.J. He just lay there sprawled out, propped up on his elbows, with his eyes closed, and a few beads of sweat glistening on his brow, obviously off in his own trip.

Then there came Dan, a picture of serenity in death if ever I've seen one. There on his back, lying just outside the light with his face in the shadows, he didn't move. As I sat there cross-legged, I realised I'd have to adjust my body position to see if Dan was still breathing. As I willed my body to lean backwards, to peer around M.J and look into the shadows to see if Dan was in fact dead or not, I discovered the new toy of the Mushrooms.

It was not only vision and colour it could play with, but movement as well. As I went to lean backwards, I realised everything had slowed down. I was a swimmer moving through water. For the first time ever I was aware on a mental level of every tweak and contraction of every muscle and fibre in my body, as it adjusted to my willed command to move. It was weird, but kinda cool.

In the shadows, I became aware of two brilliant white globes staring out into the heavens. Dan was cast in darkness, just a silhouette in the night, but I could see that he had his eyes wide open, and that his chest was moving. In that hazy dreamlike state of mind, where the boundaries of reality seemed no longer fixed, rather that they flowed and danced in waves with the music, his eyes seemed like giant saucers, as they remained fixed on the starry sky above. He barely blinked at all. I wondered where he was? The possibilities seemed endless.

Then there was 'Chief,' 'Headbanger,' 'Japan,' whoever he was I liked him. It can't be easy being in the middle of nowhere with the likes of us, especially what with not knowing any of our language. He seemed happy enough though, obviously having discovered the beautiful combination of movement and vision and how it had changed all of a sudden. For he sat there experimenting with both, staring at his outstretched hand, allowing it to dance and writhe to the beat of the drums. He moved it slowly and always intentionally back and forth, side to side, placing it first in front of the light, then into the dark, seeing it stamped upon a backdrop of blackness, all the while smiling.

Only Benny Boy seemed out of sorts. I realised he was staring at me, having been trying to catch someone's eye, to gain their attention. He was blatantly uncomfortable with something, that full 6 foot 5 giant frame of his was rocking back and forth furiously. On recognising that somebody else was back with reality, he appeared genuinely relieved.

'Man, I really need to do something, I've got too much energy, I need to do something. D'you wanna do something? Go for a walk maybe, or I don't know. There's beer in the car, we could go and fetch some.'

'Just chill out and relax mate,' I tried, surprised at how my voice sounded as it echoed through my head.

I wonder what I sound like to everybody else? Is my voice really so different from that which I hear? Or is it just the drugs playing yet another new game? Still, there was no time to explore that thought right then.

The last thing I wanted to do was go for a walk to be honest. I was enjoying just taking the trip easy, just smooth, calm, chilled out. Dealing with someone being hyperactive was not something I really felt I could deal with at the time. I didn't want the prospect of a bad trip hitting me, flipping me out. This was all new to me, and I'd found something comfortable to sit back and enjoy, without anxiety, happily in control. The last thing I wanted was to bring extra-unknown eventualities into the equation.

It seemed that as we remained in our group, some strange kind of barrier had been forged invisibly around us. We were protected around that fire, seemingly safe somehow, I can't really explain it, but to break the connection seemed in some strange way perilous to me.

Still the pain and anguish in Ben's face as he heard my response was heart wrenching, as was his reaction. Looking desperately around the group, he asked a little louder, but with a slightly shaking fear and uncertainty, 'does anyone want to come for a walk with me? Please.'

There was no response from the others. Dan just lay there, continuing to stare upwards into oblivion, on his rocket ship flying through the stars. M.J kept his eyes closed, and that funky little Japanese guy, just continued to get his groove on, dancing along in his own little world.

I don't know whether they heard, but I could just tell they all felt the same as me. I don't know how or why exactly, but have you ever noticed that bizarre but brilliant characteristic of human nature? The way we seem able to tap into each other's emotions, without having to say or do anything. How often is it, when you spend a certain amount of time with someone, that you can just tell that something is wrong? So it was, that I knew no one really wanted to deal with this, they wanted to chill out and just sit safely around that fire.

Thus, Benny Boy's plea was met with silence. I caught his eye one last time, as the fire flickered on, crackling, and the waves washed in, breaking onto the shore, all under the gaze of Mistress Moon, who seemed in that moment to have somehow fattened and fallen in closer to watch us. Catching his eye across the fire, as he rocked back and forth, I could have sworn I saw a single tear steal free, sparkling like a diamond as it fell to the sand.

'Sounds like a plan mate. I could murder a cold beer.' I suddenly heard myself saying.

Far more to my surprise, was that I now found myself stood upon my feet. How did that happen?

Ben was up like a shot, dancing now on the outskirts of the fire, moving crazily to the music, singing some ditty about cold beer, and how 'yummy it was gonna taste in his tummy.' I was glad to note him break loose from his potential bad trip. His mood seemingly having instantly changed at the prospect of doing something, rather than just sitting there exploring his mind alone.

As I gathered up my rucksack, I gave M.J a gentle kick in the side and told him we were off to get beer. His responding grunt and nod seemed enough confirmation that at least on some level he was aware we were off on a mission for a while, in case he suddenly came around and wondered just where the fuck we'd buggered off to.

Looking out into the darkness I could see Ben racing around on the beach, playing in between the dunes, then sprinting down to the sea's edge, only to throw on the brakes, come to a complete halt, wait until the last second before the water washed back in and touched his feet, then sprint off inland again.

(Standing there, I was reminded for some reason of my old Labrador, 'Wilson,' and how he'd race around like a headless chicken on the beach, chasing his own tail, or caught up in some other strange game he'd formulated himself. I was instantly aware again of the connection between all animals. We are ourselves direct descendants from apes. Some of us less descendant than others mind you! And despite all our creations, we are alas no more than subject to the whims of our animalistic needs at times.

I for one have always found drugs, well, alcohol in particular, particularly fascinating. Have you ever noticed that we are capable of so very much, the arts, mathematics, philosophy, we seem at times to have evolved so far from our past, but there is no denying in the end, just where our roots lie.

As I said, take alcohol for example. Give some guy enough pints and just watch how all traits of humanity are instantly stripped away. He becomes no more than his ultimate animalistic needs, to want to have sex, or prove his masculinity by beating off the other males in his presence, like some great Silverback Gorilla. An idea I more commonly refer to as the, 'Fuck or Fight,' theory.

Trust me, next time you're out pubbing and clubbing, just take a brief time out and sit back and watch those around you for a while, You can instantly see the men employed in their Fuck or Fight philosophy. They're either leaching onto some poor girl, or trying to gain control of the males surrounding them by throwing out challenges. Interesting isn't it? Though when you see it, try not to laugh out loud too much at its now blatant existence, else you might find you're the person the Silverback Gorilla wants to beat the crap out of!)

Anyway, I didn't want to risk Benny Boy sketching out again, so bending down, I rummaged though the contents of my small day rucksack (Hooray, not a travel iron in sight!) until I found my portable C.D player and speakers.

(Trust me, it's the most important thing a traveller will ever need. Well, apart from a spare roll of toilet paper. For all the brilliance music brings, it can never quite substitute the essential roll that toilet paper fulfils in those tricky sticky situations. Trust me, I know!

Anyway, personally I feel music really does make the world go around. It can fill every mood, picking you up when you're down, echo your sadness when all you want to do is cry, set you in the mood when you're getting dolled up for a night on the town, or just chilling you out after a long day's toil.

I even love the way it can even remind you of a certain person or place in time. They say your sense of smell is that most closely linked with memory.

Well, that may be true, but I love the way you can be standing in some random store in years to come, or be driving down the motorway with the sun shining, the windows down, and the radio blaring, when all of a sudden a song comes on, and you're instantly transported back in time, to the sandy shores of the Bahamas, or the arms of a lost lover. Wicked isn't it?

I even remember a particularly bizarre lecture I sat in on at uni. I swear the lecturer was constantly puffing away on the old marijuana. Well, he asked us how many of us instantly get home and as soon as we set foot through the door, enjoy nothing more than sticking the stereo on? A huge proportion of the students put their hands up, myself included. He went on to explain that this is because the place we live in is no more than a collection of 'things,' They all exist in their own individual right, but are forever separated from each other, by the space in-between. So they exist, stopping at the edge of their physical walls, as is exactly the same with ourselves. So, we're stood there, separate from our surroundings. However, put your music on, and suddenly the airwaves between us become an extension of ourselves. Thus, we are no longer separated from our 'things,' the music in the air between connects us to everything, we are all harmonised, and therefore, our house is instantly transformed into our home. Well, I thought it was an interesting concept anyway!)

I pulled out a CD with dance tracks on. Sticking it on, I put the player in the outer pocket of my bag, the speakers in the side holders, and threw it on my back. Instantly, 'Stereo Bag,' was created, and wherever Ben and I walked, our own soundtrack for the experience would follow us.

I even pulled out my ever-faithful Tin-Bear-Scaring-Whistle. Not because I was particularly concerned about the possible imminent attack of a pack of Ninja Karate Bears armed to the teeth with Shruiken Death Stars and Samurai swords, but because it gave Ben much entertainment to dance about around me, whistling away in time to the music.

As we set off along the beach, and the music briefly quietened, Ben pulled up alongside me.

'Thank you for coming along with me,' he said hesitantly.

'Ah. No worries mate.'

'No, seriously, I was wigging out big time back there. I just needed to get moving, but I didn't want to go on my own.'

'Seriously, it's not a problem. I didn't want to get moving at first, but I'm quite enjoying it now,' I said honestly.

Wandering along that beach late at night, with the sands illuminated by the moonshine, I was feeling rather peaceful. It was weird but I kind of felt like I was standing on a conveyer belt, oblivious to the movement of my legs walking, I felt like I was just floating blissfully along. The intense hit of the first batch of Mushrooms seemed to be over, and now everything just seemed to have some strangely mystical feel and haze around it. Everything felt like it had been lovingly wrapped up in cotton wool, and it just felt nice to be alive and wandering along the waters edge.

Although the crazy range of colours had disappeared with my eyesight remaining in focus, every colour I could perceive now seemed to burn as brightly as I'd ever seen it before. I also noticed things for the first time. Our progress was particularly slow. I kept on stopping to pick up shells. I just felt that I'd never really studied them before. Not properly. I saw just how beautiful everything in nature really is. I saw every pattern on every shell, and the million different subtle shades of colour they held seemed for once to stand out startlingly.

'Can I tell you something?' Ben asked a little sheepishly. Before I answered he went on, 'you see, I figure I'm like twice the size of everyone else, so I decided to eat all three portions of Mushrooms in one go, so I'd be in the same place as everyone else.'

(Well I guess that explained why he'd been hit with the unsettling need to do something, that his brain was on overload, whereas we'd just been sat there quietly.)

'Have you done the rest of yours yet? Go on, take the next lot, it'll be cool,' he advised.

I stopped and thought about it for a while, before I slowly answered, 'you know what, I don't think I will. I feel pretty cool already.'

The original hit of the experience had been interesting, but all a little too intense I decided in hindsight. I liked what was going on then, on the back end of the trip. Everything just seemed far more beautiful and quiet, slow and peaceful.

So we wandered on. Benny Boy still full of energy, prancing around all over the place, and I trudging along in my blissfully euphoric little state.

We finally reached the point where the path cut up briefly through the trees to the jeep. Pulling out the flashlight the nearest tree immediately caught my attention. Moving up for closer inspection I slowly ran my hand over its bark. It was so intricate, so full of shape and colour, so intriguing. Spirals of patterns wound their way up its trunk everywhere I looked, and the trails of some small snail glistened away before me. I think I finally realised where the term, 'tree hugging hippie,' had originated!

As we pushed on, the branches overhead blocked out the moonlight, pitching us into complete darkness bar the faint beam of the torch in my hand. Despite Ben's giant frame he deemed it best to allow me to carry the flashlight and lead the way. (Cheers mate, how very brave of you!)

So it was that we pushed our way along the track, winding slowly uphill towards the road above. I probably should have been a little scared, but everything was still wrapped in that warm safe cotton wool kinda mood. Plus I decided that Ben seemed to have the whole fear thing covered for the both of us, judging by the way he basically walked on the rear of my heels, continually holding onto the back of my sleeve. Well, it was good to know now at least that my acquaintance was nothing more than a big girls' blouse, more prone to sit down and blubber for his mummy, whilst sucking his thumb and holding his security blanket, than stand up and fight any Ninja Bears or the like!

I think my favourite part of the journey was when the batteries briefly died on the torch. As I stood there doing the whole, 'if something electrical doesn't work just smack it hard enough and it'll fix itself,' technique, I could feel Ben standing directly behind me.

As the beam flashed into life, Ben screamed, 'what's that?' And all 6 foot 5 of the fat bastard jumped onto my back, hugging his arms round my neck, trying to strangle the life out of me it seemed.

Struggling to breathe with his big old hairy arms wrapped round my windpipe, let alone talk, I managed to force out, 'it's ...just...a... tree.'

Finally releasing me, and stepping back down to earth, he just said, 'oh, sorry. I thought it was a person.'

Ah, what a truly brave soul he was!

The return from the jeep passed without event, and we eventually reached the others with fresh cold beer. Everyone was finishing off their mushroom trip, so we all settled for just sitting round, chatting, and drinking beer until the sun came up. Just enjoying being wrapped up in the peaceful comfort of the cotton wool feeling the whole world had taken on.

PART FIVE

COURAGE IS ADMITTING YOU'RE SCARED, BUT SADDLING UP FOR THE RIDE ANYWAY

ASSESS. MANOEUVRE. ATTACK. SUMMARIZE. REPEAT. CHECKMATE

AS THE campervan pulled into a car lot in Cairns a couple of weeks later, M.J and I jumped out and said our goodbyes to Ben and Dan. They were already behind schedule and were shooting straight off up to Darwin. From there they planned to drive straight down through the heart of Australia, via Ayers Rock and its barren deserts, before eventually completing their loop back at Sydney at last.

I'd be lying if I said I hadn't been more than just a little tempted to join them, but M.J and I had plans of our own.

The goodbyes and hugs were long and genuine, but this is the traveller's life, a life of hello and goodbye, but at least we had had one hell of an adventure.

Shooting up the Eastern coast on a whistle stop tour, we'd shared a lot of laughs I'll never forget. In Airlee beach Dan had managed to fall overboard whilst pissed as we'd toured the Whitsunday islands on a three-day yacht cruise. The coast rescue helicopter crew were not amused.

In Bingarra we'd gone to the beach late at night to watch baby turtles hatching. They'd all laughed at me when in my particularly stoned state of mind I'd decided to dive into the sea in all my clothes, with the newborn turtles in tow.

You see, as they hatched, climbing out of their nest in the sand and making instinctively for the ocean, one of the group had become separated. All the damned tourists on the beach had almost crushed the poor little guy. So I'd taken it upon myself to follow him all the way down the beach to stop him being trampled on by the rabble.

Watching over him all the way, I'd felt we had connected in some strange way by the time we hit the waves. He was my little friend, and so when he washed out to sea, I dived in alongside him, just feeling like it was the right thing to do. Much to the amusement of everyone around may I add!

As we wandered around stoned in the zoo at Rockhampton, Dan had decided to prod the tail of a crocodile with a stick and almost lost his hand.

We'd also hooked up with a couple of girls and burst into hysterics when we reached the chimpanzee cage. You see, one of the cheeky little chimps was lying on his back over a rock, the most amazingly human eyes staring straight out at the girls, all the while masturbating. Us lads all found it thoroughly amusing, the ladies for some reason seemed far less amused.

Oh yeah, and whilst at Dingo cattle ranch we'd all found ourselves inadvertently line dancing with all the locals. They'd made us get up, and at first I was just messing around in my drunken stupor, then from nowhere, as if I were a man possessed, I was bewildered to find myself actually line dancing! I was doing all the proper moves and everything! All in my ever-trusty snakeskin cowboy boots. How bizarre!

It has to be noted though, that my self-destructive stage was still far from over. It took different forms from cigarette ashtrays on my chest and experimentations in mind exploring drugs, but the ghost of Beth and the scars I bore were still far from healed. I was still tearing myself apart at times.

I was soon forced on from Townsville after I became briefly addicted to gambling. I lost over two thousand dollars at the poker table in the casino there. I would've lost more if M.J hadn't caught me trampling in one particularly bad morning. I hadn't been home all night, and was coming home with an empty wallet, and a white strap on my wrist where my Rolex used to sit.

All I can say, is that whilst sat around that green table, cards in hand, nothing else existed. It was the perfect form of escapism. Whilst I played my life and the world around me finally filtered off into the background. There was nothing else to ponder or worry about except the cards in my opponents' hand. It was almost as if I'd placed myself in a vacuum, and the bliss of the ignorance of my life, was a welcome, but very expensive respite.

Oh, I guess I should also mention the fact that I spent a few nights in Airlee Beach jumping from bed to bed. I think my reasoning behind it all was that I could fuck away my memories of Beth.

There were numerous girls. Two sisters in one night (though not together unfortunately!) was particularly interesting, as was pulling the stripper we'd booked for Benny Boy's birthday bash.

Perhaps the most eyebrow raising of them all was when I managed to screw a 33-year-old girl who'd been a lesbian for 15 years. Although I know this classifies as impressive man points from the guys, all it actually led to in reality was a large amount of shame on my part, and a visit to the local STD clinic to have a needle shoved down the part of my penis that things are only really supposed to come out of. Luckily the results were clear, which was quite a relief and a surprise to be honest.

Still, these were the darker parts of those days after Beth. Often I'd take two steps forward and one step back. Such is the nature of the beast. Such is that ability in life to reach inside ourselves after agony and press the self-destruct button.

Still, from darkness springs light, and from sorrow springs hope.

Yes, M.J and I had our own plans. I was expected back home to take up my job as a lawyer in just over a month's time, so we had planned to spend three weeks in Thailand, and the last two in New Zealand, and it was here in which my fresh hope blossomed.

Ever since Destiny and I had hugged each other goodbye back in those early days of travel on Bondi Beach, few days had ever gone by in which she and I hadn't conversed. In that short space of time we'd been together, we had connected in some weird and wonderful way and from friendship I felt something more had grown. We had spent hours since departing discussing everything in our lives via email. I had told her about all my travels and tears, about all my joyous crazy antics, and all my melancholic inner fears. In her I had found a true friend for life, and a particularly gorgeous friend at that!

Yes, as time had elapsed, I had found that I would approach the local Internet café with a slight tinge of apprehension. As I handed over a handful of dollars to the man behind the counter, and took up the seat at my appointed terminal, logging in, I would watch the green bars at the bottom of the screen take an age to load up my Internet account. The whole time I would wait with hopeful anticipation for my welcome screen to blink into view, and instantly I'd scan the page for Destiny's name. When I saw it there, I would be incapable of stifling a brief smile of joy to break from my lips.

On the few occasions in which it didn't appear, I must confess as to having felt a brief cut of disappointment slice across my heart. Not entirely sure what that was all about? I suspected I may have an idea, but wasn't quite willing to allow myself to explore that possible avenue of emotion yet.

Anyway, we seemed to have been lucky enough to have discovered in each other one of those few people you meet along the shores of life, who you can happily, readily, and with full faith, reveal your heart and innermost thoughts to.

As to the question of whether she was a potential, 'soul mate,' in the sense of, 'Beth,' or one of those, 'soul mates,' as M.J and the like, was yet to be seen. All I knew was that in my heart of hearts, somehow unexpectedly, hope had blossomed. All fuelled by the fact that Destiny had invited us to stay with her and Chloe for a while in New Zealand. So in three days time, M.J and I were due to catch a flight from Cairns to Bangkok, and then three weeks later, from Bangkok to Christchurch to see the girls once more.

For our last two days in Oz, M.J and I had decided to play a little game. Leaving each other to our own devices for an hour, we were to book up something to do in secret. Without breathing a word about our potential exploits, we'd wake and place ourselves into each other's hands, no questions asked, and just see where we ended up.

That evening we decided to just take things easy, and save our energy for our unknown adventures. On the back patio of our hostel, a man with a 2-foot tall black chef's hat emblazoned with the words, 'diner's do so at their own risk,' charred up a barbeque. For some reason M.J made us wait at the back of the queue. Apparently, 'patience is a virtue,' true indeed, although I can categorically say it's a virtue I most certainly don't have, and despite the words of prophetic warning displayed by the chef's hat, I was bloody starving! Alas, I relented to M.J's instructions, and waited. That which is waited for, often tastes all the sweeter, quite literally in this case.

As we finally handed over our plates to the cook and asked for, 'ten of everything,' I was ecstatic to see a 16 ounce T-bone steak, 3 sausages, 2 burgers and half a chargrilled chicken dumped unceremoniously on my plate. (Oh, as I mentioned before, Australia doesn't do things by halves. True that its spiders and creatures will scare the shit out of you at there sheer size, but if you do escape their mangy clutches, the celebratory dinner will consist of a whole cow on the barbeque just for you! I say celebratory, though forever in the back of my mind I always wondered if it was merely a case of the farmer feeding up his fattened cow for the feast. In other words, were we the tourists the actual feast? As we followed each other round like cattle and sheep. Were we the ones who in reality were being herded through gates and into pens by some cunning sheep dog for some reason beyond our grasp?)

I decided not to continue that train of thought, opting instead to stop at the, 'help yourself,' counter and pile buckets full of fresh salad onto my mountainous plate. I particularly enjoyed exploring the enterprising game of, 'how much can a plate hold before it physically breaks?'

Exactly why do they always give you such a peanut sized plate at a help yourself shindig? Knowing full well that everyone around you is gonna think you're a greedy pig if you pile anything more than a pickled egg on it. (Ha ha, I'll show them this time! I really had ceased to give a shit about what others thought of me. In this full plate of food, I was going to make up in one go for every bit of food I'd ever missed out on before that moment. Missed out on because I believed those around would judge me. They'd dub me as 'greedy' for putting that extra piece of chicken wing on my plate, or extra 21 pound lobster!)

Anyway, it was whilst wobbling around, attempting to balance my enormous plate load of tucker, that I realised M.J had stopped for conversation with the local culinary artiste.

Without even an introduction M.J launched straight into it, 'know where I can buy some weed mate?'

I waited for the man to yell, to order that we be thrown out of the hostel, (I'd already in an instant worked out an escape path through the picnic tables, kicking a hole through the rotten fence panel before vaulting over the barbed wire surrounding the premises so as to get my plate of food to safety) for the police to be called.

To my surprise the man simply answered, 'how much d'you want?'

'We've only got a few days here,' M.J explained, 'a quarter of an ounce will be plenty.'

Without another word said, the cook rummaged through his pockets and pulled out a plastic baggy originally used by banks to carry coins, now used to carry cannabis. M.J handed over some dollar bills along with his plate, and the chef handed over the cannabis along with some sausages and steak.

As we sat down having procured our, 'draw,' and dined upon a feast fit for a king, a chessboard took pride of place in the centre of the table. Fingering the pieces in hand, we decided to battle away. I thought it best not to mention the fact to M.J that during my time at uni we had whiled away many an hour at a friends house, drinking crates of beer, and playing chess. In all those years I'd only ever been defeated twice, and I wasn't about to change the habit of a lifetime.

Some people are blessed with looks, some with a talent for the ladies, I was given the role of 'village idiot,' but also a natural ability concerning chess. (Yippee for me. Trust me. The women don't really want a popular attractive guy they want a chess champion!)

I had taken great enjoyment in beating some smug Canadian bastard further down the coast though. He had beaten every challenger as I'd sat around watching the Aussie Rules Football match on TV. As it finished, he stood up and proclaimed to the whole room that he was the 'greatest man in existence, and how he doubted whether there was 'anyone out there man enough to take him on.'

Standing up, I said I'd give it a go, as though I'd never really played before. Where you are strong, always appear weak, for those who live a life of self-love, are always susceptible to defeat.

The guy was far better than I to be brutally honest, and I was forever on the ropes for the first half hour. Yet he became too cocky, too confident, he believed he had me in his hand, and knew my every move. Placing his queen in an advanced role, he never believed I'd take it, for I'd lose my queen in return.

So I took it. Sometimes we must sacrifice much to get where we want in this life. Sometimes we must leap into the unknown, despite our fear. For sometimes a leap of faith is the only thing left available to us.

I took his Queen, and lost my own. My greatest strength was gone, but sometimes, it is only once we have seemingly lost everything, that we finally manage to discover ourselves. What often defines us is our ability to find the good in every bad situation.

So it was that my opponent buckled. He had lost his main attribute, he had believed he could see and anticipate everything, he had realised that he had become blind in his arrogance, and so he was annihilated. Alas, I fear we are nothing more than kings or pawns upon this chessboard known as life.

Though for now, it was actually the queens that were causing M.J and I consternation in the game we played. I thought you could only ever have one queen on the board at once? So I allowed a second pawn to reach my boards edge believing it to make no difference, but M.J went to exchange it for another queen. I was not convinced. We decided the only true and fair way to continue was to go and smoke a joint somewhere.

The best place we decided was the local cinema. We watched a couple of instantly forgettable movies in a row. What was memorable though, was when we disappeared during the brief interval for a smoke. The only place available was an upper storey outdoors car park. The only problem was the fact that the car park was regularly patrolled by a couple of fluorescent-jacketed attendants. We'd eventually found ourselves lying underneath someone's vehicle in the deeper recesses of the car lot, hoping the owner wasn't about to come back and drive away, passing a speedily rolled joint between ourselves as we waited for the next movie to start.

BURST BLOOD VESSELS MAKE GOOD TOOLS
FOR SCARING YOUNG CHILDREN

WAKING the next morn, I gave M.J a shove and told him to hurry up and get ready. He inquired as to clothing and breakfast? To the former I signalled that tee shirt and shorts would more than suffice for the day's task, but breakfast was probably not the best idea. Raising an inquisitive eyebrow, he eventually shrugged his shoulders in quiet resignation and jumped down from his upper bunk.

Stood in the early morning heat out front of the hostel on the already sizzling tarmac, I was happy when an unmarked minibus pulled alongside the kerb. I didn't want some crappy distorted picture on the side of a run down old bus to give my game away.

A portly man struggled to remove his stomach from where it had momentarily become jammed under the steering wheel, eventually broke free and catapulted out the door to fall at our feet. As we helped him up, barely suppressing a chuckle (another wake and bake morning!), he eventually produced a clipboard with our names on as he dabbed at his sweating forehead with a handkerchief. Ushering us into the back of the bus we eventually found ourselves on our way.

I knew M.J must have been wondering just what in hell he had let himself in for? Times they were a changing and I had become somewhat of an unknown entity as of late. So the mystery was doused in intrigue, for I had been unaware myself just what I was doing until I'd put the phone down the previous day and it had sunk in.

Steering through melting suburbs we soon hit the outskirts of the city, and after a brief blast through thick undergrowth M.J was ultimately put out of his misery.

Just before we reached our destination, a bloodcurdling scream broke through the closed windows of our minibus and I fancied I even caught M.J stiffen in a brief moment of fear. As our fat friend behind the wheel dropped half his Subway sandwich down his pants, the bus momentarily veered off course as he took his hands off the wheel in a struggle to rescue his meatball filling that now rolled under the chair. Just in the nick of time he pulled us back onto the road, but was still unable to prevent the wing mirror from catching the metal signpost, which whirled round like a target on a 50-cent

116

fairground shooting gallery. With a high-pitched metallic 'ping,' it spun round seeming to emphasise the words engraved upon it, 'Cairns Bungee Jump.'

M.J turned around and eying me almost impressively, stated the obvious, 'so we're doing a bungee jump are we?'

'Nope. We're doing a days unlimited jumps,' I replied!

As we circumnavigated the lake beneath the bungee tower we stopped briefly at the railings to watch the troubled soul miles above pitch off into oblivion. With a chilling scream they fell towards the earth. For a moment we wondered if the rope would tense, but at the last moment the soul in question pinged back up into the air, retracing their flight path briefly, before just bouncing back and forth. As the cable was lowered from above, the boatman set off from his bank with a long fishhook pole in hand. Steering with craft below the dangling form, he held up the pole for what we now determined was a grinning girl to grab hold of, and pulled her into the safety of the dingy.

As we stood there preparing ourselves mentally, the next poor victim stepped up to the plate. This guy had opted for the full body harness off the tower roof option. We saw him stop and stare over the precipice. He seemed to take an age. Although we couldn't hear what was going on from so far away, obviously all was not well up there in the sky.

Eventually we saw him step back out of sight, obviously deciding to take a run at it. As he sped back into view the guy slammed the brakes on at the last second, blatantly having had second thoughts. He teetered on the brink, arms propelling like windmills in reverse, like some crazy cartoon character as they run off a cliff, trying to propel himself back to safety.

Hovering on the edge, we were astounded at how he seemed to be evading gravity itself as he leant forward off the thing. Gravity always wins though, and with an unceremonious 'plop,' he just fell like a big fat raindrop from the heavens above.

It would have all been rather amusing, if we weren't about to be attempting the same thing ourselves! To my endless enjoyment, I could actually see the slightest tint of fear in my dreadlocked companion. Surely this crazy hip-cat was incapable of such an emotion?

Just to be sure I mentioned, 'you know I heard a tale on the news not so long ago of someone dying doing this in Europe. Apparently you could decide to either do a 150-metre jump off one side of the bridge into the chasm below, or the 100-metre fall to the other side. Well, is seems like there was some sort of mix up. Someone accidentally attached the 150-metre rope to the 100-metre drop. Poor bastard. He waited for the rope to tighten, but it never did. Just ploughed straight into the ground below. Terrible thing really.'

Yep, M.J's face definitely turned a whiter shade of pale!

There seemed to be an uncountable number of metal steps leading up toward our goal, and for some strange reason, I found myself racing up them. I guess the adrenaline had already started to flow.

At the top was a small wooden bench upon which I was told to lie down. Two burly blond haired hippies strung my ankles together and before I knew it I was hopping towards the gangplank leading out from the bridge and into oblivion. I remember hopping up to the plate going as carefully as possible so as not to fall over the edge. After all, it was a bloody long way down! It was then and only then, that it dawned on me that this was the whole point of the venture!

I can tell you, stood up there high above the trees, the sea a distant blur on the horizon, gazing down at the people below that appeared to be no more to me than ants, I was feeling pretty bloody weird. On the one hand, I was bricking myself with fear, I mean, the whole thing replicates a suicidal act of motion, but then again, the sheer amount of adrenaline your body creates to compensate, is overwhelming. I felt invigorated, I felt alive.

The guy told me to wave to the camera, and the film crew, and I spewed forth some random thought or another along the lines of, 'live with all your heart in every moment, 'coz it might be your last,' and with that the guy screamed, 'JUMP.'

I flexed my shoulder muscles, threw my arms back with clenched fists to propel myself forward, and then, in one heart wrenching moment, I realised that my feet had refused to move. Hmm? Interesting? Not entirely what I was expecting. I was pretty sure I had told them to jump, but there they still remained, rooted firmly to the spot. Apparently a new approach was required.

Looking over my shoulder, the guy looked a little non-plussed at me, before I just said, 'give us a count down mate.'

Now, there are certain moments in your life that demand a countdown I believe. Don't ask me why, but it seems I wasn't going anywhere without a countdown.

'No worries mate. Ready?'

'Three.'

(Okay there are people watching, it's starting to get embarrassing now. Whatever you do don't freeze up again, don't freeze. Look down you wimp. Look down. Face your fear. You're stronger than any emotion. A life lived in fear is no life at all. Don't freeze. Don't freeze. Just jump.)

'Two.'

(Why? You don't have to jump. You don't need to do this just to prove something. Perhaps it is the bigger man who can back up and just face those people and explain, 'I can't do it.' 'I just can't do this.'

Let's face it; roughly take the length of a football pitch and then imagine yourself falling down it. Imagine yourself falling down it with just a piece of rope tied around your ankles. Something goes wrong, these are your last moments on this earth and you know you'd rather have chosen life.

You wanted to see and do everything. You wanted nothing more than to see your children grow old one day. So you don't have to do this. Just think about this logically for a moment. Your actions here could end everything, and what for?

Look down indeed, and face the fact that death is only 2 seconds away)

'One.'

(Fuck you. Death could always be no more than 2 seconds away. Its what we do in those few seconds that define who we are. Fuck you fear.)

'JUMP.'

(It's all just a leap into the unknown; it's all just about keeping the faith.)

I threw myself off the platform this time. I threw myself from the edge and fell to earth with no more than a bit of rope to stop me ploughing head first into the water below. Instant death.

I fell and a yell of excitement escaped my lips. I loved it! That's all I can tell you. In moments like that your brain overloads, and its just pure adrenaline. Pure excitement. Pure pleasure. It was fucking amazing!

The rope didn't snap. Neither did it on any of the other five jumps I did that day. Funnily enough though, if anything, every jump became all the harder. It seemed that the body is certainly a fast learner. With the knowledge of what is to come, slightly less adrenaline is created whilst stood on the brink, and ultimately, you rely on sheer strength of mind instead.

Things did take a slightly interesting spin when I burst all the blood vessels in my right eye mind you. For weeks afterwards I had no white in my eye, just blood. Quite entertaining really. It gave me hours of entertainment in shops and the such, staring at small children and then removing my sunglasses to reveal my devil's eye. Not sure how impressed their mothers were though when the child barrels into their legs in fits of tears?

I didn't realise I'd done it at first to be honest. On my penultimate jump I'd asked the guys at the top what the craziest possible jump was. They explained that if I stood backwards, and leapt off in the vertical position watching the platform move away above me at impossible speeds, the brain simply melts down.

I think my favourite piece of advise was when they told me to hold my neck with both hands as I fell, forcing myself to stare upwards. Not so much to enjoy the experience, rather that it was a necessary precaution to prevent my neck from snapping.

Well, it certainly was some pretty messed up shit I can tell you! My mind melted indeed.

They'd promise to dunk my head in the lake at the bottom of the fall just for good measure, and I think that's where the blood vessels burst. My brain had been so overloaded I didn't close my eyes as I dipped into the water. Obviously the pressure change from falling at such speeds to going under water was simply too much to take, and things just popped.

That's what I reckon the reason was anyway, though science has never particularly been my forte, always been more of a sports fan myself.

Like I said, this was on my penultimate jump. Any regular person would have quit at that, but sanity like science, has always been somewhat of a struggle to master for me. I didn't want a little thing like a buggered up eye to prevent me from taking my final planned jump. I wanted to fall from higher!

So I soon found myself in a full body harness on the roof of the tower bridge. This was the final and hardest test. It took two countdowns to get me going. Oh, and the arrival of a brunette beauty to overlook proceedings. (Finding your bottle and your balls is evidently a slightly easier task with the knowledge that a girl is watching you!)

Man, that was fun. You sprint across the roof and it's only at the last possible second, once you have too much momentum to stop, that you see over the side, that you see just how far down it bloody well is! Very, very fun!

The beer in the bar later that evening had never tasted as sweet. We didn't stay too long though, as M.J announced we'd need our rest for the next day. I was rather excited to find out what it was he had planned, though he wouldn't even give me a crumb to wet my appetite with.

Oh yeah, in M.J's defence by the way, he'd done just fine that day. If he ever felt any fear it never showed, and he performed some textbook swan dives. Bastard.

'O'

STOOD at the harbour in Cairns the next morning, I closed my eyes and tilted my head towards the sun. With the sound of gulls in the air, and the tide washing against the quay, I remember sighing contently and thinking that life all in all, is a pretty wonderful thing. I was extremely aware of the fact that I was really, really looking forward to backpacking around Thailand the next day. Oh, and that I most definitely couldn't wait to see Destiny again after that.

In the mean time however, that very day itself was gonna be pretty damn cool. As our ride pulled up, we jumped onboard the old Pearl Trawler, and pointing our nose out towards the great open sea, and the Great Barrier Reef beyond it, the largest living organism on this planet.

We lunched that day on a succulent smorgasbord of fresh sea delicacies. Everything tasted amazing, especially as M.J and I had a major case of the 'munchies' after partaking of a sneaky joint off the stern of the boat as we chugged along our merry way. The sun was blazing down, there wasn't a cloud in the sky, and the sea was as blue as the most picturesque postcard you've ever seen. The major point for this little trip though was not merely to feed my ever expanding waistline, but to scuba dive.

Our captain killed the motor and anchored a short distance from some small tropical islands, announcing that, 'the coral in these parts make for some of the best scuba around.'

M.J and I didn't have the time to become fully qualified divers, or the money, though it's something I will get around to doing one day. The opportunity did exist however, to dive without any training as long as we never let go of our guides hand (A little gay I agree! But we just wanted to take this brief chance given to us to sample what it's like).

So, after a huge ten-minute briefing session, we were kitted out and released into that wonderfully warm water.

My Dive Master did give me a little longer to adjust to the apparatus I wore thank goodness, as I originally struggled with the whole feeling of breathing under water merely through my mouthpiece. It was instinct to either hold my breath in for as long as possible as I submerged beneath the waves, or try to breathe through my nose, which blatantly achieved nothing.

It surprised me all a little actually, as having grown up by the sea, I thought the water had become somewhat of a second home to me.

(My parents still delight in telling anyone I introduce them to about one of my first childhood ocean experiences. I was too young to remember it but apparently as a small boy my father had taken me down to the sea's edge to show me how to skim stones across the water. We'd rummaged around through all the pebbles looking for flat rocks perfect for skimming.

Not being particularly old or particularly bright the whole concept had apparently eluded me. I instead delighted in trying to pick up the biggest fattest rocks I thought I might be able to carry, and just 'plopping' them in.

Anyway, so there we were, paddling in the sea, trouser legs rolled up past our knees, with my old man showing off and trying to teach me at the same time. I'd stood there, fat stone in hand, ready to throw it in, but being the incredibly smart little button I am, I'd pulled back my arm to launch the rock as far as I could, only to completely forget that I was supposed to let go of the thing, and pitched myself head first into the sea as well!

Hmm, its funny how parents delight in telling everyone your most embarrassing childhood memories. Parents hey, some children do 'ave them!).

Others around me were having similar problems it seemed, one girl even refusing point blank to go through with the whole shenanigan. Still, just as with everything in life, all you need to do is try and find a little bit of peace sometimes. So, after a little, well I wouldn't say panic stricken, more a struggling to get to grips with things, period of time, I finally decided to go walkabouts in my head to sort things out.

The ability to disappear inside oneself and meditate is quite regularly the key to this life. The ability to create an area of calm when everything around you is flailing is a true trait indeed.

M.J had started me on its exploration months before, and it was one of the reasons we were heading off to Thailand. For there an old Buddhist Monk, a friend of M.J's from long days gone by, had agreed to guide us around the jungles of the Golden Triangle region. An area of dense dark foliage, tucked away in the mountains on the Thai, Myanmar, Laos border. A jungle hidden away from the modern world, filled with ancient intrigue and wonder, filled with the unknown. There he planned to not only be our guide in the physical world, but the spiritual one as well.

As the sun began to rise over the treetops, we would find ourselves practising Tai Chi around the mud and straw huts of a remote hill village, with the indigenous tribes people surrounding us.

Anyway, once again I'm getting ahead of myself. Where was I?

Ah yes. As I lay floating in the waters of the Barrier Reef, I found a little peace and clarity, and the trick to the whole breathing thing soon came to me.

In the age-old universal symbol of, 'everything's good,' (the whole curling together of thumb and forefinger to create an, 'O,' shape) I signalled that I was ready to dive.

Driving myself downwards with small kicking motions from my webbed flippers, I discovered in an instant a whole new world beneath the waves. In those shallow waters the light broke through and illuminated the scenes below. We dove in and around the coral until my belly pressed upon the seabed.

My instructor signalled for us to sit for a while, and so that's what we did. I sat at the bottom of the sea, with my legs crossed, the odd infrequent air bubble slipping away above me to pop on the surface, and 'under the sea,' from the Little Mermaid playing in my head! I took everything in.

My breathing had become slow and unrushed, for I was existing on some level or plain removed from this world. I was in some euphoric state of tranquillity as I watched the underwater world go by.

To my right a mass of virginal white coral burst with life, from the end of its strange trumpet shaped stalagmites many flowers seemed to grow. Out of one trumpet tooted some party blower, as the flower inside allowed its scarlet red streams of petals to willow and blow into the surrounding sea.

Everything teemed with life and beauty. As we sat there a massive shoal of rainbow coloured fish swam towards us. As the light hit them they seemed to flash and change before me like some great chameleon, as the proud creatures revelled in showing off the full range of the spectrum that their flanks could replicate. Swimming straight for us they broke at the last possible moment, literally just before they brushed against my face. So there I was, sat cross-legged at the bottom of the Great Barrier Reef slap bang in the middle of thousands of brightly coloured fish. Very, very funky!

We exhausted the last of our oxygen tanks swimming with the underwater creatures, playing games with them. We'd tag onto the back of a shoal, chasing after them as they darted about the coral. We'd glide over the surface of the flora and fauna, before diving down through natural arches and caves to the sand below before bursting into a fresh shoal and breaking off to play with them. All the while the colour and light danced through my vision and my internal voice was silent, its incessant tongue stilled for a moment in time.

So I was tired, happy, but a little disappointed when my guide finally pointed to his wristwatch and pushed towards the ocean's surface.

Finding M.J draped on the forward deck, lounging in the sun whilst breaking claws off the lobster on the plate beside him, I collapsed in exhaustion. Neither of us spoke a word; there really was no need to.

Eventually I filled my own gurgling stomach with fresh fruit to regain my strength and leant back in the sunshine. It baked my salty faced as I plucked ripened and fat strawberries from my plate, and delighted in biting into their succulent flesh as I hung overboard, with my eyes closed, and my ears filled with the soft lapping of the waves against that ancient pearl trawlers hull below. I was indeed a happy and contented old soul.

Yeah, I can say with true conviction that Australia had certainly been an eye opening experience. Still there was no time to look back at all that right then, because before I'd even had time to stop and pause for breath, the wheels of our airplane were screeching down onto tarmac, and I was being thrown out of the frying pan and into the fire.

PART SIX

WE SHOULD GIVE LIFE MEANING,
NOT WAIT FOR LIFE TO GIVE IT TO US

BANGKOK. PAPIER-MÂCHÉ BRAS WITH RIFLES. NAKED MEN'S KNOWLEDGEABLE SMILES. BUDDHA MEDITATION DOWN GLITTERING AISLES

M.J and I's flight had been instantly forgettable to be honest. You know how it is; long and tedious, just wanting to get where you're going.

We touched down in the region of Don Muang, home of Bangkok International airport, a little after midnight. After months of sleeping on Mother Nature's carpet, old mattresses in Youth Hostels with questionable stains included for no extra charge, and the back floor of bright orange campervans, we had decided to push the purse strings out a little for our few days in Bangkok.

Our hotel sent a guide to 'meet and greet' us, before taking us on to our four star lodgings. After booking in, we saw a massage parlour was on offer. Now, I'd already heard many a story of the notoriety of Thailand's massage parlours. Well, in a country whose second highest income earner after tourism, is prostitution, I was more than a little wary about taking up the offers of a massage in fact, being pretty sure that there were plentiful 'extras,' to be had.

(Oh, and I think Thailand leads the way in, 'country with highest amount of sex changes' by the way, so be warned, you may be getting more than you paid for!

At one point in my travels I ran into a couple of Americans in one bar, and as we sat around chatting, a Moulin-Rouge-esque kinda dance thing started up on stage. Well, one of the dancers kicked her legs up, took a little interest in my lanky friend from Chicago, and moved over to our table.

Lost in lights, music, short skirts, glitter and masks, he was completely bewitched by her. Her top was nothing more than a small dish cloth, covered in brilliant silver sparkles, and being rather intoxicated, he seemed incapable of staring at anything else bar than her breasts.

Eventually she kissed him on each cheek before landing a huge wet smacker on his lips, waiting for our other American friend to camcord the situation, and for all the eyes in the bar to be on them. Right in front of his bulging eyes, she slowly, seductively, undid her buttoned top.

As she ripped her shirt open at last, my friend's expression was unforgettable as she revealed her, well, actually now we realised, his, muscular hairy man's chest! Yep, she was a he, and the huge breasts the top held were nothing more than papier-mâché below the glitter line! Priceless!

Unfortunately, it seemed like some of the drunken punters wandering by outside were not being given a chance to realise their mistake. I saw one he/she stop and chat to a fat red-faced aged man, obviously the worst for wear for alcohol, and pretty soon they were disappearing arm in arm to the rooms downstairs. Boy was he in for a surprise when he rolled over the next morning! Talk about the world's worst hangover!

Oh yeah, and the massage parlours and clubs in the Patpong district also boasted such extravagant shows as women shooting ping pong balls out of their, well, you can guess where, and also using the same part of their anatomy to open beer bottles! Now, just how a woman discovers she has the ability to do these things is slightly beyond me, but there you go.

Of course I never actually saw these things happen may I add. Someone told me about it, I'd never frequent such places naturally. Yeah right!)

Anyway, M.J twisted my arm, as he always does, and so I took a massage and I had an unbelievable time! The woman was amazing! At massage that is thank you very much; get your mind out of the gutter! After my recent escape from an STD clinic with a still disease free anatomy, I really didn't fancy risking it all again with some, 'me love you long time,' girl (or boy if I was unlucky!) in Thailand.

No, I settled for a massage, and it was amazing. She did such bizarre things as walking up and down my back, using her toes as well as her fingers to relax my knotted muscles, and it was oh so relaxing. Doubled up with a steaming hot bath later (a truly rare thing in the backpacking world) and a huge double bed, I slept like a baby that night.

The next morning we met up again with our guide from the night before (Marco). He had mentioned that today was his day off so I'd asked if he might show M.J and I around the city, and being an extremely kindly guy, he said he would. This was a real sign of kindness to be honest, because he didn't even ask for any money, he just let us pay for his lunch or entry fees, which we insisted upon, feeling that it was the least we could do.

It was really nice of him to take his day off unpaid to do this. For as I wandered the streets that day I very quickly realised that so many people out there just looked at us and saw dollar signs in their eyes. I guess it's kind of understandable really; we Westerners are so rich in general compared to them.

I guess the best example I can give of the strength of the dollar or the pound compared to the Thai Baht, and how a few pennies to us, is a fortune to them, is in visiting a McDonalds out there. A Big Mac meal, upgraded to the largest size available, will set you back around 12 British pence, that's about 20 American cents including tax!

Anyway, we met Marco in the hotel lobby at 9am and our first stop was the river. We procured the use of a riverboat and set off down the canals. It was along this stretch of water that we got to glimpse the, 'real,' Bangkok. i.e. the poor areas that Tourists didn't often want to bother seeing; one bedroom wooden shacks on stilts in the river, which hosted dozens of family members, often spanning four or five generations, and their pets, for example.

Wild dogs ran around. Women both young and old sang along to themselves as they washed their clothes in the river. The brilliant greens of the trees dazzled us as they reflected off the water, fattened coconuts crashed to the floor, and all the while Marco explained what we were seeing.

I think the most penetrating image from that boat ride was when we glided past a wrinkled aged man, washing himself naked in the river. As he swam, taking his early morning bath, he looked up and shot us a huge genuine toothless grin, and waved.

As I waved back, I realised something fundamental. This man had almost no worldly possessions. He shared one room up above our heads on those mossy rotten stilts, with his entire family. He had no mod con's, not even hot water, thus he bathed and washed in those filthy tepid brown waters. To the men from the west, he seemed to have nothing. To him though, he knew he had everything in this world that really mattered. So he smiled the broadest, most genuine smile of happiness I think I've ever seen.

This started the little grey cells of my mind in motion, set them on a voyage of discovery that would take me the length and breath of Thailand to fully grasp and clarify.

In the afternoon we headed to a local Buddhist temple. A lot of Thailand's wealth is placed in its holy shrines, and this was definitely apparent as I gazed up at the huge golden statue of Buddha sat cross-legged in front of me.

My nostrils were filled with the aroma of incense burners and in the distance; the sound of preaching could be distinguished. The only other noise was the rogue love song of a nesting bird; else the other few visitors were silent in prayer.

Without shoes I knelt in front of Buddha. Marco showed M.J and I what we were to do. On knees I must put my hands together and bend to the ground three times, firstly for Buddha, secondly for the story of Buddha, (which intricately adorned the walls around the temple with ornately detailed pictures) and lastly for the Monks.

As I knelt there, the peacefulness of the situation washed over me. It seemed I was capable of blocking out the troubles and woes of the external world, and ascend onto some greater plain of existence for a while. It was almost as if I could just turn off and stop everything that rushed hustled and bustled about me, not just in the surrounding world, but also in my internal heart and soul as well. The tranquillity of the situation means that when you do finally open your eyes again, you feel enlightened.

I guess the best way to explain it is that in the every day monotony that life can sometimes throw at you, you long for a break. You go on holiday to recharge the batteries, to spend a little time away from the craziness, troubles and intensity of your home life. You make the world stop spinning for a while, and exist a little outside the realms of time, so that when you do return, at least for a short period you feel rejuvenated.

Well, when I opened my eyes, I was rejuvenated from my short trip away from it all, in which I stopped the world from spinning, and had made old man time rest for just a few minutes.

You see, prayer is often a form of meditation, and I've found meditation can be a key to happiness. How often do we find we don't have the time, the money, or just far too many responsibilities to take a break and recharge in some exotic location?

Well, I'll let you in on a little secret, you can go wherever you want when you meditate, and come back just as enlightened and relaxed. It's an incredible way to relax and find a little clarity.

Hmm, guess I should at least try and show you a glimpse of what I'm talking about, else you'll just think I'm a complete nutcase!

Hmm, well, the simplest meditation technique I think I know is this. Lying down is probably best, put some relaxing music on if you think it'll help.

Close your eyes.

Now the key to all meditative techniques is breathing. The best explanation I got from one of the Buddhist monks I met was this.

When you come out of your mother's womb, you're not actually alive. The mid-wife has to give you a giant slap on the back and this action makes you breathe for the first time. Your very first action in this mortal realm, is to breathe in and fill your lungs with air. And so, rather fittingly perhaps, our very last action before death is to breathe out and let the oxygen escape one last time. So every breath is re-enacting life and death.

Every time you breathe as you lay there with your eyes closed, concentrate on it. As you breathe in, picture a ball of energy and life passing in through your mouth and nose.

Just like your very first moment in this world, this action of merely breathing in, is what is keeping you alive. Every intake is life itself. So see this life and energy as a ball. As you breathe in see that ball pass down into your lungs and heart, now hold that breath. The key is slow breathing.

Hold that breath and feel that ball of life spread out from your heart into your blood stream. Feel it pass through the blood around your body, gradually filling every part of your matter with existence, with energy, with life.

Now exhale. This could be your last breath, this action will be the last you ever perform I promise you that. Feel all the energy and life draw back in from around your body to your heart and lungs, return into a ball, and then pass up to your mouth to be released back into the atmosphere.

Again hold it like that. Savour how it is to die briefly. For this is a replication of your final action ever. So now you see, when you breathe in, it tastes much the sweeter, it's all of a sudden so full of energy.

Once you've got the whole deep breathing thing sorted, once you've focussed on it for a few minutes, then tense every muscle in your body.

In your mind's eye, visualise that you're lying on some warm beach, some tropical paradise you've always dreamt of. Feel the warmth of the sun on your face as you lie there down by the surf.

Now, visualise the tide slowly rolling in. As it washes in, just pulling in over your toes, relax the corresponding muscles in your feet.

The water rolls out and back in a little further this time, reaching your ankles and calf muscles. Relax them.

Once more the tide rolls out, and every time it washes back over you a little further, so relax those muscles it reaches. Keep doing this until every muscle in your body has been catered for.

Feel the sun on your face, feel the life washing in and out of your lungs. Just stay like that with your eyes closed for however long you want to.

It's one of the simplest techniques, but if it works for you, there's a whole new world to explore. Worlds and plains you never even knew existed.

Another short ride took us past street vendors cooking up some strange exotic food or another, (perhaps it was best you couldn't ascertain the origins of the meat they roasted, what with the sheer amount of wild dogs running around the roads and yet no other seeming presence of fresh meet available) and lepers and cripples, struggling along, holding each other up, with their hands extended for some form of aid.

(Actually M.J asked the Tuk Tuk driver to pull over so he could drop a number of notes into their thankful hands. They smiled broadly and mumbled, 'Buddha bless you.' M.J answered, 'what goes around comes around my friends. Plus, another God once said, 'do as to others as you'd have done to yourself.'

M.J was always coming out with little quips and proverbs like that. He seemed to have a inexhaustible supply to cover a limitless amount of scenarios. I think those two to be my favourites, because time and time again whilst walking through life I've seen proof of this karma in existence.

Though thinking about it, his proverb, 'man who go to bed with itchy bottom, wake up with smelly finger,' is also a front-runner in favourites!)

Soon we were arriving at Marco's. His family were amazing, kind and generous, his wife, young and beautiful, made us a wonderful supper. His kids were full of intrigue and playful natures. I had a lot of fun with Nan Puk, (his 12 year old son, who like his father spoke wonderful English) teasing him about the girl who lived across the road, Ghan. She kept appearing as we played soccer in the street to poke her tongue out at him, or tackle the football away. So I teased him saying that he loved her and she was his girlfriend, so he'd beat me up, wrestling me and pinning me on the ground to get me back for my cheek. Yeah, I really enjoyed my hours there at dusk.

As the heat of the day finally dissipated, (I hadn't been able to play football too long as I was sweating buckets in the humidity) M.J, Marco and I flagged down a Tuk-Tuk to transport us to the local Muey Thai Kick-boxing arena.

I thought it was wicked that we were able to get ringside seats, though I soon discovered why they were still available. In Muey Thai combatants are allowed to use their knees and elbows. Due to this, with noses breaking, eyes swelling, and large gashes being rent open wide for the brilliant white of bone to protrude from beneath, with particularly peachy punches we were doused in a stream of fresh blood in our ringside seats.

There's something particularly strange about tasting the blood and sweat of a stranger on your lips. Something strangely invigorating as well truth be told. You soon find you're on your feet with the rest of them, screaming aloud, 'fucking kill him!'

M.J and I only spent another day in Bangkok. I've never really been a city boy and I was itching to escape the confines of its walls.

I guess the only other thing worth noting, apart from how nice the Emperor's Grand Palace is, was that M.J and I had to replace our backpacks when we kinda got kidnapped. Well sort of anyway.

You see we'd sat around in the hotel bar sipping copious amounts of Chang beer, getting quietly tipsy, when we'd decided not to heed Marco's sagely advise. Whenever we'd gotten taxis with him he'd always insisted that we make the effort to wander around the side of the building and flag down a licensed taxi or Tuk-Tuk.

On staggering out of the front doors, neither M.J nor I could be particularly arsed to go walkabout and settled for one of the private drivers always touting for business on our front steps. So we ended up falling into the back of a regular car with blacked out windows, and setting off for the bus station.

Or so we thought.

You see the driver had other ideas. He kept on tapping the little red light on his dashboard and exclaiming that he had to go and find fuel. In the mean time, he'd drop the two of us off with some friends of his. As we turned off the main street and started bumping down dilapidated and abandoned back roads we realised the entirety of our mistake.

The driver refused to be bargained with, he refused to listen to our orders to stop immediately and let us out. He was quite happily protected behind the glass between us, and so he just kept driving.

Suddenly, in no time at all, I found myself in a particularly bizarre and fucked up situation that I realised I had absolutely no control over whatsoever. It was a little mental to be honest. I guess it just goes to show how life can change in an instant.

Anyway, as we took a left turn, barrelling through hanging sheets that had been left to dry on the washing lines above, strewn between the buildings, alien graffiti of blood red warnings flashed us by. An immediate sharp right turn at speed dragged us into a dead end.

At the end of this road, M.J and I suddenly became aware of three short squat men carrying some sort of rifle. Despite my panic I remember wondering with rather absent-mindedness for such a situation, 'I think those guns are Ak47's,' before a flash of silver to my right brought the seriousness of it all to the foreground. M.J had unsheathed his ever-trusty Bowie knife and it was glistening away with dastardly intent and finality.

I really couldn't be arsed with a fight to be honest, so I just told M.J to put his blade away and as the car started to slow, threw my passenger door open, pulling M.J out of the moving vehicle with me.

We hit the ground rolling, hurting ourselves a little in the fall, but the adrenaline pumping around our systems blocked it from our minds. Before the car could stop, before the bullets could start to rain down around us, or anyone could even start to give chase, we were sprinting away from the scene.

We always kept our passports, credit cards and cash in money belts tucked down our cowboy boots, so it didn't really matter in essence that our backpacks were still in the back of the 'taxi's' trunk. However, I must confess as to having been just a little bit pissed off because I was looking forward to giving Destiny a beautiful jade necklace I'd bought for her at the Damneon Saduak Floating Market, and now that dick-head had stolen it.

Oh yeah, and he'd run off with my travel iron as well the little bitch! Oh well, shit happens I guess.

Needless to say, once we reached the main street, more than a little out of breath, we deemed it best to flag down a licensed Tuk-Tuk after all.

A quick stop off at the Ko San Road (completely dedicated to tourists) gave us replacement rucksacks, clothing, (I was now looking oh so very different from the guy who stepped off the plane back in Australia all that time ago) and of course, most importantly, (no not a travel iron and Tin-Bear-Scaring-Whistle!) a new walkman, speakers and tapes.

We did eventually make it to the bus station, and by late evening we were on a choking spluttering old crate carrying us to Phuket.

GREAT WHITE WOLVES IN THE FIRES OF HADES

M.J. and I stood awaiting our ferry from Phuket to the golden islands of southern Thailand. I would've been bored and more than a little irritable if I'd been back home, what with the fact that the boat was supposed to have left over two hours ago, but that's travel for you. More to the point, that's Thailand for you.

Long waits had become somewhat second nature to me however, mainly because I'd found a way around it all. It basically involves losing yourselves in some game or another that you've created for yourself. In doing so, you kinda forget about time somewhere along the line.

Well, a wandering street vendor that passed our way as we waited inspired my first game. Procuring a plastic bowl of chicken flavoured noodles from him, I decided I'd test myself by throwing away the fork. The aim of the game was to pluck the noodles up with my lips, twist the lengthy strands around my tongue, and eat the full contents of the bowl without getting my face dirty.

This proved rather difficult to be honest. The only way to get your lips to grip the slimy strings was by literally sticking your face right inside the bowl. Of course this meant that when you pulled back up, you always found a vast amount of noodles stuck to you. They were now dangling from your forehead, your ears, or had become entwined in your long hair, forming some kind of crazy chicken dreadlocks in imitation of M.J. In fact, I mentioned as much to my travelling companion. Though, stood there with my face covered in dried yellow noodle juices he just kind of looked at me as though I was a madman, muttered something under his breath, and turned back around to gaze at the sea. Oh well, suit yourself.

Anyway, when the gates finally opened and the Thai guards started ushering us forwards to the boats, I was almost sorry to go.

The latest game to preoccupy my mind was trying to puzzle out whether the stunning Thai beauty in front of me was actually a man or a woman. He/she had an unbelievable pair of legs that seemed to go on forever, they were a luscious creamy brown colour, and were barely concealed beneath a tiny white mini skirt. The tits looked unbelievable but as my American friend had discovered back in Bangkok, this can be particularly deceptive. Papier-mâché or not? Despite all this, my instincts screamed out that there was something not altogether right about this belle. So I was sad when we had to leave him/her behind because I'd just worked up the courage to go and find out for sure.

Whenever I walked down the side streets of Thailand I'd had to keep my hand at the level of my head, and I am being rude here by the way! It was something you had to learn to do, because when the lady boys stood outside the bars saw you, they'd automatically grab at your privates, 'you wanna ha' fun?' Man, you had to bat their hands away else they could get a bloody tight grip!

So, I'd pretty much decided that if it was fine for them to do it to me, surely I could do the same in return? Hell, it was certainly a sure-fire way of being certain just what a person is packing!

Each ferry had a capacity of perhaps 300 people at a rough guess. Stacked to three tiers above water, and a couple at least below, I was relatively impressed to be honest. A lot of things in Thailand don't exactly reek of confidence, but these ferries were quite posh really. The hull was painted beautifully in a deep red which didn't even seem to be flaking. Someone had even gone to a great deal of effort to finish the top or the red off with a line of aquamarine blue. Whilst the top half of the vessel was your regular, though freshly painted, cotton wool white.

The thing was pretty chocker block by the time M.J and I pushed our way on. Literally, we were pressed right against the metal railings at the stern of the ferry.

Personally I seemed to have managed to find one of the rare few native fat fuckers in Thailand to stand behind. She insisted on continually bending over, and every time she did so, her gigantic arse (which I firmly believe was at that very moment causing some consternation to NASA scientists, believing that a small meteorite had just landed in Southern Thailand) would push me up and over the steel bars, so that I was literally hanging overboard, hands spread wide grasping in thin air. Not exactly your romantic Leo and Kate scene from Titanic.

Much to my relief a guard pulled down the cord preventing people from gaining access onto the ferry docked beside ours, and ushered M.J and I forward. This was an invitation we happily took, especially as this overflow ferry now consisted of only around 50 of us. Personally, I would've thought it better sense to share the loads between the two, but who am I to question?

So, our spacious cruise set off first, along with ferry containing fat arse woman in close tow.

I contented myself with a cigarette upstairs as we pulled out into the open water. The cool fresh wind in my face was a welcome change after the sticking dead heat of being stood on the mainland. I watched it move away from view, slowly becoming no more than a speck on the horizon. I had nothing better to do to be honest. So I just chain-smoked my Marlboro's enjoying the sun on my face, and the sound of the spray below.

Flicking my fourth fag out to sea only half way smoked due to my lungs unhappily throwing me into a coughing fit, I eventually removed myself into the confines of the downstairs seating decks. With the gentle swaying motion of the boat rocking me to sleep, I slipped my headphones on and closed my eyes in rest.

I was broken out of my dozy dreams as my mind locked into the fact that something was most definitely not right.

Pulling out one of my earpieces, I realised that seriously, all really was not well.   I was alone and the ferry was drastically changing course, we were turning through a tight 180-degree angle back the way we had come.

Throwing my stereo back into my bag, I quickly skipped up the metal steps in twos towards the upper decks. Locating M.J amongst the other sea farers, I saw that he joined them in staring off to starboard, with anxious looks in their eyes.

Pulling up to the rails beside him, in an instant I could locate the cause for concern. We had turned around and were shooting back towards the jam-packed ferry M.J and I had been previously removed from. It stood stock still now, no more than 1000 metres away to our northeast, and the front was crowded with panicking people. It seemed everyone on board had rushed to the bow of the boat. The reason was blatantly evident. Tall flames stretched skywards from the stern of the ferry, dark, dirty black smoke billowing away into the cloudless blue above. The engines at the rear had somehow caught alight.

My immediate reaction to all this? Well, I'm ashamed to say almost. It all seemed so surreal to be honest. It just seemed like a reel from a Hollywood movie, somehow I was completely separate from it all, just a viewer. So yes, I'm afraid to say it, but I pulled out my camera and joined the other passengers aboard our vessel in taking photos of the incident.

 Hell, one American guy was even filming it all on his camcorder! To us, it just seemed like some exciting event to tell people about. None of us really thought that there was any real danger. How were any of us to know that it would ultimately end in such disaster? For now, it was just a crazy snap shot to add to the photo album, and a funny story to tell in some pub in years to come. Sometimes humans can be so fucking clueless.

As we neared, many people were already leaping into the sea below. The flames had started to lick their way further up the boat, and it was evident that the stern was slowly sinking deeper below the water. I heard someone say, 'you know what, I think that boat might actually sink.' As more people jumped overboard, I think we all started to realise that this wasn't some scene from a movie, and that the shit was really going down, literally.

Pulling up as close as we dared, the sinking ship to our right, I could fully evaluate the extent of the situation. The back two thirds of the vessel were alight; I could feel the heat even from where I stood some distance away.

Now, I've personally always been somewhat fascinated by fire. I can often be found gazing into its dancing flames with a smile upon my face, as I camp in some deserted wood, hand outstretched holding a forked stick, marshmallow gently roasting away, but there was nothing fascinating about those flames.

Their reds, yellows, and whites where the intense heat surged, were coughing up so much black oily smoke that it seemed the very sky above was being choked. The stern was lying severely low in the water, and the fizzing it caused where the tide gradually began to wash into the very rear of the flames, was throwing up crazy amounts of steam. The noise was horrendous, almost deafening. There was a deadly, haunting cacophony of burning flames, hissing steam, and human screaming.

By now, almost everyone had thrown themselves into the sea, and were struggling to swim towards our vessel. For our part, we pitched red and white life rings down to them, heaving at the ropes, dragging them to the safety above.

By this point in the proceedings, I was operating on autopilot. Your mind and heart desert you and you're numb to everything. Something carnal, animalistic almost, something that lies inside that only rears its head in times like these, roars its way to the surface and takes control. I was a man existing outside of myself. Throw rope over, pull someone onboard. Rush around, exert super human efforts when required. You have no time to analyse anything, to ponder anything. All of a sudden I was a man possessed.

The boat burned, in the sea below floated almost 300 people. Men, women, children, mainly Thai, screaming, begging to be saved. Strange words filled my ears, a strange language, chattering on in a scared alien tongue, and yet I somehow knew what they were saying.

Jumping onto the back of M.J's rope as his strength waned, we hauled a Thai man to safety. He hugged us and jabbered on. I pushed him away, somehow understanding and yet shouting back in English to, 'chip in and help.' He looked into my eyes, instantly knowing and understanding somehow what I was saying, turned, and fled to help the men preparing the life rafts away to our right.

It was only after we'd rescued most of the bobbing bodies that I saw them. I had stopped all of a sudden, my mind finally returning with the situation almost resolved, and it was only in that moment when I stopped to take a gauge of the proceedings, that I saw them.

Back onboard the doomed vessel; a lonely Thai mother and father stand by the side railings halfway down the decking. She holds a small child in both arms, the babe's head resting on her bosom, I know from the judder of her shoulders that she is crying.

That shot is forever imprinted on my soul. She is stood there, dressed simply in a long flowing black dress, the baby is wrapped in a bright turquoise blanket, it screams aloud.

The father has taken off the jacket of his suit. His lightweight cream trousers cling to his frame, his leather sandals stained by the blood from a gash upon his torn right knee. His salmon pink shirt is now dark and doused by sweat.

They're stood at the entrance to the lower decks, and he's smashing down his jacket into the flames that leap out of the doorway. Like some strange matador he brings the rag down time and time again onto those impossible flames. They show no sign of extinguishing.

Even as I watch, one of the fuel tanks finally explodes nearby. Everything goes into slow motion.

The heat blast sweeps the couple and the child off their feet, off over the railings and toward the sea below. Even as they fall, I see the impact of the blast.

The man falls backwards, his arms outstretched. The explosion strips his flesh clean off his body. As he turns his face away from the heat, one side is cremated to black; the other side is stripped down to the very grinning skull below. The eye pops and explodes smattering the crystal white bone. He lands on his back in the water below me, his arms still outstretched, yet no more than disgusting skeletal fingers point upwards now.

She, she is instantly cauterised into one with her baby. The two fused together in a sickening display of smelting. Even the waves cannot extinguish the flames, and so mother and child float facing upwards, no feature of either recognisable. I watch them float there. I watch the black melted ooze of the woman and the child she bore burn away still. Even as they float there below me, I watch the flames dance from the flesh of their former faces.

I vomit. I double up and vomit all over myself. I retch, and I continue to retch even when there is nothing left to bring up. Still my stomach convulses. I dry retch. Maybe half a dozen times.

The next thing I know is that M.J is grabbing at my sleeve screaming something. Through my shut down mind, I finally piece together his words to make a sentence.

'There's still people on there!'

A number of people, both Western and Eastern, are already diving off our ferry into the water; M.J is not far behind, climbing onto the railings, and swan diving after them. I wipe my mouth with the back of my sleeve. The smell of acid burns my mouth and the stench of burnt flesh and vomit assault my nostrils.

I vaguely remember shaking my head to try and gain some form of self-control again.

I can hear the screams onboard the other boat now. Some part of me registers the fact that the burning parents floating below must have been trying to reach and save someone. So I dive overboard to join the rescue mission.

I reach the sinking flaming behemoth last. There is no crystal clarity, there is no gentle calm inside me, there is only instinct and adrenaline, driving me on.

The bow is already jutting out at an awkward angle above the water, as the stern sinks beneath the waves. Still, the bow is where I head.

I vaguely remember catching hold of a rope that hung down into the sea, an unoccupied and useless life aid still attached. I can't even register the aching in my muscles from the continual concerted effort. All I know is instinct and adrenaline, instinct and adrenaline, no mind, no thoughts, just reaction, flight or fight.

I find myself standing alone on the tilted forward deck of the doomed vessel.

The crackling of flames is deafening. The sheer intensity of the heat is almost unbearable. I slide down to the door in front of me, pulling it open.

The front glazed room is small; barely half a dozen rows of seating fill it. They are now stood at 45-degrees as the boat continues to barely bob above the waters. I slide down sideways on the insides of my feet, I'm surfing again. The second door opens to a world of pain.

The complete rear wall is alight. All the windows have been blown out, and the thick black smoke is funnelling out of them. There is no way forward, but I can still hear screaming. There is only a flight of stairs leading downwards, further into the belly of the beast. I take them two at a time, slipping down the metal steps, barely catching myself on the wooden handrail.

This room too is awash with flames. Everywhere I look I see red. Everywhere I look I see fire and death. I am in Dante's 'Inferno.' The hairs on my arms stand on end; I try and turn my face away from the heat. I wonder if even now my flesh is being stripped away from my bones like it did to the couple outside?

I should turn back. What the fuck am I playing at? Just where the hell am I? What in the Devil's name am I doing here?

The plastered white ceiling above me is bubbling. Even as I look up, one bubble grows in enormity, like some little kid blowing at chewing gum, and explodes. Fire drops from the room above, falling through the newly created hole. I watch the flames fall. As soon as they touch the carpet, they light it like a taper; a match to a cigarette. The rug beneath my feet ignites.

Now is my choice. I still have no control over any of this. There is no reason, no careful contemplation, no weighing up of the pros and cons. Who I am bares no choice in any of this. Everything I've learnt has no part in all this. I am nothing but the animal inside. I am a great wolf howling scared. I am a great white wolf bursting forth, bursting to the surface, raising its head. In times like this rationality deserts us, and we are no more than instincts, no more than the animal inside.

The carpet beneath me catches alight. I watch the little flame spring up. I watch it grow in stature as it flies towards me over the rug, gathering more fuel and oxygen to destroy us all.

I am in Hades. I am in Hell.

The burning Devil strides up and with long welcoming flickering flamed fingers, pulls itself up to its full titanic height around me, reaching forward to envelop the white wolf cornered before it.

Now is my choice. Turn tail and run. Run for my life. Run back the way I came whilst I still can.

No.

I can distinguish the whimpering cry of someone still calling out from below. The whole room now seems to be ablaze, the noise is deafening, the smoke chokes my lungs. Just as the Devil's forked tongue licks down at my very feet, I move.

I jump forward to the last flight of steps. They lead me down in the direction from which the cries have come.

Once again I descend into the belly of the beast. This time I do fall down those white metallic steps, for the stern of the boat is now fully submerged beneath the ocean, the bow is fully above the surface, and so I fall. I land hard taking the skin off my knees, elbows, chin and top lip.

This time, with the taste of my own irony blood on my tongue, the wolf inside me howls in rage. I pull my sorry arse to my feet, somehow finding stability in that insane, manic and crazy hellhole, and there I find him.

A small Thai boy lies draped beneath the benches. I remember, despite not exactly being myself for any of those dark hours, every detail about him. He is barefooted; his dark skin is dirtied and bloodied. A pair of khaki shorts hang down his skinny legs to his knees. He wears a bright yellow Brazilian soccer shirt, the small blue ball of its badge shines forth. His long black basin hair cut is matted to his forehead with blood and sweat. His eyes are not open, his long dark eyelashes flitter back and forth, and he barely cries now, merely letting out an unconscious whimper.

As I reach him, he barely reacts as I sweep him up into my arms, and looking down at his dwindling face, he reminds me instantly of Marco's son, Nan Puk. Although, perhaps he was a little younger, only ten or so I remember thinking.

I pull him up into my arms and stagger as best I can back the way I came. The steps are now at crazy angles, like David Bowie's, 'Labyrinth,' or Escher's artwork.

Reaching the bottom of that flight I realise there is no way forward. I can already see that the room I came from above is completely enveloped by fire.

Looking around, it's only now I notice the shallow film of water brushing at me toes. The fire at the stern has been extinguished by the rising water level, and the sea has rushed in. I can see it running down the steps at the back of the room, but this is the only way onwards now. Onwards and upwards.

Splashing at a run to the back of my prison cell, the young boy in my arms grows quiet. Glancing down I see him giving up the fight, and yet his chest still rises. So I race up the steps into new surroundings.

Once again I find myself barely standing at drunken angles. One end of the room points upwards, the distinctly lower end is half full with seawater. Double doors lie wide open as the water rushes in, almost filling the doorway to half way.

Taking a snap decision, I struggle upwards. The door is a single one with a small glass window. Peering through I can see the enormity of the flashing flames beyond, and yet, hope! There is a discernable way through and to the side door leading outside! Even as I look I catch the flash of blond dreadlocks disappear through that open doorway.

'M.J,' I scream.

Hope!

Throwing the boy over my shoulder, holding him securely in one arm, I grab the metal handle.

I recall instantly in pain. 'Fucking hell!' The thing has been heated so much throughout the proceedings it's like putting your hand into a furnace!

I go to touch it again, to pull it open and thus free us, releasing us into safety, but I don't seem to be able to. My reflexes take control and every time my hand gets to within an inch, it withdraws. Still, I look on through that window. I look on and see our escape route diminishing. Slowly the gap is being eaten up.

With our hopes, and our lives, disappearing before my eyes, someone speaks inside to me. Is it the animal, or is it my mind returned?

'It's better to burn out, then to fade away!'

The cry screams throughout my head, reverberating all around, and with a scream of, 'fuck this shit,' I force my hand down onto the handle.

I hold it there through all the pain. I hold it there despite every sane part of me (if there was indeed any left) begging for me to pull away. I hold it there, smelling my own flesh cooking away below me.

Using every ounce of courage in me, every fibre of will power, all the strength that the animal inside can lend us in times of need, and every part of the man that I am, I pull the handle down.

The door doesn't budge. The door is locked. I failed to notice the keyhole. I cannot open it. I cannot open it. We cannot get out.

So eventually, conceding defeat, I have to release my grip. Steam escapes from my fist as I open my palm. My skin bubbles just as the ceiling did before. The pain washes over me and almost claims a hold on my consciousness.

Some part of me opens up. Some part of my memory banks slip the image of me back in Bondi, getting stung by that Blue Bottle jellyfish, into the screen projector in my head. I almost laugh at the memory.

The image once again brands the flanks of the wolf inside me, and he roars in defiance. Once again I push the pain inside, and use it to force myself onwards.

I race back to the far end of the room. By the steep angle of things, time is obviously of the essence. The water quickly rises, and I soon find myself wading through those thick double doors. The seawater reaches my stomach as I hold the boy out at arms length above its level. The salt washes into the scrapes on my knees, washes into all my wounds, and it stings like a bitch man. I grimace in so, so much pain. Can I continue?

My adrenaline is almost spent. For an instant I feel the overwhelming urge to lie down and sleep, but then I notice the boys chest stop moving. I stop in turn, watching and willing with every part of me for his lungs to fill again with life.

They eventually do. His breath is shallow and comes at such long intervals now I know he is almost dead. This spurs me on. In an instant I forget my pain. In an instant I burst on, wading through the water as quickly as I can.

Through the double doors I find myself in another box room. From here I take an immediate left, through another door wide open and awash with water, and then I'm in the Bar.

Suddenly, I'm out of options it seems. This room is thin and long. I can see fire dancing at the windows of the doors above, and below me, the doorway back there is completely filled with water.

'Shit, game over, you're dead man. You're dog meat pal. Not a chicken's chance in Thailand bro.'

Then I see it. The wooden hatch doors off to my right, the slope leading up to them. I suddenly realise this is the hatchway they lower the beer kegs through to the Bar.

The boat is now at impossible angles to properly stand upon. So I lay the boy down, pull myself onto my back, digging my back into the small ruts and grooves of the ramp the beer barrels are lowered through, raise my foot, and smash forwards with every ounce of strength in my body at the latch of those doors.

I draw all the strength left inside me and through the ball of my right foot; I swoop down with redemption at the flimsy frame. I deal a blow to smite the very God's. In my minds eye I can already see the splinter of wood, and the burst of sunshine above. My foot is Thor's hammer. It comes down with more force than a mortal is possible of.

The doors don't budge. They don't fucking move, let alone smash open.

In sheer frustration I scream aloud and keep smashing away at them. I keep raising my foot and striking it down, as the boy lies dying behind me. The flames lap laughing above me, and the water gurgles welcomingly below. I keep banging on and on, till all my energy is spent.

So, I rely on something more in the end. Never underestimate the power of the human mind. Never underestimate the strength of will power. For we are nothing more than atoms are we not? Everything in this world is made up of space and atoms. If you can get in tune with all things, anything is possible. It's just a matter of faith. So I willed those motherfuckers to open.

To my complete and utter surprise, they do open. Awash with all that has happened, I really thought for a moment that they had opened simply by me willing them to.

But no, above me M.J and another man's face appear, obviously having been attracted by the sound of my hammering, and they reach out a hand screaming, 'come on, this whole thing's going under any bloody second!'

Before I take M.J's arm with my one good hand, I sank unbelievingly back down to the ground below.

'Come on! For fuck's sake man!' He shouted.

I didn't bother answering. Instead I turned, scooped the boy up, and pulling us up the ramp, held him aloft for them to take. The other man grabbed him, and M.J grabbed my hand.

We leap into the water below as the flaming wreck standing on end behind us, sinks fast.

I couldn't leave the boy. He was my responsibility. The others seemed to realise this, so despite my exhaustion, they allowed me to pull him from the other man. Laid on my back in the sea, I held him in my arms above me, and sculled backwards towards the sanctuary of our boat behind.

Eventually I found myself hoisted to the deck above. Someone was attempting to give the child mouth to mouth but without thinking I barged them out the way. The person looked at me with wide eyes as if I were a madman. And so I must have appeared, burnt, blistered and bleeding, but I didn't care. I simply barked,
'he's mine.'

So I performed CPR. I pinched his nose and breathed into his mouth. I linked my fingers and pushed on his chest, but it was all in vain. It was all for nothing. He was dead in my arms. He was dead. Dead. He was fucking dead man! I'd failed him. I'd failed him.

I wept. I cried big fat tears of sorrow. I completely lost my shit. I couldn't do anything more in that moment bar weep sheer tears of sadness. He was dead. I'd failed him.

I have no real recollection of that moment. I have a snapshot of me sat, legs buckled underneath me, holding the boy's dead matted head in my arms and me weeping.

You know what? Sometimes this life is really fucked up mate.

Anyway, somewhere along the line the mixture of too much smoke, and sheer exhaustion, must have overcome me. For when I came to, I was laying in a comfy hospital bed back on the mainland.

THERE IS A LIGHT AT THE END OF THE TUNNEL......
AND A TATTOO

M.J slept on a chair next to me, head rolled back, mouth wide open, gently snoring. My mouth was so dry my tongue felt like sandpaper in my throat. A glass of water stood on a bedside table, and instinctively I reached out to pick it up. As soon as I wrapped my bandaged hand round the cup a small gasp of pain escaped my lips, and the water clattered to the floor below.

The noise woke M.J with a start and he gazed at me with worried, exhausted eyes. I could tell he'd barely slept.

'Sorry mate,' I croaked.

'No worries,' he smiled wearily.

'What's the deal?' I tried to ask, but my liquid starved mouth gave up on me.

Pouring me a fresh glass of water M.J filled me in on events as I drank long and hard.

Apparently I was being kept in for a few days for observation. I'd inhaled quite a lot of smoke whilst onboard it seemed and the doctors just wanted to keep an eye on me.

My hand had suffered no more than a little superficial burning it turned out; in fact it was already on the mend. I just had to take a bit of care with it for the next week or so. They'd release me the day after tomorrow if all was well. All I had to do was just keep my hand dry and change my bandages regularly. Whatever I could do with my remaining good hand, I should, M.J explained.

'Yeah, no jacking off for you for a while,' he joked.

'Ah that's alright, I always was left handed anyway,' I started to laugh back, but the smile died on my lips as a cutting memory pierced my thoughts. Charcoal and tears.

'You alright mate?' M.J asked concerned.

'Yeah fine. I was just wondering what happened to the others?'

He told me that seven people all told died that day. If it's all right with you I'd very much like to pay tribute to their memory by naming them here.

Anantha Chulalok
Ghan Mahidol

Tunpicha Mahidol
Somlee Mahidol
Adithep Mahidol
Larkana Vatanawongsiree
Michael Ryan.

Somlee was the young boy who died in my arms.

The doctors were right by the way, my hand did heal quickly and the burns were mainly superficial. However, I was left with one really noticeable scar from the burning. At the top of my palm, just below the joints to the fingers, a scar runs directly below my little to index fingers, perhaps an inch wide. Some time later, I felt it only fitting to cover over that scar. So I had my young tragic friend's name, Somlee Mahidol, tattooed over it.

Over the next couple of days, once I'd convinced M.J that I was fine and that he should go and get some rest, I had a lot of spare time to ponder over events. Lying in a hospital bed for hours on end can get rather tedious at times. Still, I think it was the best thing possible to come to terms with events.

After hours of contemplation, unfortunately I could come up with no greater reason for things than, 'shit happens.' It seems a little flippant, but that was my universal truth. Sorry. Sounds a bit harsh really doesn't it?

Now I know such things have to happen, hell, we all have to die sometime right? It's just hard to come to terms with when it happens to someone so young, it all seems a little pointless really. I know Mother Nature and God ensure such things happen; else our planet would be even more crippled than it is with over-population.

Hell, that's why every time we find a cure for something, Mother Nature conjures up something afresh to keep things in proportion. Smallpox for example, used to claim thousands of lives, we cure that, and then all of a sudden AIDS comes along and hits us just as hard.

What I don't understand though, is why do bad things happen to good people? Somlee was no more than an innocent ten-year-old boy. In all rights he should be running around, kicking a soccer ball with his friends. Scoring the winning goal and kissing the emblem on his bright yellow Brazilian football shirt, just as he'd seen his heroes do on TV. Before his mates pick him up cheering, and carry him aloft and out of their stadium with wide toothy smiles.

He should be running home to tell his parents all about it over dinner, re-enacting every part of his brilliant goal enthusiastically whilst his mother tells him to sit at the table and calm down. His family most certainly shouldn't have been pulled out of the sea with long fishhooks, charred and scarred beyond recognition.

Oh yeah, the age-old adage, 'a problem shared is a problem halved,' really is true. Talking about things really does put all the crazy thoughts bouncing around your head into some kind of manageable format to analyse effectively.

Even if the people you talk to are just the Thai policeman and interpreter sent in to interrogate you about events. They were pretty kindly and understanding actually.

Anyway, so yeah, basically 'shit happens.' It is the best I've got I'm afraid. Maybe I'll find some grander design for it soon, but I guess I'm a bit of a coward at the end of the day the truth be told. I'd decided that was all the thinking I needed to do on the matter, I'd addressed the situation enough for the time being, and so I locked it up and tucked it away. The snapshots of burning bodies, and lifeless young soccer heroes was put on the slide projector in my mind, and spun round to the very back of my head, so that they wouldn't rotate back into view for sometime. How much of a coward am I?

That's the genius thing about travelling actually. With constant new horizons and adventures, your surroundings forever changing, it becomes very easy to forget.

So for the rest of my time in hospital, I had a love affair, removing the bad thoughts with good ones. Coward.

What with everything that had gone on, to be really honest, all I fucking wanted was a hug. Sounds a bit gay really, but oh well. So I had a love affair whilst laid under those crisp clean white sheets. A mental love affair that is.

I couldn't wait to see Destiny again. I realised as I lay there just how much I fancied the pants off her! In my minds eye I played out our love affair. Our eyes lock over the conveyer belt in luggage claim, and we instantly kiss each other. We hold each other tight before sneaking off into some abandoned office to shag each other's brains out. (Ah come on, let me off, I had to beef up this section with a bit of manliness after the 'hug' comment above!)

We'd become so close over the Internet, talking for hours, and I was missing her. Ok, I know being sat there mailing each other millions of miles apart isn't exactly a healthy relationship, but still. As you're typing at your terminal chatting to each other, all the miles float away and disappear. It's almost as if you're sat right next to each other talking, and so I was looking forward to getting out of my ward and speaking to her again.

When you're feeling blue, it seems important somehow to have someone out there to love and care about you. In reality we'd spent only a handful of hours together. Though this was all I needed it seemed, whilst coupled with the hundreds of e-mails, for me to realise I was falling for her, and had been for some time.

I played out our love affair whilst staring up at the ceiling of my cell.

We meet again, we love each other, we marry, have children, maybe call one of our sons, 'Somlee.' No, scratch that. Don't want those thoughts flooding back in again. Maybe we'll call him, 'M.J.' Yeah, that's better. Hmm, wonder how many people he and the others managed to save? Damn it, there I go again. Right. M.J, Chloe, Destiny and I, naked piggyback fighting in the shallow waters of Bondi beach. Yeah, that's better. Hmm, much better. Yes, most definitely. I can feel myself drifting off to sleep, and her smile dances in my mind. Ah, to sleep perchance to dream of her once more.........

Anyway. After I got released I did email Destiny straight away. It seems she was getting quite worried about me because I hadn't mailed her for a few days, and we were half way through talking about something serious, so she was concerned over what might be going on.

Worried about me hey? That's a good sign right? Maybe she does love me? Or am I reading too much into things as always, and its just the same kinda concern M.J showed, mates like?

Ah well, fuck it. Time will tell 'cause I'll be in New Zealand soon enough. For now though, there was a hell of a lot of Thailand to explore still.

It was advised that I shouldn't get my hand wet for a few days still to help the healing process. Although when I took a sneaky peek under my bandages, I couldn't believe how quickly it was mending itself already.

Still, M.J phoned his friend in Chiang Rai and let him know that we'd be there a little before schedule. Having decided to come back to the brilliant blue sea of the south to snorkel and scuba after we'd trekked around the jungles up north.

ALIEN CONSTELLATIONS, CEASELESS CRICKET CONCERTO. BACK TO BASICS. BACK TO HAPPINESS

WE CAUGHT a bus to Surat Thani, before picking up a day train back up to Bangkok. Neither of us had any particular inclination to stay longer than we had to in that city, so we just hung around the train station, waiting for a late sleeper train to pull up and whisk us off to Chiang Mai and M.J's Buddhist preacher friend. Apparently he'd procured the use of an acquaintance's motorcar, and would drive us on from Chiang Mai to Chiang Rai. Bloody long few days travel, but such is the life of a backpacker.

The overnight train reminded me somewhat of a prison train from the movies, or perhaps one of the old west engines that would whisk young men to the front line to build the railways. My 6-foot long bunk swung down from the ceiling above, where I could pull a dark dirtied piece of cloth along the washing line provided to box me in and give me some privacy. M.J slept in the bunk below.

It was certainly strange wandering along the empty gangways in the early morning hours. Everyone was sectioned off by their own little curtains, with only the odd flash of torchlight illuminating a silhouette here and there as I walked towards the rear doors.

Here, I left the sound of deep snoring behind and stepped outside onto the metal grated balcony to watch the sun rise. Still dressed in just shorts and t-shirt, I enjoyed the feel of the early morning chill on my goose bumped skin, knowing full well that the day would soon take on the heat of a sauna. Sparking up a cigarette, I just took pleasure in watching the paddy fields roll by, waving to early morning workers as we chugged along our peaceful way.

Ping Pong met us as we vaulted off the train in Chiang Mai later that day. Exactly what our small Buddhist friend's real name was I never found out, nor why M.J called him Ping Pong. When he introduced himself I raised an inquisitive eyebrow, but he and M.J merely laughed and said, 'don't ask, it's a long story.'

Ping Pong was forever a mystery to me. He spoke little of his personal past, or trivialities, often only responding to my questions with the quip, 'the Wise Man can say more with a word than the Fool can with many.' I guess he reminded me of that old dude from Karate Kid, or maybe a human equivalent

148

to Yoda! One thing I did learn was that this guy was extremely wise and learned. I think he'd taught M.J for a short time, before allowing my dread locked friend to go and discover his own truths in the world.

I haven't got a bloody clue how old he was. His knowledge suggested he had seen many winters pass by, but his energy, dexterity and nimbleness, made me wonder if he was no older than myself.

In appearance, well, I guess he merely reflected all members of his religious standing. He wore sandals and the long orange robes of Buddhist Monks. His head was shaved and he possessed a pearly white smile. Bar this, there really were no other particularly distinguishing features about him. I guess he didn't need them, for all he was shone through from inside.

The car was just a small clapped out old Fiat parked opposite a small open and abandoned expanse of inner city wasteland near the station.

As I went to climb into the back seat, my eyes caught hold of the wrinkled lepers cooking a half plucked chicken, with feathers still hanging off its limp form, over a small fire they'd made. It was the crackling raw red flames that made me stare. As I sank down into the ripped and torn, padding bereft seat, closing the door, I was incapable of removing my eyes from that glowing fire. It's dancing movement held me transfixed.

As we pulled away, M.J up front in the passenger's side, chatting away as we drove, for some reason the enormities of all that had happened over the last few days caught up with me. I barely heard a word M.J said, all of a sudden all I really wanted to do was spark up a big fat joint and smoke away my memories.

Unfortunately this was not an option, and I'm glad that was the case, because I was about to find out for certain that there are natural highs that can melt away your troubles far better than drugs can.

Anyway, M.J and I were to be teetotal drugs wise for our entire journey throughout Thailand, (well, almost) mainly because of the severity of the law in that country. If you're found with any drug on your personage, then the options are either five years imprisonment for marijuana, (and trust me when I say that their prisons make the one's we know in the Western world look like a fucking holiday camp) or for all other drugs, life imprisonment. However, if you're really really lucky, they may sentence you to the death penalty instead. Funnily enough, I didn't particularly fancy any of those options.

We spent that night in a sparsely furnished house in Chiang Rai. I call it a house, but it really was nothing more than a one-roomed hut really. Apparently it belonged to a friend of Ping Pong's, though I never established where the owner was residing at present.

We cooked a simple meal of rice and vegetables, a diet I was soon to become very accustomed to, not by choice mind you, rather by necessity. In a country full of poverty, everything bar rice and veg come at an extortionate price, unless you were rich, or a man from the west. Although my taste buds weren't initially impressed, I'd come to find that meal more wholesome than anything I'd previously known. You see, whilst we trekked around the jungles for the next few days, in that heat, and those conditions, all we could carry food wise was rice, chopped vegetables, and a few herbs and spices. After trekking for hours on end, starving hungry and in desperate need of energy, those meals would be heaven sent.

Anyway, we cooked the rice up on a small portable gas stove in the corner of the room, before eating off plastic plates with chopsticks by candlelight, sat around cross-legged on straw mats upon the floor.

In Thailand there's no real need at night for blankets, so we just curled up on the floor after our food, wanting to turn in early in preparation for the hard days ahead. Using our packs for pillows, we slept like babes.

(N.B. This is a journal entry from the Diaries of Me – May 25th. Year – Well that would be telling wouldn't it!)

'Today? Today has been one of those days even a case of amnesia could not erase from my memory. Take now for example. I'm writing this entry by candlelight. Outside there's no thunder, but a constant stream of lightening illuminates the night sky. Above I can see the stars as bright as they've ever been before, and yet the constellations are alien to me. A clear visual example of what a different world I'm in now. The lightening is not the only source of light in the night though. There is a constant flow of fireflies meandering through the air, nonchalantly aware of their beauty, happy to hold the eye with their fluorescent greens and yellows. Outside it is the crickets' time, as they play a ceaseless concerto to dominate the dusk.

As you can guess I am at perfect peace here. Back to basics, back to our natural state, back to being at one with nature, rather than the parasite modern society has become to our world. Back to raw feeling and raw emotions, beautifully brilliant in their simplicity.

Anyway, I digress as always, events of the day? Big breakfast, early start. Setting off in the Fiat, our first destination was Mok Fa waterfall. A huge cascading beauty. The mandatory tourist photos, followed by a short climb on foot through the jungle, using fallen branches as we crossed rivers on route, until we reached the caves halfway up the waterfall.

Inside I made the mistake of sparking my lighter to take a look around. The deafening roar of wings instantly greeted my ears, as a host of giant bats brushed past my face with their privacy disturbed.

More mandatory tourist mug shots before a light lunch. Rice and vegetables for a nice welcome change.

We continued up the mountain via Ping Pong's car. A number of dangerous ascents on narrow mud paths, shear drops off to the sides, and the rear wheels sliding away precariously due to the rain, had me ready to leap out of the vehicle. Fortunately it never came to that, though there were times when I did start to wonder!

So our trek into the jungles of the Thai section of the Golden Triangle eventually began. We walked all day, pulling rainproof ponchos over our heads and backpacks when the skies opened. It was, all in all, a very, very surreal experience.

The rain beat down with the intensity of a tribal drummer man beating down upon his bongos. Oh, and trust me when I say you don't really know what rain is until you trek through the jungle in a monsoon. Man, those big old fat raindrops were the size of hams! It fell through those brilliant green chlorophyll overdosed leaves to smack down on my head almost knocking me sideways!

Winding along an animal trail, Ping Pong would point out through a thick, highly accented English guttural rumble all the local points of interest. The flora and fauna that adorned our path. Apart from this, no one really spoke, we just listened to the cacophony of wildlife that cried all around, completely mesmerised by the entire situation. It was beautiful. It was amazing.

As our trail wound down into a gorge shortly before sunset, I suddenly started feeling very uncomfortable. The monsoon had stopped as suddenly as it had started, and I'd found myself wandering through felled landscapes on the side of the mountains. Farmers tilled their vital fields as we approached the straw huts of a hill tribe village, and I was feeling out of sorts. I had no right being here, I realised I was no more than a rich westerner treating this place like a zoo. So I thank the people for letting me pry into their lives.

Upon that descent I was instantly reminded of the old man washing in the waters of Bangkok. As the chickens ran around aimlessly, a couple of elderly women and their daughters knelt by the rivers edge, scrubbing their clothes clean. As we wandered by, they looked up and smiled. So, I decided to go meet them. I didn't want to just stand around gaping and staring at them like it was some zoo after all.

Ping Pong and M.J went to meet the hill tribe's leader, Loet La, and sort out accommodation for the evening. I removed my sweaty and stinking sleeveless shirt, and bent down alongside the ladies in the shallows of the wide running river.

'Sawàt-dii,' I said.

The ladies just smiled without making eye contact, obviously a little embarrassed and gently nodded their heads, before returning to their washing. The young daughters giggled as they watched me dipping my shirt in the water, rubbing the cloth together without really getting anywhere.

Luckily, the oldest of the daughters, perhaps no more than 18 or 19 years old, decided to put me out of my misery. She waded over to my side, squatting beside me, and handed me a small chunk of what could only be some form of homemade soap.

I gratefully took it from those long bronzed callused fingers, and looking up into her deep brown eyes, nodded in thanks. 'khàwp khun.'

Holding my gaze, she again said nothing but merely looked up from beneath long eyelashes, and smiled just a little.

'Khun chêu arai?' I tried.

As she parted her lips to respond, tucking a few strands of long black hair behind her ear, I realised how unbelievably beautiful this girl was. Before she could answer though, her mother called her after her as they departed, leaving me to scrub away at my clothes in that dark rippling river as dusk descended.

Now I'm laying here writing on my straw mat, as the hill tribe leader talks to Ping Pong. He has a harmonic voice, the fire is warm, and I have lots of food filling my belly. The heavens have opened once more, yet being warm and dry inside has a soothing effect on my soul, and so I find myself drifting off into a peaceful state of slumber.'
End of Entry.

Waking early, I wandered back down to the water to wash myself, rather than my clothes this time. Sat on a rock, drying off in the early morning sun, I watched the locals collect water from the river, before heading off to work. It reminded me of the Jungle Book. 'And I must go and fetch the water, till the day that I am old,' ran on the vinyl inside my head.

Feeling more than a little useless, I made my way back to the village to see if I could be of any assistance. The only responses I could get from people though, were appreciative smiles, but shakes of the head. I was an outlander here, and perhaps understandably so, the people shied away from me.

Still, as the suns rays really began breaking over the mountaintops, I happened upon Ping Pong, M.J, Loet La, and a number of the more aged men, performing Tai Chi on the hill slopes. For a long time I just watched, before joining the back of the group, and trying to feign their movements. I soon discovered, once again, that the key to all forms of meditation, is breathing. Each movement coincided either with the inhaling or exhaling of breath. Tai Chi was simply a more physical exercise of meditation, working the body to allow the tranquillity of the mind. So we remained for many a minute, until a cry for breakfast echoed around.

As I stood in the doorway of the breakfast hut, watching the natives go about their every day work in the early morning sun, a call of trumpets roused me from my contemplation.

Placing my emptied bowl of rice and the chopsticks back on the straw mat behind me, I watched the chopsticks dance and jiggle, tinkling away in my breakfast bowl, with an inquisitive brow. The trembling of earth around me, the loosening of soil in the roof above that fell in a light shower upon my hair, and another great chorus of trumpeting forced me out into the daylight to investigate.

Blinking up into the dazzling rays with squinted eyes, M.J beamed down at me from his elevated position upon an elephant's back.

'Climb up then shit face,' he said, greeting me with his usual, ever so friendly, insult (Remind me again why I was friends with this guy!).

As the elephant bent down on its hind legs, allowing me to place a foot upon its knee, I accepted M.J's outstretched hand, and pulled myself up onto the creature's back.

Before I had the opportunity to give M.J the customary punch in the arm for being cheeky though, our ride was straightening back up, causing me to fall into the back of our wooden seat. You see, the saddle to this great beast was a short wooden bench with room for two to sit abreast, and it was the hard wooden backrest of this seat that I fell against.

Clever thinking really, else I would've just toppled straight of the elephants back to the ground below, before climbing back aboard and repeating the same falling off process again and again. A game that could've got pretty boring pretty quickly I figured!

Anyway, M.J leant forward patting the coarse hairy sides of the beast, and as she let out another great bugle, he told me, 'welcome to our wonderful steed for the day. Her name's Mette Bo and she's a sucker for freshly picked bananas.'

As if in response to this introduction the cheeky cow reached up over her shoulder with her long trunk, plucked the banana M.J had just passed to me out of my greedy hands (well I was relishing the natural sugar of fresh fruit after no more than rice and bloody vegetable for meals on end), and placed it into her grateful chomping jaws.

'She's a beauty 'aint she,' he commented.

'Yeah,' I returned with a rather perplexed (well, even for me this was a particularly surreal situation I thought) tone in my voice. Then as she started to lumber forwards, I glanced over the handrail on my seats side at the ground some distance below, before throwing as an afterthought, 'she ain't exactly small is she?!'

M.J just laughed, 'ah she's just a teenager. You wanna meet her mother mate.'

Pointing forward, I followed the line of his outstretched finger and my jaw dropped as the hugest bloody living creature I've ever laid eyes on, burst out from the tree line off to our right. I swear this thing was a cross between a Woolly Mammoth and a Killer Whale! Shit. Now that's impressive I thought.

Mette Bo broke into a little gallop (not entirely sure that's the right terminology for the trotting type thingy of an elephant, but then again, I didn't even know until I found myself bouncing up and down uncomfortably on my balls that elephants even had more than one speed!) towards her mum, and as they pulled in beside each other, Ping Pong leant over from his perch aboard the mother, and shouted out, 'Loet La has offered us the use of his elephants for the day.'

Loet La merely nodded at me in greeting, before turning his and Ping Pong's elephant around and heading off towards the jungle's edge, Mette Bo falling in instinctively behind.

Yeah, so I found myself crashing through the undergrowth on the back of our young brilliant elephant on the northernmost borders of Thailand.

After bouncing around uncomfortably for a while, grazing a nasty gashing rash on my bum cheeks, I soon found I got in tune with Mette Bo's movement. It's kinda hard to explain, sort of a rolling circular movement I guess.

I particularly remember the sharp treacherous descents, more than a little hairy I can tell you. I really didn't fancy being pitched head first under Mette

Bo's trampling feet, especially as I fancied she wouldn't hesitate in stomping happily on my prone helpless frame, just for shits and giggles.

You see, we were already building up a good relationship. Basically it consisted of me attempting on numerous occasions to eat the bananas M.J had brought along. That little bitch, I swear I was gonna slap her some time pretty soon. She cottoned on to the fact that, unlike herself, I needed to peel the fruit to eat it. Well, as soon as I'd started to remove the skin she'd "accidentally" walk through a pothole causing me to lose my balance and grab hold of the handrail. That was exactly the moment when the little whore would strike, plucking the banana out of my hand as I rolled around defenceless, and after munching away, she'd release a mocking trumpet call from her trunk, taunting me. We were gonna have some harsh words when I finally got down, I can tell you. Women!

Nah, only joking. Mette Bo was brilliant, and riding through the jungles of the Golden Triangle on her back was such an immense experience. I could see every shade of green, and before me lay such beautifully brilliant wild flowers, blossoming away in every colour of the rainbow, even I could do nothing but gaze in awe and wonder (and that's saying something! I'm more your kind of guy who would gaze unblinking with open jawed mouth at the football play-offs, or maybe playboy bunnies, rather than flowers!).

I could see from my perch at the top of the mountainous hills, nothing more than sprawling miles of rainforest. We had left humanity behind, and it was humbling. Awe-inspiring. I sucked away on my cigarette, and watched a world I'd never even imagined roll by. It was pretty cool I can tell you.

We spent the night under a bamboo windbreaker, there really was no need for any extra shelter. Loet La, Mette Bo and her mother headed off at first light, leaving M.J, Ping Pong and I to trek on alone.

Now, despite my recent chain smoking, I still like to consider myself pretty damn fit. However, our first arduous climb up the mountain slopes in the stifling mid-morning heat had even me bent double, struggling for breath. Not quite as straight forward as I first thought this jungle trekking malarkey.

Still, when the path levelled off somewhat, and I was allowed to take in my surroundings rather than concentrating on placing one foot in front of the other, I realised how immense it all was.

Ping Pong continued to astound me as he pointed out the local flora and fauna beside us without even faltering for breath during the climb. I asked him how the hell he managed it? Smiling, he pointed at the cigarette I'd sparked up whilst I'd stopped to get my breath back, and he said, 'not smoking is a good start.'

Looking down at the glowing cancer stick in my fingers I laughed, 'I've tried to quit but it never seems to work, just weak willed I guess!'

'Not at all,' he replied. 'Just remember though, to never stop trying, because every human being has the ability to better themselves.'

I paused to contemplate this thought, before shrugging my shoulders and taking another drag of my fag.

Anyway, for me, the most intriguing discovery that afternoon was some kinda edible herb that grew about our trail. Its leaves were extremely sour, but bloody tasty. For the rest of the day I would be continually munching away merrily on my surroundings.

We stopped for lunch in the middle of nowhere. Ping Pong had somehow led us to a lonely hut, hidden away mysteriously inside the jungle. To say I was hot by this point would be an understatement; I was so incredibly boiling you could've thrown a few rashers of bacon on my stomach and cooked yourself a fry up!

Much to my relief though, a glistening stream ran alongside the shack, with a little miniature waterfall for the weary traveller to happily stick his head under for long moments in a futile attempt to lessen the heat in the day. I didn't want to move. The pleasure of the cold water splashing over my sweating face, running down the back of my sticky shirt, caused my hairs to stand on end. I closed my eyes and lost myself.

The next thing I knew was M.J calling me to lunch. They'd thrown up a sumptuous feast of wild oxen, chicken, French fries, chocolate gateaux and cold beer. Oh no, my mistake, rice and vegetables again. Oh goody. No, I wolfed it down as if it were some great feast. My grumbling stomach was certainly happy for a feeding, as were my aching muscles happy with the boost of energy.

We spent a number of days trekking, all running along the same theme. Heavy duty marching through the jungle in the day, then at night, Ping Pong would often preach to me, or teach us more meditation techniques, all under a blanket of wild stars. The guy was fascinating.

Oh, the major point of interest for me besides all this was on our penultimate day before setting off back to the hill tribe's village.

Well, basically, at the time the late Princess Mother of Thailand, along with accelerated law enforcement, had striven to push the opium that took so readily to those mountainous slopes, back into Myanmar and Laos.

So, officially for the record, and after wise advice, I'd like to state that I most definitely did not trek through rich pastures of opiate poppies on that penultimate day, lovingly tendered by their rich owners. My guide merely misled me into mistaking that which I saw. My guide merely misled me to believe that I'd strolled dumfounded through harvested opium fields. I certainly was misled into believing that I'd seen armed guards and farmers mixing tobacco together with the home grown opium, roll it into cigarettes using the banana leaves that grew all around as Rizla paper, and spark up merrily without a care in the world.

Yes, these were officially no more than hallucinations caused by the onset of exhaustion and heat stroke. Yes that's it. The flowers I saw, if any, were no more that large daisies perhaps, or possibly buttercups, yes, that's right. Nothing more. My mistake.

Our trek ended with the river. Ping Pong, M.J and I cut off twelve long sections of bamboo plant and strung them together with vines. We then floated down stream for some time, back towards Loet La's village. All the while passing huge water buffalo, and watching river snakes darting in and out of the hollowed bamboo beneath our feet.

So that was our northern adventure. I was sad to say goodbye to Ping Pong at the train station, but extremely happy to rush into the nearest restaurant and gorge myself on hamburgers, mint choc chip ice cream, and ice cold Sprites. The Thai jungle meals were nice, but meat and sugar never tasted so good.

ALL YOU NEED IS LOVE

MY HAND was suitably healed for me to not even bother with the bandages again. Sure, it was covered in some cracking scabs that took all my will power not to start picking at, but it was definitely good enough to go swimming with.

As the ferry passed once more from Phuket, carrying us to Ko Phi Phi, my thoughts understandably carried back to the events that unfurled on those waters just a few weeks before.

I remained quiet, lost in contemplation the whole voyage, merely staring out to starboard, allowing the ghosts of before to play out again before my eyes. The voyage was rather melancholic, with M.J merely leaving me to my own devices.

I was certainly relieved to jump onto hard ground at the end of it all without mishap. I was certainly happy with throwing myself into the hustle and bustle of port life society with exaggerated enthusiasm to hide my dark thoughts and memories away inside again.

Ko Phi Phi was a dumbbell shaped island, the major point of society being the thin strip of land that formed the handle of the dumbbell. I say, 'was,' because I barely know how much of it still exists. It was hit badly twice by the great Tsunami disaster of 26th December 2004. I hear whole hotels were washed out to sea. Really strange that such a small piece of tranquil paradise, my favourite beach in the world, only exists as I remember it in my mind. What a disaster that was. Floating bodies, tears and death filled the waters once again.

Anyway, I didn't want to stay on the main tourist strip. I was pretty sure M.J felt the same; we just liked it to be as isolated as possible so that we could formulate our own opinion of things. Rather than be surrounded by rich, fattened and sunburnt old white men, being massaged down by 'me love you long time,' girls.

It's not easy to formulate a real opinion of a place with that in your face all day, everyday. So, wandering down the slatted wooden runway of the port, I veered off towards a number of Longtail boats that rested in the surf far off to the right. Moving away from the squawking chicken cages being unloaded from the boats, away from the Thai people with dollar signs for pupils who tugged on your sleeves with reels of postcards and other Ko Phi Phi junk memorabilia hanging from their frames.

Approaching the owner of the nearest Longtail, his face remained in shadow, just a pair of glowing white eyes discernable from beneath his straw hat.

I pointed at my map, tapping at Hat Yao, the beach furthest away from the dumbbell handle tourist strip of the island. It was only accessible by boat; with just a handful of small huts for accommodation. No shops or anything similar. We'd be pretty much left to our own devices out there, with maybe just a few more adventurous travellers for company. If there's one thing you can rely on with the, 'Tourist Monkeys,' (as a Dutch friend of mine, 'Edo' dubbed those fattened white massaged men so aptly, in his staccato English accent that made him sound like Mr Burns from the Simpsons. 'Rotterdam de Nederland,' 'your soul is mine,' ha ha, man you used to crack M.J and I up something chronic!) is that they're generally so bloody lazy they wont go any further than they have to.

Approaching the pair of eyes I saw them light up as I spoke that most loved phrase as I pointed at my map, 'thâo raí?'

I can't remember what price he charged now, but it seemed alright. M.J and I only generally bartered on things when we felt we were really, really being ripped off. You'd be amazed how much a couple of bucks extra can purchase for people in those parts of the world, and fifty pence or whatever doesn't exactly make much difference to us Westerners a lot of the time.

Anyway, we jumped into the shallow confines of the front of the boat, dumping out backpacks next to us. The Longtail basically consisted of no more than a narrow 10-metre hull, with a small flat piece of roofing, maybe 3 metres long, at the rear. There was also a small outboard motor. Even now our captain was wrenching upon its starter cord, so as to get the ancient device to splutter into life.

With a cough, a whine, and a vomiting forth of toxic smoke for good measure, the engine eventually pushed us forwards. We were soon picking our way through the maze of vessels to shoot over the coral to Hat Yao.

The islands were so stunningly picturesque it's indescribable. Cigarette hanging from my bottom lip, bouncing up and down on the waves, face upturned to the sun, I watched the golden shores shoot by.

The sand was a brilliant white, and the steep cliffs that consisted of the rest of the islands were covered in lush emerald green vegetation. I don't know if you've ever seen, 'James Bond, The Man with the Golden Gun,' but a lot of it was filmed out here. How nice are those islands?!

I think even Bond appreciated their beauty, and he had scantily clad girls to gaze at instead if he'd wanted to!

An old hag of a woman watched us jump into the knee deep water at Hat Yao, bags on shoulders, pay our pilot before he turned tail and fled, and head towards the far end of the beach.

We took the two straw and bamboo huts nearest the cliffs, removing the keys of B-1 and B-2, before having a quick look at our prospective lodgings for the next week. This didn't take long.

The glaring brightness of the sunshine outside had us squinting into the darkness. All we could see briefly were dead bugs and dust floating in the beams of sunlight. Finding a light switch (rather impressive actually, not really the kinda establishment you'd associate with electricity) I tugged at the cord and a single dull uncovered bulb clicked into action above, illuminating the scene.

The hut consisted of no more than two rooms. The room I stood in was perhaps ten foot square. A double bed lay underneath a heavy-duty mosquito net, and the mattress sagged in the middle. Still, in my experience, a bed is a bed, wherever I could find to rest my head I would. There was just enough room outside the netting to dump my pack and still walk about without tripping over it.

Attached to the back was a little doorway through which you had to stoop like a limbo dancer to gain access to the bathroom beyond. It consisted of no more than a toilet. I should point out here by the way that when I say 'toilet,' I mean a Thai toilet. As in it was no more than a round hole in the floor leading to a pit below, which you had to squat over to do your business in. Sanitation was not your pad of bog roll, but your regular Thai bucket of tepid filthy water in which to splash your hand in and wipe yourself down with once the deed is done. It was always fun to sit there and bat away the army of flies swarming around you and your lovely bucket.

No, none of this bothered me to be honest. It's amazing how quickly a human can adapt to the conditions surrounding him. I mean, up North I'd been shitting in the woods and using leaves to wipe myself off with. I'd been sleeping on the ground, using the mossy carpet of the rainforest as my mattress, and why? Because it was the only option available. You do what you have to. Always remember in this life, things can always be better, but they can most definitely be worse!

As Ping Pong would preach, the mark of the enlightened One is the person who can appreciate the cards they've been dealt. The One who can step outside and find perspective, see things in their entirety; see the good in everything. For the cards will always change, and you never know what the next hand to be dealt will be like.

Personally I loved my little hut. I had shelter, a bed to sleep on, and somewhere to crap, what more d'you need?!

My favourite part of it all though, was the little veranda outside. There was a small washing line so you could hang up your wet clothes to dry, and a little rocking chair to sit in the shade upon. You could sit there for hours just gazing out at the beautiful azure ocean beyond. If you did get too hot then, and I measured it out so I can be exact in this, it was precisely 29 steps to the waters edge.

As I slouched down into the rocking chair, undoing my sandals to take a much needed dip, the old hag who'd watched us come ashore approached. In broken English she asked for a few baht for rent, and explained that there was a large hut with hot showers at the opposite end of the beach.

M.J and I could never be arsed to find them actually, preferring to wake and wash in the boiling sea instead. The water was so warm it was amazing, we'd spend whole afternoons just floating around relaxing, exploring the coral with a mask, though we barely needed one with how transparently clear it all was, chasing after shoals of brightly coloured fish as they darted around our toes.

It was so easy to forget the trials and tribulations of life whilst staying on that beach. It was so easy to see and understand everything our Buddhist friend had tried to teach me whilst lounging there on the shore. It seemed I could finally sort all the thoughts that had been bouncing around in my head, all my discoveries, into some kind of concrete format. I found for a short time complete peace and clarity.

Hmm, sometimes my journal extracts from the time explain things better than I can now.

'Tonight, as I watched the sun set, all my thoughts and insights of the past few months seemed to finally come together. I stayed and watched the stars take over as the reds and tangerines of the sinking sun finally dispersed. Walking bare footed in the waves, I danced. I threw my arms up, my head back and just laughed, spinning round and round as the water splashed up around me. Everything seemed to have finally fitted into place, the last piece of the jigsaw of my life slotted home and I've never felt so content.

For a long time, I had struggled to explain why I was here? Just what it was all about, what the point of this life was? I was searching so hard for answers, I overlooked the simplicity of all the things that really matter.

I realised at long last that the universe is multi-dimensional. An old science teacher told me that if we set out walking in a straight line away from planet Earth, we would eventually return to it, without ever having completed a loop. How the hell is this possible?

Well, basically, our brains simply can't compute the vastly multi-dimensional level that the language of the universe is written in. We're simply not capable enough, its not a matter of intelligence, even Einstein realised that his amazing mind was unable to process the information at hand.

So you see, the laws, the language, the questions and the answers of the universe exist in their own entity that we as humans, could never compute. In truth, it is impossible to even really understand the question, let alone the answer!

It seemed I could search forever for the meaning of it all, and never get any closer. My problem, in a way, was solved. This is how it is, and in all probability, how it always will be. Realise this, and instead concentrate on that which we can attain, that which we already have, and then we will see all the happiness we need.

Toothless old men smiling in dirtied rivers.
Beautiful young girls washing clothes in jungle villages.

All the body requires is three things; nourishment, shelter, and oxygen. Everything else is a bonus. If we realise this, we can be happy with this alone.

Suddenly a stain on a new top, the loss of a new purchase, or the lack of riches, is put in its rightful place. It really shouldn't depress us, as in the grander scheme of things, it really doesn't matter. You can't spend money nor stare at your trinkets when you're dead.

Nourishment, shelter, and oxygen. If we have these things, we have everything, for they are the essentials to life. Happiness is often a matter of perspective. Happiness is not materialism.

As for the soul, in the words of The Beatles, 'All we need is love.'

Firstly, in Faith. Something exists, some force outside us all, trust me on this one, I've seen it at work. Personally I choose to use the word, 'God,' for it, but that's only because I don't really know what other word to use. I don't believe in any set religion, for I believe all 'gods,' all names, are one and the same thing. God, Buddha, Allah, Mohammed, Mother Nature, whichever name we use for it, life so often is nothing more than a matter of keeping the faith, in having faith, for at times we must all leap into the unknown.

If we can only control 5% of things in life, make damn sure you control that whole 5%, then the other 95% is just about having the balls, the courage, to leap out into uncertainty, and believe. Courage is acknowledging ones fear, but saddling up for the ride anyway.

Love thy Lord, and your faith and courage shall be rewarded. Trust me. You may not realise it at first, but everything in our lives happens for a reason. The loss of a loved one may actually end up uniting us with our destiny. Inconceivable events are forever in motion behind our lives, so make your decisions, and then go with the flow. Your faith will take you where you need to be. I've seen these things, I've witnessed these wheels in motion, so have faith, have courage, and all else will follow.

Whatever you do, don't be a victim to fear, don't let it rule your life. For a life lived in fear is a life half lived. It turns you into no more than a shadow of the sunlight you wanted and dreamt of. Be able to turn around and say at the end of it all, 'I lived out my dreams.'

I mean, the fear we have of death, is to die knowing that we never really experienced everything, that we never really lived life to its fullest extent. So go, live your life; what's the point in having dreams if we never make them happen? After all, at the end of the day, it's not the years in your life that matter, but the life in your years.

Secondly, for nature. For if we continue to destroy our surroundings, eventually those three vital things our bodies need to exist, will no longer be available. I really feel I've seen the Seven Wonders of the World, and they're all natural. They're so amazing; they fill our minds and hearts with breathless beauty.

Thirdly, in Other People. Family, (who I love so much they'll never really know.) friends, (M.J, what can I say bro, you gave me life when all seemed lost) and of course, in a Partner. When you don't know where you end, and they begin.

That's it. Our brains lack the depth of dimensions to understand the universe, its questions, and its answers. So don't depress yourself with what you could never have. Concentrate on that which you can attain, on those things you've already got, and the happiness they'll bring you. This you'll soon realise is all you really need.

Your body; Air, Nourishment and Shelter.
Your soul: Love. For God, Nature, and Other People, in particularly Family, Friends and Partner.

I could never really describe the blissful euphoria of this point of my life. When your brain switches off, and you can just feel the beauty of a sunset, because you realise all that you have. I reckon I'm not doing too badly. The only hint of a thing missing is a Partner. Ah, Destiny! Still, 'half a dozen right people in this world, but only one right time and place.' Maybe the right time and place is closer than I think? I mean, not long to New Zealand now?

Oh well, if not then one thing's for sure, 'shit happens.' Sometimes it has to; else we'll never get to where we're going. Still, it's how we act when the shit does hit the proverbial fan, how we analyse those situations when all is bad, and use them, drawing upon their memory in the future, that really makes a difference. Anyway, yeah, instead of getting down about the Partner thing, I recognise everything I have right now and I just think, 'I'll have to bring my wife here someday.' That'll be cool.'
End of Entry.

I DIDN'T NEED AMPHETAMINES
TO TELL ME THIS WAS LOVE

ANYWAY, ah that's it, the guy charged us 30 baht to catch a boat from town, and I was damned if I was gonna pay that all the time when I had beneath me a perfectly good pair of legs as a form of transport. I know the guidebook reckoned you could only reach Hat Yao by boat, but the whole island was connected by land was it not? So I figured there must be some kind of way of walking there.

On the third day, missing Destiny and an Internet café, I set out to prove my theory right. It took like, three hours, but in the end I was indeed correct, (bloody hell! That's a first for the books! Generally my crazy theories have a tendency to work out in theory, in my head like, but never in practise!) I found a small trail that wound up and through the forest heading inland, before spitting me back out on the rocks of the seashore around the cliffs of the headland.

Finding a little café to indulge myself with a cold beer in recognition of my days achievement, (any excuse for alcohol hey?!) how chuffed was I when I read my emails? With my excursion to New Zealand less than two weeks away, Destiny let me know that she couldn't concentrate on anything at the moment because she was so looking forward to seeing me again. (I reckon that can only be a good thing right?)

I think her exact words were, 'I love spending hour upon hour chatting to you on line, I've never met a friend (Damn that word! Still I'll overlook it at the moment.) I could open up my whole heart to as much as I can with you. I just can't believe it's only going to be a few days until we can actually chat face to face at last instead of monitor to monitor. Not only because I can't wait to see that cheeky smile I've been unable to forget again, but I also reckon your face is sexier to chat to than my monitor. Only just mind you! Ha ha lol, only joking, you're not the only one who can be a cheeky lil' chimp! You know I'm only messing around anyway. The monitor's far better looking than you are! Lol.'

It all sounded quite hopeful I thought, seemed to possibly belie some sort of feelings for me, it certainly caused me to smile in hope anyway, because between you and I, I have a sneaky suspicion I might have had a little crush on her.

163

Well, quite. Anyway, she happened to be online at the time on instant messenger so I told her she was a, 'cheeky bloody cow, and she wasn't too old yet to be put over my knee and spanked.'

Well, I probably shouldn't repeat what her answer to that was, bit rude actually. Almost gave me a tent in my shorts truth be told! Oopppss, I hope I didn't just write that down! Hmm, methinks a change of subject is hastily required, now I've gone all red and embarrassed like.

Did you know that the animal that can go longest without water before dying is not actually a camel, but a rat. Interesting hey? No, alrighty then. Get on with the bloody story? Right you are, my bad.

Well, by the time I left the Internet café, it had somehow become rather dark outside. Kinda forgot where I was for a while back there, lost in conversation with Destiny on line. Think my table strewn with a dozen empty beer bottles might have had a little something to do with my absent mindedness as well mind you. Especially when I found out at a later date that some of the local beer they serve in Thailand has trace amounts of Amphetamines in!

Ah , the wonder that is Thailand. One of the only places I know where drugs are so illegal you can get strung up and hung for possession, and yet merrily sip away at your alcoholic beverage only to discover that there's a little somethin' somethin' extra in there. Trust me, you have one, and you feel like you've had twenty!

It was back on the beach on the way home, staggering around from side to side a little worse for wear, that I discovered my problem. That little mistress moon had decided to be cheeky, and apparently having looked down upon the scene unfolding below, found it highly amusing to veil her face and leave me in darkness. Oh, and one of those tropical storms decided to kick in just to make sure my adventure home would be entertaining.

I couldn't see a bloody thing, and only had a rough clue as to what direction home was. Plastered from head to toe in raindrops, it made little difference that the slippery rocks at the waters edge decided to pitch me into the sea on numerous occasions. Yep, I went arse over tit into the surf so many times I lost count, but in my inebriated state, I actually found it all worth a giggle!

How the hell I ever found the trail back through the trees is beyond me. Reckon it must have been gone 4am by the time I managed to get back to my hut, but waking the next morn with a dry mouth and slightly groggy head, I couldn't particularly remember even how I got home, let alone what time.

M.J and I spent our last days just chilling out, relaxing, and generally feeling blissful about everything. We'd cook little meals at night over a small fire, swim all day admiring the coral, although come to think of it, I think it was the swims as night that I actually enjoyed most. We lay there floating in the still warm sea, the moon illuminating things, giving everything a slightly heavenly glow and tint, chatting amongst ourselves.

A couple of Swedish girls joined us one evening, which was cool, they were pretty interesting, and pretty pretty as well! Apart from that, we had the place to ourselves, our own little tropical paradise. It was immense.

The only other thing of real note worth mentioning whilst on Ko Phi Phi was that M.J and I went on a scuba dive. Man oh man, if I thought the scuba at Hat Yao was good, if I thought the diving at the Great Barrier Reef was good, out at sea around the islands of Southern Thailand it blew my mind. Everything was beautiful. Wooden shanty boats, girls in bikinis for the boys, guys in small shorts for the girls, golden sands with just a handful of exotic Longtail boats washed ashore on, deserted islands filled with lush green vegetation, the clearest blue water, every colour of the spectrum in the sea life.

At one point I was so content that I just sat at the back of the boat on the steps alone whilst everyone went to shore. I just sat there feet in the water, sun on my face, listening to the music on the Thai radio above, swimming in the ultramarine sea whenever I got too hot. Really, when the word 'paradise,' was created, they must have been referring to here.

Well, yeah, you get the picture I guess! Sea blue, colours pretty, sun bright. I know what I am and what I'm not, and one thing I'm not is a writer, just someone with a story to tell. So I really do think it best that I stop trying to explain the paradiso of it all with heavy handed expressions, and let your minds eye do the work!

BOB MARLEY, LONG JOHN SILVER, SOME MONKIES, AND THE LOCAL AUTHORITIES

IN THE end, we left the heaven that is Ko Phi Phi with many a wistful glance back over my shoulder for my part. We spent another uneventful day in transit before reaching Ko Samui.

Ko Samui was instantly forgettable. I really wasn't a fan at all. It was absolutely crawling with 'tourist monkeys,' taking over the place. Night clubs pumped out hip hop till the early hours of the morning, the Thai bars stayed open for however long it took for the punters to run out of money and put their wallets away, and everywhere was devilish chaos. Western yobs smashed beer bottles on the streets, screamed out loud, punched each other's faces in, and threw up on sidewalks. I really couldn't see the point of coming half way around the world, just to indulge in the same things as you could do on a Saturday night back home.

My only attempt at a conversation failed at the first hurdle. I asked some lads where they'd been? I won't say what country they were from because it doesn't really matter and I don't want to piss anyone off. They told me that all they'd seen was the strip joints in Patpong Bangkok, then the rest of their weeks they'd spent here in a drunken stupor. They'd done nothing bar get pissed up all night long, barely seeing the waking sunlit hours.

I really couldn't see the point to be honest, but who am I to judge? It's important in life I think to realise this. Each to their own hey? What is it the Bible says, 'before offering to remove the splinter from your brothers eye, first remove the plank from your own,' or something along those lines anyway.

All I felt I wanted to do was perhaps point them down some amazing avenues worth exploring, the jungles, the coral reefs, the Buddhist temples. Don't get me wrong, everything in life is an experience with a lesson to teach, pub life in particular actually, but I just wanted to point out to the Ko Samui drunkards that they'd obviously done the bar thing, so why not take a peek at something else? If it bored them, then go back to the bar, but at least they'd discovered something about themselves in doing so, right?

I don't know, I'm probably just babbling and talking shit as always. I mean, if at the end of the day, they were truly happy just to forget where they were, just bring their Saturday nights from back home somewhere hotter, then it's only fair that I respect the choices they make for themselves. Still, I didn't quite understand it all to be honest. Wankers.

No, no, no, each to their own remember. Ping Pong had been right to preach that. I mean, he'd also reinforced my philosophy that I should, 'never respect anyone, who didn't respect me,' and that this should work in reverse as well I suppose.

Yeah, each to their own. For M.J and I, Ko Samui simply wasn't us, so we didn't stay long. But, (I still remember Ping Pong telling me, in the dwindling shadows of the sunset, as we slept beneath the ancient red ruins of a temple overtaken by jungle creepers, telling me with a lop sided grin of both humour and wisdom, that in this life, no matter what the situation, whether good or bad, we must realise that there is forever a 'big but' to be found) I still managed to find something memorable whilst in Ko Samui.

M.J and I booked a day trip exploring the Ang Thong National Park. The morning mainly consisted of snorkelling and scuba. Same as Ko Phi Phi really, bar a few more wicked underwater caves to explore.

It was the afternoon in particular that sticks out in my mind as a good memory. The Thai boat crew spoke little English, but as soon as they'd caught sight of M.J stepping onboard, they'd smiled and used pigeon English to try and chat to us. Pointing at his dreadlocks they'd say, 'Bob Marley, Bob Marley,' and by the time we stopped for lunch on one of the islands we'd gotten as far as, 'smoke, smoke, come come.'

So M.J and I set off down the beach with three of the guides. One of them seemed to have taken quite a shine to us, perhaps it was because his pigeon English was slightly more advanced than the others, and we could almost get through whole conversations, kinda.

I can't remember his real name now, but he seemed a genuinely nice guy. Plus we figured seeing as M.J was, 'Bob Marley,' we all needed similar nicknames. So our friendly guide was, 'Silver,' (as in, 'Long John Silver.' On account of the light blue bandana he wore holding back his long black hair, darkened goatee, and silver hoops he wore in one ear) and as for me? Well, I was, 'Kurt.'

I think he was probably around his mid-twenties if I had to guess, that's probably why he took a liking to us. The other Thai's were in their forties at least, and I've regularly found some kind of unity and invisible bond exists between cultures when the people involved are around the same age group.

I think perhaps its something to do with the patterns of thought it triggers. The whole, 'this person's the same age as me. If I was born here, in this culture, is this what I'd be doing now? Is this person in some strange way a reflection of my life and myself if it wasn't for an accident of birth? Is this some circus mirror, some strange portal that gives a glimpse of an alternate universe?' For obvious reasons, you start to ponder over their history, and all in all, the empathy invoked seems to create a feeling of unity, of friendship, between you and they.

So we wandered down the beach together, till the rocks sunk down to touch the sea. Scrabbling over boulders, Silver beckoned us towards a long cave in the cliff face.

Watching him set off hunched double, scuttling along as if a crab, we kinda just looked at him more that a little perplexed. Turning to see us just stood there watching him, he signalled for us to get down and stay as low as possible. We would've just stood there if it hadn't been for the evident look of fear in his eyes. So we dropped down, and imitating him, scuttled low between the rocks.

No sooner had we done so than a Police cruiser sped around the headland. Remembering this country's outlook on the possession of drugs, I could see Silver's point. I mean, it was really he who was in danger, rather than ourselves. If the shit went down, we had the aid of government bureaucrats and diplomats, western money and lawyers to fight our case. What help would someone like Silver get? I doubt anyone would bat an eyelid?

Cursing my ignorance, I took greater effort to ensure that I was invisible to the naked eye out at sea from there on in.

We merrily polished off a couple of spliffs between the five of us. I hadn't smoked for a while and was grinning away insanely like some Cheshire cat. Then I caught sight of the piece de resistance. Silver took from his bag a handmade bamboo bong and held it aloft as if it were some great deity that was to be worshipped.

As his countryman drew on its tube I asked to take a photo. He spluttered smoke and shook his head vigorously with genuine worry. Pointing outside to the police boat and us, it was obvious he didn't trust M.J and I. Understandable really, we could have been anyone.

Still, Silver just smiled, and taking the bamboo bong for himself, held an imaginary camera to his eye, clicked the button, then pointed to himself. Truth be told, I think that might actually be my favourite photo of them all.

More than a little baked by now, and with a major case of the munchies, M.J and I returned to where the expedition group were chomping away at a picnic lunch.

After stuffing ourselves to overflowing, (only problem with weed, makes your stomach expand) we eventually decided on a gentle stroll to sort ourselves out. A wooden signpost pointed to a large cave and so we set off in exploration. For some reason I'd expected a nice easy meandering trail, what I got was a fully-fledged fucking rock climb!

So it was, sweating profusely, we eventually reached an expansive cavern filled with stalactites and stalagmites. I couldn't even see parts of the ceiling it rose off so high into the distance!

Still, somehow in our stoned state of mind a game of, 'who can climb the highest without falling and breaking their necks,' got decided. I think we both surprised ourselves with just how high we got before finally looking down at the floor below, realising a fall onto the stalagmites would skewer us like a pig, and deciding to call it an honourable draw.

By the time we returned to the ground, Silver had arrived upon the scene. A few guy line ropes for stragglers to rely upon wound up to the caves entrance, and above them the trees climbed high and green. Spotting a wild monkey in the lower branches, Silver cupped his hands and made some kind of call.

We were soon surrounded by half a score of the things! Mothers with new born babies hanging from their bellies, the younger more adventurous ones walking along the guy lines right towards us. About two feet tall, black, with white hair on their heads sticking upright, never in an animal had I seen such intelligence. The eyes were almost human. Even as we stood there more monkeys arrived upon the scene to look at the freak show – us! They were as intrigued by us as we were by them.

So that was Thailand. My last real memory of that amazing and surreal country was back on Ko Samui that night. As the sun set I played soccer with a dozen local Thai children. M.J and I captained opposite teams, and it was a great laugh.

As the last of the light failed, with me in goal by now as too many cigarettes meant that like an old man, I had to rest at regular intervals, a ten-year-old boy caught the ball on the volley.

It flashed like a bullet past me into the bottom right hand corner of the goal (Of course I would have saved it normally, but I had something in my eye. I would have made a spectacular save, had it not been for the poor light, oh, and the glare off the sea. I probably had cramp as well come to think of it, and I bet he cheated somehow) and the boy wheeled away in celebration.

He wheeled away surrounded by cheers and pulled his shirt up over his head like the professionals do. It's funny, but in the fading light, with silhouettes casting shadows everywhere, I could have sworn that in the brief second I saw his face before he turned his back on me, that it was Somlee.

PART SEVEN

EVERYTHING HAPPENS FOR A REASON.
JUST TAKE YOUR LEAPS, AND KEEP THE FAITH

SELF-SUFFICIENCY ROCKS

A COUPLE of days later we left Thailand behind. For myself it was both reluctantly, and also with excitement and trepidation at what was to come. For one part, as we flew over snow capped mountains that signalled we were now in New Zealand, I realised I was about to see Destiny again. Oh how these torn and battered hearts of ours can soon turn feelings of despair, into those of hope and, dare I say it, possibly the ability to love once more?

So it was, after the wheels of our flight touched down, wandering through baggage claim I spied Destiny. My heart did one of those tiny and annoying little jumpy things, and I thought, 'oh crap, here we go again.'

There she was, long blond hair, perfect hourglass figure, and a smile that just seemed to make any woes you may have melt away. She was the epitome of cool. A beautiful and intelligent little hippie surfer with a knack of always knowing the right thing to say.

'Hi ya,' she said pulling me into a close embrace, kissing me on both cheeks. (Damn it, not quite the meeting I'd envisaged whilst laid on my back in that Thai hospital. Oh well.)

'Grab your bags then I've got a 24 pack of beer in the car and my friend's got a hot tub we can borrow if you fancy it?'

Was this girl perfect or what?! I mean, what concept could possibly seem more perfect to two battered and weary old souls than beer and a hot tub to rest our aching limbs.

Jumping in her little Renault we chugged off to collect Chloe from the girls' shared house in central Christchurch, and then headed for our hot spa. Chloe and M.J had also gotten close when last we met and I think it just seemed only natural for all four of us to hang out together again. I mean, by the second day we'd known each other back in Bondi, we'd ended up having naked piggyback fights in the ocean! With a track record like that, we were relishing the crazy antics that were bound to come with our reunion!

After the blistering heat of Thailand the 6 degree bitter coldness of New Zealand originally hit me like a fat guy being punched in the gut. Yet the sun was still shining outside, and as the car slowly wound its way out into the country, I realised I was far too content to be bothered about feeling the cold.

As we crawled through the hills in Destiny's washed out little Renault, that coughed and spluttered like an aged man who'd smoked 50 a day for his whole life, we cranked up the tunes and all started singing away at the top of our voices. M.J and Chloe in the back howling like hyenas, Destiny and I upfront constantly catching each other's eye and smiling, or scrunching up our faces and poking our tongues out at each other. It was, 'Fleetwood Mac – Greatest Hits,' and seeing as we all knew the words and were comfortable enough together to act like complete muppets, we each allotted ourselves a different verse to sing before all joining in with the chorus!

Now personally I can't sing for toffee, people request to hear someone scratching their nails down a blackboard before enduring the ultimate pain that is my singing voice, but in some situations, you just don't give a shit! Plus, it's fun! I especially liked it when Destiny and I would lock eyes and sing the lines of the chorus together, bobbing our heads back and forth, as we trundled about our merry little way. I especially liked the fact, that it all felt so comfortable.

Our destination ended up being a small farmstead tucked away in a valley in the middle of nowhere. Pulling up as the first rays of the day began to slip away, Jonah stood out on the porch holding up his hand in a wave of welcome. Dressed in blue jeans and lumberjack boots, below a tight fitting, dirty and muddied ribbed t-shirt, his dark and muscular complexion rippled. The guy was blatantly a Maori and black tribal tattoos wound up his bulky neck and pinched his cheeks.

As Destiny threw her arms around him and he swept her up in those tree trunk arms of his to spin her around, I must admit I felt the tiny cringe of jealousy flutter briefly over me. 'Ah beware my lord of jealousy, for it is the green eyed monster that doth mock the food we eat.'

I needn't have worried though, for as he met us with genuine warmth and hearty handshakes, his wife, Sophia, appeared at the door. Tall, dark, pregnant and beautiful, for every ounce of external strength that belied Jonah's features, this wonderful woman radiated the same in inner strength.

Tucked away from civilisation, the two happily lived their existence without the needs of modern society. Running a self-sufficient farm they found there was, 'nothing needed that God's land couldn't provide,' Jonah explained, as he gave us the tour of his home. Pulling Sophia into a deep and passionate embrace he told M.J and I that, 'without her, none of it would be possible.' In his words, she was, 'simply amazing.' She could turn her hand to anything, and forever excel in the appointed task. Oh, and I can officially state for the record that she cooks the sweetest apple pie this side of the Milky Way.

There was so much more I wanted to ask of them, their very existence enthralled me, and pulled away at some suppressed longing deeply rooted inside. For now though, Jonah simply handed us a handful of towels telling us, 'mi casa su casa,' before taking his leave as they both still had much work to do before the stars unveiled.

Jumping back into our trusty little rusty death trap, Destiny threw the gear stick into first with much grinding and gnashing of teeth before sticking the vehicle down the dirt road that slid away bedside the house.

173

After about ten minutes drive, I discovered my little piece of heaven in this world. I have been to and seen some unbelievable things, but this place is the one that shall forever burn brightly in my memory.

The road slipped away into an old abandoned rock quarry. Surrounded by trees, a large stony area existed, full of old potholes and half finished drilling expeditions. Down away to our left three large rock pools steamed away in the day's last light. It was evident that I had misinterpreted Destiny's announcement at the airport of a hot tub, for these were natural hot springs. Cracks rent in the earth below that allowed boiling water to be carried to the surface above.

This was gonna be wicked.

The girls quickly stripped down to their underwear and M.J and I quickly followed suit. As I started to make off for the hot springs Destiny reached out and grabbed my hand. Pulling me off in the other direction she told me that there was something we had to do first, and that I should trust her.

Leaving the other two briefly behind for a moment, we wandered hand in hand off to the right. She pulled me up all of a sudden and leaned gently into me.

'You know that day we went surfing together?' She whispered, 'well I'll never forget that day.'

'Me neither,' I managed to reply. All the while realising that our lips were gradually moving closer and closer together. I could already see us kissing in my mind's eye.

She gently tickled my sides playfully and continued, 'I seem to remember I very kindly taught you how to surf, and all you did in return was push me off my board you cheeky little beggar!'

'Yeah, I do like to amuse myself,' I laughed.

Once again she pressed her body close into mine, and gazing up into my eyes asked so softly, 'can you remember what I promised you that day?'

I could feel her breath on my lips now, my hands were on her silky smooth skinned waist, our hips pressed and rubbed into each other's.

'No, what was that?'

'Well, when you pushed me off my board I promised I'd kick your arse sometime,' and with that the cheeky bitch pushed me off the ledge behind me to fall slap bang into a hole of warm wet oozing mud, with a great, 'splat!'

I somehow managed to keep my head above its gurgling surface but was now covered from neck to toe! She stood slightly above me doubled up in laughter with tears streaming down her face.

'Oh it looks like Mrs Funny is back again,' I shouted, and then pulling myself out of the warm mixture of water and slurping mud as quickly as I could, proceeded to chase her round the ponds edge with her giggling away.

Now, I used to run 100 metre sprint for club, and was one of the quickest wingers around for our school rugby team, add to this equation the fact that I was definitely a man on a mission now, and the cheeky cow didn't stand a chicken's chance in Thailand of escaping!

Catching up with her in seconds, I plucked her up into my arms from behind and threw us both into the muddy waters below.

Apparently when the diggers had been excavating this area, hot water from below the earth's crust had eventually broken up into those drilled sections. The culmination of this hot water and clay had created a natural mud bath. Far better for the skin than a day spa so Destiny told me. A highly interesting fact to know I thought, but I personally found more interest in wrestling with her and trying to dunk her head below the surface.

Once we'd exhausted ourselves, we both kind of just fell into a natural embrace. Then, with the moon once more popping its head around the door in interest, she sat behind me and started massaging my travel worn and weary shoulders.

M.J and Chloe eventually arrived and pulled themselves in alongside us. M.J being M.J, somehow managed that magic trick of his once more, and we were soon sat there, massaging each other in couples, whilst passing round a joint. When did he roll that?

Sometime later we made the short walk across the quarry to the largest of the natural hot springs to wash ourselves off. Dipping my toes in I grimaced momentarily in pain and recoiled, 'damn that's hot.' I then realised just what a big girl's blouse I was being, and quickly pitched the rest of my body into the water before Destiny saw my incredible show of macho manliness!

Anyway, so it was, I'd found my little piece of heaven. As I swam around on my back, allowing the waters to massage away all the bad in this world, I've never felt so cleansed, so purely filled with ecstasy. Quite simply, it was amazing.

Swimming away I watched the sun finally set around me, and it filled my every fibre with pleasure. Gazing around it was like a photo from a National Geographic magazine. The whites and yellows of the moon and its haze directly above, planted in black, with just the sparkle of diamonds surrounding it as the first few stars burnt brightly onto the scene. Then as your focus fell towards the horizon, the dark blue clouds gradually got lighter in shade where it met the purples, pinks, reds and yellow of the setting sun. Even the way the ancient and archaic mining machinery sat abandoned amongst the rocks, casting strange and wonderful silhouettes against the back drop of the setting sun behind, added such unbelievable beauty to that scene.

So I contented myself with the task of continuing to swim around on my back, slightly stoned, with my ears below the water, singing a quiet song about beauty. My voice sounded so far away and distant, which is probably a good thing when you've got a voice like mine! But no, I was in heaven.

I let my whole head eventually sink beneath the waters surface, intrigued to find that with my eyes still wide open, the view above simply hazed into pools of colour. Such beauty, so amazing.

When I resurfaced for air, great and fiery lit torches flamed away along the trail behind us. Sophia and Jonah had finished for the day, and had come to join us.

As Sophia slipped her heavily pregnant stomach into the warm waters of an adjacent pool, Jonah planted the burning stakes into the ground around us.

There we stayed for hours, long after all shades of day had slipped away, and still, just wow, what beauty. There were so, so many stars shining away

175

above. Miles and miles from civilisation, without any light pollution to ruin our view, well, just wow. Paradise. Eden. Heaven. Destiny.

I was certainly a sad man when the time came to walk away from that place. I kept on turning around, trying to steal one last glimpse of it all. I kept on trying to imprint that picture into my very soul.

As I stood there surveying the scene alone, I could only tear myself away finally when Destiny stole back to my side, gently slipped her fingers into mine, and said with a hint of remorse, 'I know,' before leading me away.

Waking the next morning I realised that it seemed an awful shame to be saying our farewells to Jonah and Sophia already. I really did rather like them. Rather envy them as well the truth be told. We had stayed up all night talking, drinking and eating merrily. I had given them quite a hard time actually, grilling them on all aspects on farmstead life, you know, how they got started, what their routine was etc. It's just that in my rather intoxicated state my mind was running away with me, and I was daydreaming of a similar lifestyle in the future for myself. I would like that.

Anyway, towards the end of the evening I had decided in my drunken state of confidence that I'd try and risk, giving Destiny a kiss. Fortune favours the brave as they say; unfortunately fortune doesn't favour the drunken fool who passes out on a bed in a spare room before even getting the chance!

COUNTING TO TEN CAN BE HARDER
THAN YOU THINK

THE next few days whirled by in a haze. All the while Destiny and I were growing closer and closer by the moment. You know how it is when you really just click with somebody. The constant flirting, the catching of each other's eye wherever you go. Whether it's across a crowded bar, or when you just glimpse into a shop window and see them smiling back at you in the reflection.

I don't know about you, but with me I always seem to start bullying the women I like as well. My favourite move in particular is the quick little poke to their sides, just below the ribs. No surprises really that I don't get anywhere with the women hey?!

No, it's all just to get them to let out a giggle and start to fight back. Then I can pick them up or throw them over my shoulder and threaten to throw them in the river or something. All the while with them squealing in laughter and the feigned belief that I am really going to go through with it.

There just seemed to be rather a lot of bullying each other verbally at first, which obviously led to physical harassment like play fighting, wrestling, tickling and then trying to find any other excuse to get physical contact with each other. Yet all the while that first kiss still continued to elude me.

I don't know. We couldn't get enough of each other, and yet neither of us seemed to want to risk ruining our friendship by making the first move. Or, silly really, but it seemed that despite the fact that both of us were so open at times it was scary, that one certain topic of conversation was still unapproachable, even to us. All I do know is that I was enjoying every single second spent with her.

Now when I travel, I love doing the touristy things, and the crazy random shit, but some of my best times are when I just hang around with friends, doing the same kinda things I'd do back home, but doing them half way around the world.

So we just chilled out over the next few days around Christchurch. We went to the movies; the girls dragged us reluctantly around the shopping malls with the promise of beer for our troubles at the end of it all. We went ten-pin bowling and played mini-putt. Hung out at a local coffee house sipping lattes' late at night as Jack Frost tried to reach in with his chilling grip from outside. Played Frisbee Golf in the park, drank at bars, and generally did the same things everyone our age around the world does. We just enjoyed doing nothing much more than just hanging out with our friends, enjoying each other's company.

Well, there was still the odd random giggle here and there.

I think Destiny's favourite memory from those days was when we wandered up to the top of the hill overlooking the waters of Christchurch. We'd attacked an, 'all you can eat and drink,' Pizza Hut for dinner, and with my ever-increasing beer belly growing bigger by the day, I thought it best to try and burn off my meal.

Wandering through the woods we discovered a little park serenely illuminated by the dieting moon, and decided to play for a while.

Being a crazy dare devilish kind of guy, as I like to call it, (although others seem to prefer the terminology, 'idiot') whilst Destiny jumped onto the swings and pumped her legs to push herself as high as possible, I danced around in front of her ducking and dodging away at the last minute to avoid contact.

No surprise really that in my efforts to display my manly athleticism, on one particular attempt to duck forwards below her swing, my foot slipped and Destiny's big old feet caught me full in the face, sending me sprawling to the floor.

Of course Destiny found all this highly amusing! I'd like to say she leapt instantly to the floor to administer first aid, kiss of life and all that, but I'd be lying. No, she opted instead to carry on swinging back and forth over my prone and dying body, creased up in hysterics. What a lovely young lady hey?!

It's alright though, there's no need to worry, although I was blatantly knocking on death's door for a while back there, I somehow managed to pull through in the end. Plus, I got my own laugh at her expense later the next day.

We'd driven round her friends' house for a smoke and ended up getting rather stoned. Destiny made sure she didn't drink anything but her driving, when we finally left just after midnight, was rather questionable to say the least. She had a major case of red eye and was hunched up over the wheel in concentration like an old Grandma, trickling along at 15 miles per hour.

Anyway, so there we were, pottering along our merry little way when turning the corner we discovered a police roadblock. They were doing random breathalyser tests. Destiny hadn't touched a drop of booze, but did it acknowledge marijuana? Looking at her I didn't think it would be necessary, any copper in the world would take one look at her and realise she wasn't exactly sober.

Rolling down the window, a clean-shaven young man took one look at her and smiling, introduced himself. That's the only problem with hanging around with beautiful women; any man with a pulse starts trying to crack onto them! Well, in this case, it actually worked in our favour.

Holding the tube of the breathalyser towards her lips, the policeman said, 'blow into this ten times and count aloud in-between please.'

Destiny somehow stumbled through the process, but the cop looked down curiously at the results of the breathalyser unit. Raising an inquisitive eyebrow he asked her to kindly repeat the process.

By this point I had virtually become one with my seat. I'd sunk further and further down on the passenger's side, my rainbow coloured hat was pulled right down over my eyes, and I was begging myself not to start giggling.

Destiny started to count again. Unfortunately she got to seven before briefly hesitating over just what number exactly came next.

Well, this was too much for both of us. The fact that she couldn't even remember how to count to ten was beyond belief! So we both let out a little smile at first, then a giggle broke free, before we both completely died in fits of laughter! Oh dear.

Luckily for us the copper thought this was all very amusing and laughed along with us. Eventually we somehow found our composure, Destiny managed to remember how to count to ten, and the results were all clear. The Policeman waved us on our way, with a twinkle of an eye, a flirtatious smile, and a dropping of his telephone number into Destiny's lap. Bastard.

Well, actually, maybe sometimes it's a good thing that men get a little too preoccupied with their loins! Whichever way you look at it, I found it all highly amusing!

M.J and I had only booked to stay on the South Island for a week, before spending the rest of our trip trekking around New Zealand's North Island. Although I didn't want to leave Destiny behind, she and Chloe had major exams coming up and I didn't want to mess that up for them.

So for our last few days together, we all decided to take some rather more bizarre trips. The first event in question was climbing the snow-capped mountains near the Franz Josef Glacier.

ONE FOOT IN FRONT OF THE OTHER.
FOREVER ONWARDS AND UPWARDS

WE ALL woke early to start our two-day trek into the mountains. Taking in a hearty breakfast before the sun had even risen, we soon found ourselves crammed into Destiny's little Renault once more, winding down the narrow roads to the valley below.

Our first port of call was the last chance saloons at the mountains base. The buildings had been there since the turn of the century. Old wooden slated contraptions that used to serve alcohol to the lost and weary outlaw, looking for a place to find a little peace from the law on the outskirts of civilisation. Or just for the hermit mountain man, who once in a blue moon would leave his cave in the wilderness, to come and steal a little news of the outside world. The busty harlot barmaid would pour them their shots of whisky, all the while dreaming of love and escape.

Gradually though, things had changed, as they are always want to do. The migration of the people away from the land and into the hustle and bustle of the industrial cities, had come full circle. Many like us now sought to migrate away from the mechanical machinations of filling the world with modern skyscrapers, and sought a return to our roots, free to roam over the land as we pleased.

Ferlinghetti, Kerouac, Ginsberg, all the Beat poets of the '60's had started to draw the publics' attention to the machine. The 2.4 children, the way we work to buy new fangled gadgets that we don't even need. We were all buying into materialism, into commercialism, and individuality was dying. We had risked becoming just a cog in the machine of society. An unrecognisable cog, an unthinking clone, George Orwell's, '1984.'

Enough people had been alerted though, the 70's occurred, and people migrated away from the skyscraper. The ruggedness and wildness of the wilderness reflected our hearts, and so the scenery at the foot of the Franz Josef glacier had changed. The busty barmaid had hung up her dishcloth and replaced it with a pair of crampons. The saloons had changed into outdoor adventure stores and so this is where we stocked up.

The one and only street of this hamlet was barely 500 yards long, but we somehow managed to waste 2 hours there! Bloody women and bloody shops hey?! No, just messing, although we were shopping, for once the cries of, 'I'll just die if I don't get this,' actually rung with truth. We all purchased an ice axe, a decent pair of crampons, carabiners and sturdy rope together, before deciding to split off into pairs to buy the rest of our things.

Personally I was in desperate need of a new Swiss army knife, and found exactly what I was looking for in a tiny downstairs apartment shop, lined with cobwebs and old dusty boxes from the 1920's. The place was deserted, and the only noise breaking the silence was the eerie howling of wind tearing though long broken windows high above me at street level.

Outside the weather had taken a turn for the worst. Black clouds had ripped the suns beautiful radiant coat away, and pulled her down beneath their blankets. Big fat old rain had come upon the scene and started dowsing down the world below. The gloom outside meant we were virtually stood there in darkness; even Destiny gave my arm a little squeeze and suggested that perhaps we go.

I'd just found what I was looking for though. Tucked away at the bottom of a warped and rotten shelf, the symbol I was looking for struggled to make itself seen.

Bending down, I picked the ancient black box up between thumb and forefinger, and blew away the dust that had settled there over long unknowing years. Oh so slowly, I undid the metal clasp, and with a little groan of pressure and resistance, the lid eventually allowed itself to be flipped open. I took it into my hands and with the flick of a switch; the blade ripped itself free, glistening away in the fading light.

'Don't make them like they used to hey?' A sudden rasping voice cut through the silence, causing Destiny to let out a little yelp of surprise and me to almost fall over as I crouched there.

A one eyed man who must have been at least 200 years old had glided up to us as if a ghost. White wild hair stood up on end, and a speckled beard fell to his waist. As I stood up he beckoned for us to follow him to the counter. Walking behind him, Destiny slipped her hand into mine and I gave it a little squeeze to comfort her.

Taking the blade from me he switched a table lamp on and inspected it under its light. Turning it over and over in his hands, he just said, 'yep, yep, yep, don't get workmanship like this these days,' before he just continued to gaze on in silence.

A few minutes had passed, and I could tell Destiny was starting to eye the door. I mean, this guy had obviously completely lost his marbles. Just like that though, he snapped out of his reverie, popped the blade back into its box and into a bag in one fluent flowing motion, before asking for the cash. Handing it over, the transaction complete, Destiny dashed towards the staircase leading to the door, pulling me after her.

As we raced up the steps, the madman shouted out, 'hey you, wait!'

Destiny and I just bolted even faster, especially as glancing down we saw him gliding with an incredible turn of speed towards us. She yanked the door almost from its hinges and threw herself into the street outside. I was right behind her, almost over the threshold, when I felt his clammy hand wrap round my ankle from between the slats below, stopping me in my tracks, making me fall.

As I lay there, the wind knocked out of me, he somehow pulled himself up from below, bringing his face level with mine. I could smell his tepid, rank and dying breath in my nostrils, making me want to retch, his eye stared at me, unblinking, piercing my very thoughts and mind.

Clenching my fist, I went to strike out at that manic, crazy, haunting skull, but before I did, he quickly whispered in my ear, 'storm's a brewing, there's death in the air tonight. Don't go up the mountain.'

My fist connected with thin air. With his chilling warning given, he'd allowed himself to drop back into the shadows below, out of sight. I heard Destiny cry my name from above, and pulling myself up and out onto the street, she threw her arms round me.

'What the hell happened back there? You okay?'

I lied, 'nothing, I just tripped, that's all. Come on, lets go meet the others.'

We eventually left those haunted shacks of yesteryear behind and drove on as far as we could towards the glacier.

Parking up, we threw our packs onto our backs, and pulled our hats down low. The rain was falling gently, and although the sun had deserted us, we found once we got trekking, that we weren't too cold. The others had full waterproofs on, rather stupidly I had set out in jeans. I realised that once they'd filled with rainwater, they'd weigh down my weary legs as I pulled on into the back part of the day, and not only that, they'd also lock in the cold as well. So I actually changed into a pair of shorts believe it or not!

Neither of us were particularly experienced climbers; we'd just wanted to explore the mountains for a few days. So that was why we'd chosen this point.

Franz Josef glacier climbs up for more metres than I could imagine, before giving access into the larger surrounding mountaintops. It is relatively easy to climb though; certainly there would be no need for rope for most of its ascent. It would quickly spit us out into the higher ranges, where the glacier fades away at its pinnacle, the ice recedes, and the granite and snow of the middle ranges begin providing a multitude of caves to rest in.

We would spend the night there, and in the morning could play around amongst the upper levels, before pushing on with the quick descent back home. For now though, we had to cover the mile or so of flat rock land that were the foothills.

Leapfrogging from rock to rock to traverse shallow rivers, backpacks strapped tightly, we took everything at a gentle stroll, enjoying our surroundings. We chatted and laughed as we went, despite the constant falling of rain and ominous storm clouds above. I also pulled out the genius that is stereo bag again to keep us smiling, and so in good voice and light hearted moods we eventually reached the foot of the glacier just after mid-day.

Taking on a light lunch of complex carbohydrates, not wishing to stand around in the cold and wet too long, and also feeling ourselves a little pumped and charged with adrenaline, we didn't hang around. Strapping on our crampons, taking ice axe in hand, we started the real ascent.

There was no need to tie up together quite yet. We pretty much just allowed ourselves to find our own paths, dependant on how we were feeling. The four of us climbed for around four hours, sometimes stumbling upon each other as two trails combined, always greeting each other with a hearty, 'hey ho,' or a, 'well fancy seeing you here.'

Every once in a while a cry of 'cooee' would break out around us, and we'd congregate on that point to see what the others had discovered.

My two greatest finds were a huge natural arch made of ice, (I have a particularly silly photo I'm rather fond of, of me stood under its curve, dressed in shorts and crampons as the rain falls around me, ice axe in one hand, and a bag of Skittles in the other) and a network of narrow tunnels that just begged to be explored, as if some monstrous rabbit had set itself burrowing a den up in the great heights of the world. It was cool because not only was it great fun squeezing my way through ever narrowing spaces on hands and knees, in almost pitch black darkness at times, but also because it proved rather a useful short cut up the mountain.

By 5 'o' clock we were happy to find ourselves not too far from the point where the top of the glacier led into the rocks half way up the surrounding mountains. The only thing I was slightly disappointed about was the fact that I knew that all the time we climbed, the views were becoming more and more spectacular. The problem being that visibility was really becoming rather poor, and I couldn't really see jack shit truth be told.

We all came to a natural stop at the top of a ridge that had taken quite some energy to conquer. Gradually we'd all found ourselves moving closer and closer together, following the same tracks as our bodies grew a little weary.

For my own part I was completely soaked through to the bone by now, I had a small pond complete with complimentary goldfish in the bottom of each boot, and I was pretty low on energy. Toward the end of the afternoons hike I'd found in the ever-diminishing daylight that I was having problems concentrating. My feet no longer wanted to go where my brain willed them, and my once oh so sure footing was now making me stumble in places, almost as if a drunkard.

A trench wound away below us and we all jumped in to take shelter for a while, and take on board some much needed food.

Whereas before we had all itched to push on as quickly as possible after eating, no one seemed quite so willing to go now. Everyone was blatantly pretty damned knackered. No one really talked.

Destiny flashed me a weary smile and then came and sat in front of me. Without saying a word she leant backwards, rested her head on my chest, pulled my arms tight around her, let out a deep sigh, and then closed her eyes. I pulled my hood further over my face to keep the rain from dripping on us, undid my jacket and pulling her close to me, wrapped it round the two of us.

Finding a little piece of warmth half way up a glacier in the pouring rain and cold, I realised I should have been thinking, 'just what the hell are we doing here?' Instead I was thinking, with my arms wrapped round her waist and her calming breathing sounding deeper and deeper, 'hmm, this is nice.'

I rested my head on hers, and thought I'd just close my eyes and rest for another minute or so before pushing ever onwards and upwards.

A crack of lightning and crash of thunder directly above us woke me. I don't know how long we'd slept but I could barely see M.J and Chloe curled up together, even though they were barely a foot in front of my face.

The storm had completely enveloped us as we'd slept, the dark had settled all around, and so there we were, half way up a mountain, with only the flash of forked lightening to illuminate our dire situation. The wind had also changed direction, now blowing a stinging and torrential flow of rainwater into my face, and slowly filling the gorge we rested in.

My arse was steeped in inches of puddle, and we knew there was no way we could stay there the night. We'd either drown or die of hypothermia before morning came.

Assessing things, I didn't need another flash of lightning to determine the worried expressions that etched my friends' faces. The consternation and anxiety was more than evident in their trembling voices, and I realised, in my own as well.

'We need to find somewhere to spend the night,' M.J stated simply.

No one moved. Destiny just squeezed my hand. No one moved.

'Come on, it'll be fine,' I tried. Only to hear my voice fade on the wind, lacking all sincerity, swallowed up by a deep resonating roar of thunder that shook the very mountainside.

Still no one moved. The rain continued to lash into our faces, my hair stood on end, and I shivered in chill. I could hear Destiny's teeth rattling away beside me as we cuddled into each other.

Even as we stood there, the wind picked up, forcing us to turn our battered faces away from her shriek. Her shrill scream continued, a torn pocket of flimsy material flapped in defiance under her attention, before it lost the fight, tore itself completely loose from our pack, and disappeared over the side of the mountain and off into the night.

We couldn't stay; we'd be signing our own death warrants.

Chloe moved.

Taking one of the lengths of rope from M.J's pack, that little movement alone seemed to spur us all into action. Passing the rope through the carabiners around our belts, we all grabbed flashlights. Everyone was drenched, freezing, and exhausted. Yet the adrenaline induced by the situation forced us into action.

So it was, we found ourselves stepping out of our trench and back onto the face of the glacier. M.J pushed out first leading the way, before the rope passed down from him to Chloe, on through Destiny's belt loop, and then finally to me, bringing up the rear.

We stepped out into insanity. The wind immediately greeted us with open arms. Whipping up all around, it seemed capable of literally plucking us up into its mitts and pitching us out into oblivion. The lightning once again bore down with a tongued fork of torment, and his brother thunder laughed all around. All we could really see was the ground directly below our feet, looking up and gazing out only stung our eyes, and even in the few futile attempts we tried, the darkness just swallowed the beams from our flashlights.

It was then, and only then, that M.J made the first and only real mistake that I've ever known him make.

'Look, out there, I think I see a cave.'

We all huddled round and concentrated our torches in the direction M.J pointed.

'I don't know,' Chloe deliberated.

The spot in question lay relatively far off to our right, the major problem being that the crossing would be particularly treacherous. I don't think I'd want to attempt it even during the height of a beautiful summer's day. One thing I'm not, is a recognised mountaineer.

'Well, we gotta try right? We're dead out here otherwise,' M.J insisted.

Did his voice waver for the first time ever?

It came to a vote. I mean, this wasn't entirely a trivial decision to make. It wasn't your regular case of, 'what ever you fancy doing mate, it's up to you.'

Get busy living, or get busy dying, right? We all took the leap off to our right, into the unknown.

As it turned out, we made the crossing relatively easily. Well, as easily as you can get in those situations. It was merely a number of roughly 5-15 foot climbs, up steep ice faces that spanned, perhaps 2 people wide. Luckily there were foot holes available, our crampons were sharp, and our ice axes dug deep.

Progress was slow and arduous, but we focussed, and eventually made the half-dozen climbs needed to get to where we wanted to be.

No cave. Nothing. Shit. Shit, shit, shit. Screw me backwards and call me Spanky. Shit.

Now we were well and truly fucked. There was no way in hell we could go back the way we came. Descending the steep climbs we'd just made in the storm could only lead to one thing. Of this I was sure. There was no way we'd survive. So in a unanimous decision we pushed on.

As we pushed on into the storm, we started to lose the battle. I stumbled a number of times, only catching myself at the last minute.

The climbs were becoming more and more dangerous, we were shaking with cold, and could no longer have any faith in our movements. We were completely unsure about how exact and precise we could be in our present state. Our footfall no longer had the accuracy that was being called upon time and time again now.

Concentration was fading. Things were looking bad. We were all caught up in our own private inner struggle over whether we could really do this, just where this was all going to end. Trying to block out the reality of it all.

Still the storm crashed down on us.

I feel I'm struggling to explain just how things were in those moments. Imagine the kind of storms that you see in the movies, the ones that sink boats, that kill people, now imagine you're one of those people. One of those extras that never have any other role in this great show except to gaze up and face their doom, to know they're about to die. Now you're getting close.

Now put yourself on the edge of a mountain, tied up to your best friend, the woman you now ironically realise, you are so completely and utterly head over heels in love with that you can't believe you never did anything about it, and they're all going to die the truth be told, along with you.

You really want to know what I was thinking though? Sure I felt more tired than my body's ever felt before, I was slowly freezing to death, the storm wouldn't relent, I was scared as hell, but the one thing I remember more than anything about that day, is that I was pissed off as hell. I was so angry you would not believe. I couldn't believe I'd come back from the brink of death, hanging from that tree, seemingly lost from the world, and yet through all the shit and dirt that I thought was my life, I'd eventually found something worth living for, and now it was all going to be taken away.

M.J stopped. He sunk to his knees upfront. He physically couldn't go on. He'd literally seen the end.

Centuries of exposure to the harsh elements on the unprotected face of the mountain we'd now traversed, had created a wave like effect in the ice. The ground had risen until it formed a point in front of us. The surface area to tread on dwindled into no more than a knife-edge. The sides of this wave slid smoothly at great angles down into the shadows below, who knew how far they fell?

We had reached the point of no return. We couldn't go back, and yet we couldn't go on. Try and stand on the apex of the ice, the pinnacle, the tight rope line that wound away in front of us now, and you'd give your crampons so little surface area to bite into, you were almost certain to fall.

Or, with this storm being a complete and utter little bitch, just as you stepped out onto that line, she'd recognize that all she needed to do was blow one sudden gust of tempest, and we'd disappear down those slippery slopes into the chasms below.

We all drew in together around the crouching form of M.J. Looking up through drowned dread locks he caught each of us by the eye, and spoke frankly and honestly.

'I'm so sorry, I can't do it. It's too much. I'm so, so sorry. I can't believe I lead you to this.'

I realised it wasn't the rain pouring down his cheeks now, but tears.

'I've let you all down, please forgive me, though I never will.'

Chloe wrapped her arms round his neck, and there on the brink of everything, she leant forwards and kissed him passionately on the lips as he wept.

'There's nothing to forgive you for silly,' she smiled.

At the end of it all my friends found, whilst stood there oblivious to everything, despite the thunder roaring in rage and the wind hurling itself at us, something stronger than the elements. The lightning actually struck the rocks off to our left in anger, but in that instant, as M.J and Chloe kissed, I knew they were untouchable. They existed beyond all of this, beyond this mortal realm, and they were beautiful.

For my own part, that great white wolf inside of me broke free from his cage again, and bearing sharpened bloodied fangs, growled in defiance. I was barely aware of Destiny pressing into me, weeping softly, kissing my neck, searching for the same piece of comfort the other two had somehow managed to find.

The shackled animal inside was once again untameable, just as it had been that night I'd ridden my steed straight into the river. It threw back its head, howled a challenge into the night, and then leapt forward into combat.

I was barely aware of my hands at my belt, unclipping my carabiner, releasing the rope around my waist. Stepping out and around to M.J, I bent down and switched our places in this sick chain gang. Too late did Destiny realise my intentions. Too late did M.J shoot out his hand to catch me. Too late came their cries of, 'DON'T!'

Once stood on the edge, again a man possessed, I calmly turned around and giving them a cheeky little grin, I just told them, 'time to even the score M.J.' He'd saved me once before, and I wasn't going to go anywhere from this world until I'd returned the favour.

My smile then turned in an instant to one of pain and sorrow as a new memory took hold. Fire and ashes. Catching M.J's eye, I spat out in simple grit and unquestionable resolution, 'no one dies on me. Not this time.'

So, with that said, I loosed myself from the rope around my waist and stepped out.

Boom, boom... Boom, boom. Heart beating. Boom, boom... Boom, boom. Time...stands... still.
Time stops.
The storm fades away.
There is only the beating of my heart.
Tick, tock...Tick, tock.
I step out.

I wait for my crampons to strike the glancing blow on the hard ice below that is surely bound to come, I wait to fall.
If I fall, what would happen to the others? Would I hit the ground and come to hours later, to find myself completely alone, and rely only on a search and rescue helicopter to inform me of my friends' fate? To know that they had been found hugging each other, frozen together for all time.
As kids we'd had two rabbits. In winter we'd cover their cage up with blankets. One night we'd forgotten. We'd discovered them in the morning cuddled into each other for warmth, frozen solid.

No, no one dies whilst I still draw breath. Not this time. I had failed Somlee before. I'd never fail anyone again. Especially my friends.

I stepped out.

The crampons bit.

Now it was all about balance. I lifted up my left leg and stuck it into the spike of ice in front of me. Walking that tight rope line up above the world.

So it continued. So it continued until I reached the other side and the ground once more became flat and secure. Fuck me that was intense. I still wonder how I did it looking back on that dark day.

Once I reached the far side, I removed the spare rope from my pack, embedded my ice axe in the ground below with all the strength that still remained within me, and tied the slack around its handle. I passed the rope around my waist, through the carabiner, and threw the loose end to the others. (Good job old habits die-hard. Even half way up a mountain, in the worst storm I'd ever known, across a great chasm, I can still hit the mark every time with a rope.

I'd once spent a summer ranching with friends and once again that experience proved invaluable. How long had I practised? Take your lasso in hand. 'Boy you get that word out of your vocabulary! Proper cowboys only ever refer to it as a 'Rope,' they'd shout at me. Take your Honda and Spoke then rope yourself a water cooler, or the dog, or the cattle, or eventually, your friends).

So I roped me my friends, and high up above the world we formed a handrail to hold onto. It was now up to them. They had to find some inner reserve. I just hoped the taught handrail I'd created would do the job.

It did. Eventually they all reached my side of the crevasse without incident. It was only then, that I allowed myself to collapse in exhaustion.

I'd love to come out of this story as some kinda hero. I'd love to say that I well and truly saved the day, but that only really happens in the movies. Truth be told. I lost it after that point. It seemed I'd depleted any strength I'd drawn from within. The wolf lay panting and tired, and I bordered on become a gibbering wreck.

For the next two climbs I was incapable of stopping myself from shaking. I was reduced to moving at a snails' pace, gripping the ice with my body, hugging onto it for dear life.

I thought I was done for when my left leg seized up with cramp. We were now attempting a sideways ascent in the steep side of a vertical iceberg. Dangerous because once more, our crampons had such little surface area to bite into. Only the spikes on the very left of our boots could be utilised in any kind of way.

Yeah, I really lost it after that crossing, but I had no other choice but to push on. Destiny, Chloe and the rather abashed and ashamed M.J were relying on me. (I really don't know why he was giving himself such a hard time about breaking down before. I tried to tell him what a plonker he was being. I mean, how many times had he pulled through for me? Still, he was having none of it. The poor guy was tearing himself up. I tried to tell him that we all have our breaking points, we're only human after all. No, he still felt guilty for believing he'd let us down. Not at all mate, not at all. You never have and you never will. We all need someone to cover our backs at times bro.)

What was I saying?

Oh yeah, well the others were still counting on me to lead them to safety it seemed. So I had no choice but to try and hide away the internal crap I was going through, and lead us on out of there. In those moments when my legs did turn to jelly and I ended up hugging the ice face, I just lied through my teeth when I saw the fear in the others eyes, and said I just needed to rest and get my breath back briefly.

You know, despite everything, I remember those moments more than most. M.J would pat me on the shoulder, Chloe would ruffle my hair as I tried to recuperate, and Destiny would bend down forgetting the cold, and rub the life back into my weary cramp filled leg muscles. I remember those moments when she'd stand up, hug me and looking with complete trust and expectation into my eyes, lean forwards, whisper 'thank you,' and kiss me on the cheek.

Those little things gave me the strength to lead us on. So, we all saved each other in a way. All four of us, friends to the bitter end, pitched in and guided our sorry arses out of there. I was no more of a hero than anyone else.

As the glacier finally passed into the sides of the rocks of the mountain, we found our cave. The mountain was regularly climbed, and this was blatantly a regular stop-off point. A deep and enormous mouth led away into the mountain, protecting us from the harsh elements outside. Oh how they rumbled and shook themselves in fury at our escape.

A plentiful supply of dry logs aligned the walls, and although we were idiots, at least we weren't complete and utter idiots. Our firelighters, matches and multitude of warm blankets had been wrapped in polythene bags, and were still crisp and dry despite everything.

In that cave, half way up a mountain, somehow safe and sound, almost unbelievably so in hindsight, we torched a huge roasting fire. We stripped naked, dried ourselves, pulled up close beside those beautifully boiling flames, and wrapped up under a million and one thick blankets. Destiny and I spooned and cuddled up into each other, naked, and fell into deep exhausted sleep.

Suffice to say, after out exploits of the previous day, we let ourselves sleep in for as long as possible. It was a small wonder indeed that neither of us had come down with hypothermia.

Now I can't for the life of me think why, but none of us particularly felt like exploring any further up the mountain that morn. No, we settled instead for a huge and ravenous breakfast, and then a gentle, long, and very, very, very easy descent back to terra firma below.

I think M.J summed it all up best when we reached firm ground. He bent over on all fours, and kissed the floor beneath him.

Yep, you know what mate, I completely fucking agree.

BETTER THAN SEX?

ON the penultimate day before our inevitable fateful farewell we all booked ourselves in for a tandem skydive. We figured we may as well pay the little bit extra and go for the 12 000 foot jump, allowing almost a minute of free fall time. Trust me, its definitely worth the extra bucks if you've got them, 'cause there ain't no better feeling than plummeting towards earth at terminal velocity. Hell, its even better then sex! No orgasm even compares, and that's saying something, especially as I finally mastered the whole Tantric sex thing I'd seen M.J practising with those Dutch girls back in Australia.

Yeah, someone close to me asked me recently, 'if you could go back in your life and do any event again, what would you do?'

Well, I've managed to squeeze in some rather random things in my years, but nothing comes close to skydiving. That's definitely what I would do. Although now, thinking about it, I wonder if I could find the balls to do it again in these my older years?

Perhaps our recent exploits in the death defying experiences helped us in this instance. For I found myself relatively peaceful in mind as the plane pulled into the air.

As we steadily climbed to cruise level, I was certainly aware that on some conscious level I was a little apprehensive, but this somehow seemed like a walk in the park now, all things considered. I mean, its not even as if I had to particularly do anything. Hooked onto the front of my dive-master, it was all rather out of my hands, he was the one who pulled the cord; all I had to do was just hang there, and I think even I could manage that!

So, third in line, the doors opened, and one by one the couples in front toppled out. We waited for the light inside the hull to change from red to green, then before I really knew where I was, or what the hell I was about to do, the instructor said, 'go.'

All of a sudden I was sat at the edge of an open door 12 000 feet above the ground, looking down. I stuck my legs over the ledge and tucked them up underneath the belly of the plane as I'd be previously told to do. I felt pressure on my back as the dive master leant forward and in the next instant I was tipping out into the sky, with some stranger tied to my back, and a parachute involved somewhere in the equation I hoped!

It was one of those situations where you just have to keep the faith, and trust in things out of your own control. Once again I was leaping into the unknown, and once again, I was bloody loving it!

One minute free falling at terminal velocity, wow man, there's nothing like it. The adrenaline just overloads your brain, nothing goes through your head, you just feel the g's, and boy you don't half know how it feels to be alive.

I remember shouting and whooping out loud, who knows what the hell I cried? Although I have a sneaky suspicion it was something rather sad like, 'I said Devil be damned what a rush!' Oh dear, never mind hey?

Shit. It was amazing. You really do reach some higher state of happiness, of consciousness, yeah, nothing compares. For that one minute every fibre in your very existence appreciates this brilliant thing called living.

I believe I thought it would end there, but it didn't. Perhaps, just like the magic mushrooms, the come down after the mind-blowing intensity of the initial rush, is just as amazing. Oh so very diverse and different in every way, but just as wonderful. As the parachute pulled up and away into the wind, I was oh so surprised to find the crystal clarity of the situation somehow continuing.

'Man, what a fucking view!'

The sun was setting, its warm rays reflecting off the lake below, the rolling hills rose to meet us, and, well, yeah, I guess its just yet another one of those things that I can't really explain. You really can't be told how it feels. You can but experience it for yourself. So go do it. Leap into the unknown, 'cause you know what, you've never really lived till you've skydived!

PROCRASTINATION OFTEN BREEDS CONFUSION

ALAS it seemed as if time was a running out for me. Destiny was called in at the last minute to do the late shift at her part time job in a small bistro down town that night.

My options, and hopes for that matter, were vastly diminishing. Decisions needed to be made, and they needed to be made fast, for we were leaving early the next morning for the North Island.

Luckily, I had M.J with me, and by this point in proceedings, I no longer had to speak my mind about what I was feeling.

As I lay on my bed, staring up at the ceiling in just another backpackers hostel somewhere in the world, pondering life in general, (okay, okay, so that's a lie, pondering not exactly life in general, rather daydreaming about something very specific, i.e. Destiny.) M.J wandered in and threw me my coat, the zip catching me a treat right in the bloody eye.

'Come on Romeo, we've got dinner reservations to keep,' he said nonchalantly, and with that turned around and wandered back out.

I guess I knew what he was up to, else I wouldn't have stopped at the mirror before I left to follow his footsteps, and tried to shape the complete long mop that had become my hair. (...'style,' I was going to say, but although indeed it was hair, by no long stretch of the imagination did, 'style,' come into play!)

Taking the stairs two at a time as I pulled my tan leather jacket about my frame, I leapt into the entrance hall almost barrelling into poor old Chloe.

'Sorry,' I blushed.

'It's alright, no harm done. Honestly, 'cause I would've decked you if you'd hurt me!' She laughed.

As her eyes danced playfully, and her cheeky smile flashed away, well, hell, she definitely almost rivalled Destiny in beauty I thought. I could completely see how M.J and she had hooked up. The two of them were like a pair of bloody super models together, and apart from that, their personalities complimented each other so much that, well, I guess they just seemed like two little peas in a pod. I was definitely glad they'd gotten together, but there was no time to contemplate that right then, I had my own love life to go sort out.

We caught a short taxi ride downtown, hopped out onto the sidewalk into the rain, (it seemed like that oh so lovely storm that had plagued us so bitterly back in the mountains, had eventually worked its way into Christchurch to haunt us) and paid the driver through the open window. The neon sign, 'Bojangles,' tried to burn its way into the darkness, all the while its diners were hidden away from the street behind steamed glass bay windows.

A doorman kindly opened the entrance doors for us poor drowned rats to take refuge. M.J gave our party's name, and we were seated at a small rounded table at the back of the restaurant, near the kitchen doors.

We had barely removed our coats and pulled up a pew when Destiny appeared in view through the double doors next to us. Her strawberry blond hair was tied back, with just a few wisps left to dangle over those divine and stunning features of her face. She balanced an enormous tray of food in front of a busty chest barely contained behind a virginal white (top buttons undone) blouse. No wonder I could barely prevent myself from drooling and frothing at the mouth like Homer Simpson at the thought of a beer and a donut! Wow! I was seriously starting to re-juggle skydiving in the importance of things!

I'd planned on doing the whole smouldering, mysterious, cool and calm, James Dean-esque approach on things, but M.J had other plans. Letting out a huge ear-piercing wolf-whistle, he whooped out at the top of his voice.

'Hey sweet cheeks! Come and give us some lovin'!'

All the suited and booted posh diners turned to stare, the 'Sam,' at the piano stopped mid tune.

Personally, I for one just died of embarrassment, and from the look of Destiny and Chloe, I wasn't the only one! Still, it all seemed rather amusing once the piano started up again, the drinks were ordered in, and we set about getting completely and utterly sloshed.

I was evidently drinking like a man from the Old West who'd just been told that alcohol was about to be outlawed. I think there was food involved somewhere along the course of things, though I can't be entirely sure, because the anxiety of the situation had completely taken a hold of me. Just how the hell was I gonna tell her I love her?

You see the place was absolutely jam packed and despite her best intentions, Destiny could barely get to speak to us for more then a few brief seconds at a time, and it was driving me crazy! I couldn't stop fidgeting, my leg kept jiggling, my fingers constantly tapped the table, and I wasn't much use in any conversation. I was spending my whole time constantly aware of Destiny's every movement, always looking for my opening. Every time she walked by I tried to catch her eye, though when I did, I over exerted on the whole smile thing and just resembled the Elephant Man in some considerable pain, or possibly constipation, and when she did manage to talk, my nervous jokes seemed to make no sense whatsoever.

Hmm, this was going to be harder than I originally thought.

So, as the hours wore on, and the countdown ticked away, oh, and my thoughts and eyesight seriously deteriorated with the contents of my wine bottle, I started getting desperate. I started clasping at straws. I decided a new approach was evidently required.

Pulling my ever-trusty journal and pen from the satchel I always carried, I started scribbling away furiously like a madman possessed.

Right, I'll warn you right out, this absolutely stinks, but I didn't exactly have a lot of time, (or consciousness for that matter, left) so I wrote the following lines. Don't analyse them, for they were nothing more then the last futile and desperate attempts of a drunkard to capture the heart of the woman he loved. Well, enough said, here it is, those terrible and fateful words I penned on the table as Chloe and M.J sat snogging the faces off each other, as if to rub in the desperation of my situation.

'Love destroys, such men as I,
 To be a lover, is to only feel woe,
 Yet to be another, is to merely deny,
 All that I am, and all that I know.

So I must face, this darkness alone,
 Must carry on, heaving a heavy heart,
 For in me, the seed of love has been sown,
 And these feelings Destiny, shall never depart.

Sorry babe, I guess all I'm trying to say, is that I'm lost without you. Oh, and in case you haven't already guessed, I FUCKING LOVE YOU!'

Yep, that was it. Not entirely Shakespeare, but under my blurred and alcohol induced hypnotic gaze it looked like it might possibly work. Oh, and there was the other overriding fact, that I was completely fresh out of ideas.

So it was, the next time she approached our table, I pulled myself up, and stumbled into her feigning drunkenness. (Well, it might not have been completely an act!) You see, she wore around her waist a small black apron, and as I fell into her, she reached up and put her arms around me to support me, and this was the chance I'd been looking for. I slipped my note into the front pocket of her apron, (I couldn't think of anything more embarrassing, anything that would make me want to curl up into a ball and die on the spot more than handing her the note and have her read it in front of me. I can't believe I thought this to be the best tactic. Though things always do make far more sense when you're pissed as a fart on far too much red wine, white wine, tequila slammers, Southern Comfort, beer and cigarettes) and with my message delivered I quickly made my way to the toilets.

I actually did need a call of nature, (when the floodgates open there really is no stopping them on a drunken night out) and I also needed to sit down and gather my thoughts alone for a while.

So I found myself sat in a cubicle, pants around my ankles, head in my hands, trying to talk sense to myself. In all probability though, and the brilliant clarity that is hindsight, I expect all I was really doing was passing in and out of consciousness!

After what must have seemed like an age to the others, I finally emerged from the restroom. Most of the other diners had finally left, thank goodness, and

Destiny stood at our table, with my journal in hand, running her fingertips along its edges.

As I staggered towards them and plonked my sorry arse down at last, Destiny placed my notepad with great care and precision underneath my gaze, and winked with a conspiratorial air at me. She then turned, upped and walked away, leaving me completely confused.

She hadn't said a word. She hadn't changed her attitude to me at all, ignoring me or the like, letting me know in no uncertain terms that she wasn't interested in the slightest. Then again, on the other hand, she hadn't grabbed me by the lapels and pulled me into the passionate kiss I'd dreamt of. She'd done nothing at all. Right, interesting?

Through the haze of my drunken stupor, I stumbled upon the answer. 'She hasn't found my letter tucked away in her apron.' Oh fuck.

Looking up at the three M.J's that appeared in my vision now, I found myself sucking away on my top lip, and blinking for long periods as I struggled each time to reopen my eyes. All the while my head seemed to have all of a sudden grown particularly heavy, and started bobbing up and down on my straw like neck. As I struggled to speak, I realised I was talking absolute gibberish.

Yeah, now I come to think about it, I was absolutely wankered, I was more pissed then a pissed man who enjoys spending his holidays on the island of pissed-out-of-his-face-arinio, whilst sipping at a cocktail.

At the realisation of this state of things, I reached for my full glass of, well, truth be told I'm not entirely sure what the hell it was a full glass of, but I do know it was of alcoholic content, and proceeded to knock the whole thing over the table and myself. I jumped up in shock as the ice cubes soaked against my skin, and instantly started to topple backwards. M.J leapt up and managed to catch me, and it seemed I was very much in need of the extra support as I slumped against him.

My last memory of the evening, was Destiny approaching and pushing my long hair away from my rolling eyes, and in an attempt to find a piece of me still in them, asking rather broken heartedly, 'well?'

All I managed to blurt out along with a long loud belch was a slurred and confused, 'well what?'

As I once again rested my head on M.J's shoulder and closed my eyes, I think I remember M.J saying to Destiny, 'I better get him home. Will you come and see us off tomorrow?'

Her response almost held a tint of sheer and utter pain and hurt in its tone, 'I don't know, I really don't know what to do,' and with that, I must have passed out.

IT'S BETTER TO TRY AND FAIL,
THAN TO NEVER HAVE TRIED AT ALL.
NO REGRETS

I WOKE up the next morning with an almighty bitch of a hangover. My head was full of dancing jackhammers, and my mouth tasted like a skunk had shat in it. Breakfast consisted of a vast amount of aspirin for my headache. As I slowly started to feel a little human again, I once more made that vow that I'd, 'never drink again.'

As I spent the majority of the morning recovering, it was only due to an incredible show of strength on M.J's behalf that my packing got done, and that we somehow got to the bus terminal on time.

By the time the clock signalled our time for departure, I was a little fragile, but myself once more, just, and it wasn't great the truth be told.

We waited until the last possible moment before M.J gently put his arm around my shoulders and giving them a small squeeze, looked at me matter of factly, and simply said, 'she's not coming mate.'

Looking back at him, I realised he knew everything, and just behind his eyes was the genuine worry of what I might do at the realisation of the obvious. That indeed she wasn't coming. She'd finally seen me for the drunken idiot waste of space, complete and utter dickhead, I really was. Why did I bother throwing away the unbelievable friendship we had again?

Oh well, it's better to try and fail then to have never tried at all, right? No regrets.

I think M.J was a little surprised when I just shrugged my shoulders eventually and replied, 'I know. Still, we'd best be moving.'

So we threw our bags into the hold beneath the coach, and stepped through the gas propelled pneumatic doors, hearing them whoosh close with such finality behind us.

As we moved to the back of the bus, it gently pulled away from the station, and we found ourselves off on the open road. I must confess as to glancing back through its large rear window one final time as we pulled away.

For the briefest of moments I even fancied I saw a blond haired girl dashing along the pathway behind us, vaulting over luggage and old aged pensioners before we turned the corner and the scene was lost forever from view. I fancied I saw Destiny, before I made myself realise that it was probably nothing more than the hopeful longings of a fanciful mind.

As we left the city and Destiny behind, I was aware of M.J constantly casting me an anxious glance out of the corner of his eye. He was obviously concerned, I mean let's face it, my track record of dealing with heartbreak wasn't exactly the most impressive. What he didn't realise, was that I had come a long way from the man he'd first met. My constant leaps into the unknown had forever changed me, and I firmly believed, or at least hoped, that those changes were mainly for the better.

So, how did I react to all this? Obviously I'd be lying if I didn't say I was more than a little disappointed. At least I'd tried though, right? No regrets, I'll forever strive to be lying on my deathbed and look back on my life and smile at all I've done, rather than spend those last moments regretting that which I never did. Wasting my time with, 'what if's,' and, 'if only's'.

So, I pulled out my journals, grabbed up my sword, and penned away my worries.

Perhaps those words explain things best. Perhaps those words reveal my heart far better than I could try and explain now. Perhaps.

'O.k. So I haven't written anything for a while so I guess this entry isn't really going to follow any kinda order. It's going to merely be a chaotic smorgasbord of memories. So where do I start?

Well at this present moment in time I'm sat on some shitty little bus like the kind of old bangers you see in the movies. I'm listening to the Braveheart soundtrack whilst sat on my highly uncomfortable chair that comes with a spring up my arse for no extra fee, but still, at least I've got a freshly opened beer by my side, and a pen in my hand.

Once again, as so often, I'm sat here alone. Yep, I'm all by myself, it's as I've always felt. Well, barring M.J of course, but you know what I mean. Besides, he makes a hideous looking lady! The instrumental in my ears is one of love, loss and longing, and I find myself surprised to discover that it is not only Beth who fills my thoughts as I once believed to be the only possibility, but Destiny now as well.

I think I came to New Zealand to find my heart again in truth. I suspect in reality I was already aware that when I booked my ticket, in Destiny I had a chance of reminding myself just how it felt to be happily in love again.

Since Beth walked out after years of being engaged, I guess my heart kinda just stopped. For a while back there I forgot everything. Who I was, who I wanted to be, what I wanted from life, and above all else, what it was to feel anything. For a short space of time the word, 'emotions,' seemed as alien and extinct to me as a blind man being told just how much beauty can be found gazing into your lover's eyes. When they act as the portals to the mind, and all the love and beauty from within bursts forth from their pupils, and you could just gaze into those eyes forever.

It's almost as if you can see eternity. The universe itself presents itself. From those small black orbs shines such light that you can see the very stars themselves sparkling forth. All you feel is peace, utter bliss, and it seems as though the whole world stops, time itself stands still, all things make sense in that moment, and it seems as though God himself is staring right back at you.

I guess it's understandable why I hit the self-destruct button back there when Beth left. All emotions had faded to grey. All in the short space of time it took for me to read those fated words on that day by the river. Just like that I had found that chapter of my life finished. A chapter of happiness, smiles, laughs, and a constant feeling that everything was just as it should be.

I can't even begin to explain how it felt to believe in that bliss, that euphoric knowledge that whatever life threw at Beth and I , as long as we had each other, nothing else mattered in the grander scheme of things. I was untouchable. I was a naive fool.

So a new chapter in my life began, a chapter of feeling nothing bar numbness. Still amongst it all, somewhere I found the means to keep going on. After M.J saved me I realised that I couldn't just curl up in a ball, roll over, and give up the fight. I realised that life doesn't place obstacles in our path that we can't overcome. So, that's why, whilst sat around the campfire with M.J and our Aboriginal friend, I had deemed it best to carry on. 'Get busy living, or get busy dying,' right?

It's relatively easy to do this, to push it all to the back of your mind and get busy living during the hectic waking hours, but personally I found it terrible when the world stopped spinning late at night, leaving me alone with my thoughts and dreams.

I hope you don't know how it feels to wake from a dream, and not want to be alive in the real world. You just want to sleep forever, for in my dreams I was with Beth again, and everything was just as it should be.

The worst part of it all is when you first awake. When your dream carries over momentarily into the real world.

I remember how I would wake some mornings, with the early morning sun casting a serene light through the drapes of whichever hostel I was staying in at the time, or the back windows of Ben and Dan's campervan. As I awoke with my dreams still confusing my groggy mind, I would watch the sunray dance through the slit in the open curtains, and for a moment mistake them for the drapes of the flat Beth and I shared back home.

I remember how I'd struggled to hang those curtains and eventually managed to somehow fall off the ladder. Beth had thought I was seriously hurt but I was just crying wolf for attention.

Yeah, it had been Beth who'd shed the tears back then, not me. She'd told me she couldn't bear to lose me, and we had ended up making love on the torn up newspaper cuttings that carpeted the floor, in-between the pots of paint we'd stolen from a neighbour's trashcan to decorate our first home.

Shit. I'd wake from a dream of her and in that hazy, ethereal light, I would forget how things really were. I would lay there, smiling, happy and content, until a strange, uneasy feeling would take hold of my stomach.

This knot of anxiety would slowly seep through my body, working its way lackadaisically, like some demented lethal drug taking great pleasure in its unstoppable task, through my blood stream, beating towards my brain. Then all of a sudden, it would hit me. I would realise that the happiness was all just a dream, nothing more. Beth stopped walking with me and there would seem no real reason to drag myself out of bed, out into the real world, out into a world without her.

When times were really bad, I remember closing my eyes up tight, and willing myself to fall asleep, back into that dream where everything was right. Surely this fucked up reality must be the dream?

As with everything in this life though, time numbs all things in the end. Eventually the dreams of Beth disappeared down the days. Eventually her face faded; eventually a new smile appeared in the crowd, shining brighter than all that had gone before. It was the last thing I was expecting to be honest, but somehow I found Destiny in the darkness of it all.

Unfortunately I have recently realised that it isn't my dreams that outline the true depths of my emotions now, it's my nightmares.

I had one only last night, a nightmare that is. Destiny had fallen for me, my heart had filled and started to beat again, and then by the end of it all, she had told me that I had just been a toy, a child's play thing that she liked to pull the strings upon like some sick puppeteer. Pull the strings and watch me, the marionette, dance to her unholy jig. She was really in love with someone else. I can still recall the horror, the pain, the quiet part of me resounding over and over again, 'please, please let this not be the case.'

I guess it was just a premonition of what I was about to feel right now, what I was about to feel when she didn't turn up at the bus station, my heart wrench when I was to realise that my love was unrequited.

Yep, my heart and my love lay with Destiny. Yet Destiny and love have decided to escape me on a winged chariot. Oh bollocks. Dick Wank Mother Fuck! Still, fuck it, however much it hurts, I will not give chase on horseback, not this time, for I have changed.

After Beth left, I locked my heart away in a small tin chest in my ...well chest I guess! Over time I have learnt to keep the lid of this chest open, and allow my heart to show again. Through this I was able to fall head over heels in love with Destiny, yet she is gone now, and it does not do well to dwell in dreams. This is what she has become to me. A dream, an unobtainable reality. A parallel universe almost.

It is good that I did not allow myself to hope too much. It is good that I kept a constant, vigilant hand over the lid of that tin chest. Ever ready to bring it crashing down and lock the clasp to protect myself, because my heart could not take such bitter disappointment a second time. I fear it may well have torn itself in two and this time, there would be far more than a deep pulsating scar, this time, the pieces could not be put back together.

Yes, some things just don't work out, however much you want them to. Every chest has a secret compartment. So I shall lay my feelings for Destiny to rest gently at the bottom, carefully replace the velvet lining, and I guess the lid can then be opened once more. Life goes on, and I know one day everything will work out as God intended. I am nothing without my faith.

Still, a plan of action for the mean time may not be such a bad idea. I mean, when the shit hits the proverbial fan, I think it's always worth having a plan.

Hmm, right, well I guess in some sense, perhaps the way has been clear to me for a while now. I am at last starting to know who I am and what I must do. I must continue to strive to be, all the ideals that have become so dear to me, whilst all the while continuing to adapt and grow.

My soul is a phoenix from the ashes of the warriors of old, of both the Samurai of the East, and the Chivalric Knights of the West. To me, it is not our status or the accumulation of materialistic wealth that define who we are. It is honour, perhaps a lost word in this day and age, that makes us men. So, the morals of old are how I must strive to live my existence. A life of honour, morality, discipline, compassion, courage and empathy. I know that this will not always be an option, but to emulate such feats where possible is where the importance lies. As there is no such thing as a perfect man, just a man with perfect intentions.

I still believe in love. Only now I realise that we can't become preoccupied with pouring it into just one person. It risks breaking us.

I find such beauty forever surrounds me. Take now for example, a brick wall faces my window as we wait for the traffic lights to change. Yet one small flower has somehow found roots to blossom there. It mesmerises my eyes, to see it dancing in the wind, as the rain gently falls.

No. It is better to pour our love into everything and everyone, than to live a bitter and resentful existence.'
End of Entry.

So that's how I vented. I let it all spill out onto the pages before me, and in doing so, not only dispensed with my inner demons, but hopefully gave myself the kick up the arse I needed to not revert back into that whole self-destructive phase again. For one thing I don't think my liver could deal with much more of the whole alcoholism thing. As much fun as it was sharing a park bench one night with M.J and some homeless Aborigines, it wasn't the best idea I'd ever had choosing to share the methylated spirit they were passing round.

No, perhaps in writing down the ideas I'd discovered along life's way, I had something in cement to try and stick to, and aspire towards.

The other thing I had to try and remember, were my words back on Ko Phi Phi, to remember how I felt back then. To remember the importance of striving to recognise all that we already have in life. To recognize the fact that without the lows, how could we ever judge the highs? It's just a little easier said than done when the chips are down unfortunately.

201

Closing up my journal, I went to tuck it back into my bag. It was only then that I discovered that someone had slipped a letter in-between its back pages without me even noticing. Tucked into my notepads last few sheets, a small blue envelope slid out.

So it was, with feelings of hope and anxiety all rolled into one, that I picked up the letter from the floor upon which it had fallen, and held it aloft in front of me. Studying it, I found my name scrawled in small letters upon the envelope's front, and I found I certainly recognized the handwriting.

Could it really be? Do I dare open it? Am I really ready? Is my spare hand held poised and waiting over the lid of the tin chest surrounding my heart, ready to close it in an instant and protect it all once more?

With trembling fingers I tore at the letter's seal. Unfortunately I found that my annoying insistence on forever biting my nails did in fact possess a drawback. Could I open the thing without ripping it, like hell I could? Stupid bloody glue, stupid bloody nails.

The one thing I refused to do was give in to my manly instincts and just tear the whole bloody thing open with brute force. I mean, this letter could be quite important, and the last thing I wanted to do was rip some vital part of the message inside, and be stuck puzzling over just what the hell the writer had been trying to say.

Allowing a brief moment of respite to think, I decided to give in to my other manly instincts. Leaning over to M.J, I asked to borrow his Bowie knife. He was forever sharpening the thing with the rock he carried around with him, and its blade slipped easily through the paper in one clean smooth swiping cut. Quite the letter opener wouldn't you say?!

As I unfolded the letter, I dared myself to read its contents....

'We are nothing more than mere grains of sand on the beach of time, or one of those infinite stars shimmering away in the blurry night sky. Quietly shining in our own little way until our light begins to fade and we are lost forever from view.

Yet some of us regular stars are blessed. For very rarely a shooting star burns brightly across our paths, and we stop and stare in wonder. They never stay for long, but whilst they're in our lives, they change us forever. They blaze with such brilliance, such passion, intensity and love, that their mere presence lifts us up when we're down, offering us a helping hand when we feel we can't go on, and that we must surely be lost beneath the waves.

To gaze upon them steals our very breath away, and stops our heart mid beat. Their light seeps in, through all boundaries, through all defences, through all walls, and so when we do draw breath again, everything has changed. The air feels fresher in our lungs, and our heart feels like its never really beaten before that moment. We're alive, and the greatest gift of all, is that we're truly inspired with hope. Hope for a better life, hope that we can become better people, and hope for a love that transcends both time and place.

It is you who are the shooting star. Without people like you there is no light, no beauty, no hope.

The sun has gone down in the west, and the day is drawing in. The snow has begun to fall, and the night seems to carry a chill. Yet as long as you continue to blaze a burning trail across the darkness of our lives, then everything will be just fine. Never lose your light, without you I'm nothing.

Destiny x

P.S. I love you

P.P.S. What is it you always say? 'Half a dozen right people in this world for us, but only one right time and place,' right? Well, fancy finding out if this is the right time and place? I know I'd like to.xx'

Reading the letter through twice to allow it all to sink in, I smiled openly. In an instant I realised the humour in it all. Destiny had been in exactly the same state of mind as I on that last night in Bojangles. We were both officially as useless as each other! Neither had managed to feel it was the right time to say something, so both had relied on a letter to let the other know their true heart. I had placed mine in her apron; she had placed hers in my notebook.

So that's why she'd placed it with a wink in front of me! Man, if only I hadn't been so drunk to see the light!

So it was that neither of us had gotten each other's letter until it was too late. I, whilst sat here on a bus far away from her, and it transpired, that Destiny had found my note whilst counting up her tips late that morning. So it wasn't my imagination, it was her racing after my bus after all, vaulting over suitcases and OAP's to catch me as we'd turned the corner.

I released one of those huge broad grins that M.J was now becoming accustomed to, which forced him to instantly remark, 'oh crap, you've got that look in your eyes like you're about to do something stupid again!'

Grabbing his shoulder I thrust the letter at him and simply said, 'she bloody loves me mate! I'll see you at the airport in Auckland later this week'

Before he had time to respond I was up on my feet and smashing through the protective glass panel with the butt of M.J's knife, yanking at the emergency stop chord.

In a deafening screech of brakes the bus crumpled into the highways emergency stop lane, and the driver shouted, 'what the bloody hell?!'

As I leapt down the isle I threw a fistful of dollars at the man by way of an apology, and explained that something terrible had happened, and I must get off the bus immediately.

Releasing the door I leapt from the coach with the driver in hot pursuit. Suffice to say he seemed pretty damn pissed off, not to mention the other passengers as well, but oh well; sometimes the end justifies the means! He grumbled away to himself, muttering obscene profanities under his breath aimed in my general direction, but eventually removed my bags from the cargo hold, and without even a, 'good luck,' jumped back on board and sped away. I just had time to catch the sight of M.J raise his Stetson off his head and nod with a smile before I was showered with gravel.

There I was, stood by the roadside in the middle of nowhere, with my thumb up, but not a worry in the world, because I was officially a man in love.

CHOCOLATE CARAMEL COATED CALAMITIES

DESTINY shared a house off campus with a few other students, and that night, I flew to her on angels' wings.

In a futile attempt at romanticism I'd stopped off at a 7-11 store along the way, and procured a single red rose and a small box of chocolates.

As I reached her house, I approached the side door and raised my fist to knock. Something stopped me. Whether it was the hip flask of whisky I'd swigged at for dutch courage along the way, or some unforeseen entity guiding me I don't know. But I stopped.

Sneaking around to the back garden, I saw a flickering light burning away at her bedroom's window. She was still awake!

My idiotic nature took control, and I longed with all my drunken heart to appear as if an apparition at her window. I longed to show the world that it wasn't completely devoid of Romeo's. I longed to show the world that such love still existed that would stop time itself in its tracks. That true love was not a thing of bygone days, belonging only to long dead poets, but that it still lived and breathed inside of me.

A glass conservatory stood beneath her bedroom, and to its right, a drainpipe. Without a second thought I clenched the raw red rose between my teeth, tucked the chocolates within my jacket pocket, and with great dexterity started to scale the drainpipe.

Reaching the level of the conservatory roof, I placed a cautious foot upon its surface. It showed not a single sign of weakness. Thus, I pulled my whole body weight onto its edge, and still the thing held fast.

By now, her windows edge was but inches away. I saw her silhouette move behind the candle's flame, and with the window slightly ajar, I fancied I heard her sigh my name. Spurred on by this, without thinking I stepped out further onto the roof to tap on her windowpane.

Did she really love me? Had she secretly hoped in her heart of hearts that her letter would bring me back to her? For the briefest of seconds I shut my eyes, and allowed the image in my minds eye to settle happily upon my soul. I saw her embrace me; I saw the passion of our first kiss at that window ledge.

When I opened my eyes again, I realised in the split second it took, that I was falling. With an almighty crack the glass panels had buckled underneath my weight, and I had fallen from the first storey of that house to the concrete floor below. Landing on my back, the shards of glass fell like the pattering of rain around me. I simply lay there, unable to move.

So it was that Destiny entered into this romantic scene of me destroying her rented accommodation. Aroused by the noise she had thrown her window open and peered outside.

As I lay there, looking up, temporarily paralysed, I saw her. Leaning out she gazed though the broken hole, and saw me in turn. Saw me sprawled battered, broken and bleeding upon the concrete floor below, the broken stem of a rose hanging from my lips, and my body dotted with chocolate caramels that had burst free. How smooth am I?!

Lying on her bed later that night, with me more than a little worse for wear, Destiny and I shared our first kiss.

It was everything I'd ever imagined and more.

Well, behind locked doors that night we shared more than our first kiss truth be told. Ah, but I'm afraid that a true gentleman never does a, 'kiss and tell.' However I've never claimed to be a gentleman!

So basically we were lying there and she pulled my tight jeans down before...ha ha just joking, rather boringly I won't actually kiss and tell. Some things, some memories, well, they're just for me.

In that time and place, we only had a few days together, but it's more than some get in a lifetime. I'll never forget them, for those hours were enough to live on in me forever, they re-ignited my burnt-out heart, and made me the man I am today. So I keep those memories for myself. I don't want to share them all, for in times of trouble, when hell itself seems to be tearing loose around me, I can still look back on them and find reason to smile. So, nope, they're just for me.

All I will say is that after months of restless heartache, I finally found peace. I'd discovered something more complete, more real than anything I'd ever experienced before.

I won't try and put it into words, I think I'd just ruin it. I don't want to run the risk of negating it all down to a number of old clichés. If you know true love, then you know what I'm talking about. If you've ever lost someone, only to find what you never thought possible again in someone else, then you especially know what I'm talking about. For me, love is more than a four-letter word, it is more than thoughts, feelings, or the stars in the sky above, love is more than all these things, as it's what I felt for Destiny right then.

Alas forgive me, I've said too much already, with every word I poison that which I talk about, placing something unique into no more than common words, words that despite their numbers, no matter what combination I place them in, will have always been said before. Instead I shall tell you of just one single moment from those days, and I can only hope that will suffice.

Outside it was no more than a regular day. It was no romantic setting, there were no candles flickering in the breeze, no smell of fresh jasmine wafting in through open doors on a warm summers afternoon, no music serenading us, and there was no crackling fire present, nor a rug before its flames for making love on (more's the pity!).

I was sat on the couch in Destiny's room. With my left hand I held the book I was reading open, with my right hand I ran my fingers ever so delicately though Destiny's hair, so as not to wake her. She lay curled up to my right, her head in my lap, softly sleeping.

For long periods I'd forget my book, choosing to gaze upon her instead. She somehow seemed more beautiful to me in that moment, than she ever had before (trust me, not an easy task!). I traced the lines of her face. Those curled long eyelashes, that cute dimpled chin, and those small pressed succulently divine lips that made me want to kiss her forever and never stop.

In our peace I loved the way our breathing had tuned in together. I loved the way at one point she stirred, reached her hand up to mine and gently squeezed my finger. As I leant over and kissed her, she smiled in a way that in an instant told me that she felt the same way to. So it was that we remained like that for the better part of the afternoon, for my own part, I could have happily stayed like that for all eternity.

I forced myself to imprint the still frame of that moment into my very heart and soul. I forced myself to remember that picture. For I knew that no matter what life had in store for me, no one could ever take that photograph away from inside, no one could take away that memory, no one could ever take away her. I knew there and then that lying on my deathbed, hopefully years from now, I can once again close my eyes, and see us there once more. I can close my eyes and smile away happily one last time before I go to meet my maker.

Sometimes I wish I were a poet, so I could help you feel the emotions I'm drawing upon when I write. The emotions I felt in moments like that, the emotions that I still in some cases, feel now. But I can't. I am no more than myself. Far better men than I have spoken of love, but trust me when I say, I've felt it too. I just don't write so good like, I'm 'Fick,' with a capitol, 'F,' and have verbal diarrhoea to boot! Anyway, I just figured I'd try and show you the moment, thought that perhaps what I was trying to explain, would make more sense then. Like I said, I hope it kinda suffices.

Then again, perhaps I should have gone with the short and sweet after all. Kept it simple. Well in that case, I'll put it another way, 'I Fucking Love Her!' Ha ha, I'm such a numpty sometimes.

PERHAPS THE GREATEST LESSON LEARNT, IS THE ONE IN WHICH WE APPRECIATE THE IMPORTANCE OF 'CHOICE'

IN NO time at all I was off to meet M.J at the airport in Auckland, ready to fly, shit, was I really flying back home? How strange?

Tearing myself away from Destiny's arms when the bus pulled in to carry me away, was the hardest thing I've ever done. Unfortunately, I just didn't feel like I had any other choice. My money was running seriously low; I'd already paid for my return flight, and really, what other option was there? I had no Visa to stay and work, no place to live in and so, let's face it, no choice.

I guess sometimes in life you just have to bite the bullet. Some things are out of your control and you just have to face those moments with strength, and get on with it. Unfortunately, that's just the way life is. For we are often nothing more than mere tumbleweed blowing in the wind, being blown on out of town much to our sorrow.

I once met a wonderful woman by the name of Ann Heckbert. This woman was amazing in every way, the kind of person who you'll always feel your life is a little better for having known. She was an old soul who knew the score, so I shall borrow her words for a while to explain myself.

'I understand that life can only be perfect in moments and that we have to recognize those moments and live in them with all our hearts. We need to move slowly through life, to absorb and savour the present – it will never happen again, no matter how much we want it to at times.'

So I made sure I savoured every moment with Destiny, lived in those moments with all my heart, for I knew the wind was soon gonna come a blowing, and move me on from her arms.

Sat on that coach to the North Island, and eventually Auckland airport, I realised I would soon be flying home. As is only natural in such times, I found myself reflecting back over my travels.

Pulling all my thoughts and ideas from the last few months into one, I realised one overriding fact. I realised that these were my answers, my own, and no one else's. We are all unique at the end of the day. We are all individuals, trying to find our own way in life. Trying to find our own little piece of happiness. Our own pieces to the puzzle of life. No one can tell us who to be, no one can tell us how to live our existence. At the end of the day, it's up to us, and us alone.

I've read many a book on philosophy, been told many a learned story by some prophetic traveller, and discovered such wise words in the most unexpected of places, my local bar back home for one! I've studied the Bible, the Quaran, and the wise prophetic teachings of the great Dali Lama, but you know what? All they are, is different pieces. It's up to us to take the best out of all of the things we learn, all the things we're told. It's up to us to take the pieces that sit well in our soul, sit well with who we really are, and slot them together ourselves. Only then can we form a whole mosaic, and no one can take that away.

A shadow soon disappears with the setting of the sun, or old mistress Moon pulling up her veil to hide her face away, but that rainbow coloured mosaic will live on throughout the ages, too bright to ever be hidden away.

Well, there is one thing I'd still implore of you actually. Like I said, the greatest gift in this world is to make someone smile. So give it, don't take it away. It may be far easier to destroy something beautiful, than it is to create it, but where is the honour in that?

All the rest, everything else I've babbled on about? Well, if any of it sits well on your soul then take it, it's yours. I mean this is merely my story. One of millions to be told. For each one is right for that individual alone. Happiness can't be found in buying completely into someone else's philosophy, somebody else's story. You have to take the best bits of all you hear, and make up your own story. For at the end of the day, what it's all really about, is not what I or any of the other millions think, what it's about, is, 'what do you think?'

Anyway, the coach eventually pulled in with me still lost in memories of mountains and scuba, bungee and sky diving, VW campervans and Mustang horses, jungle treks and rapid river raft riding, torn up lover's letters and burning bodies, and of course, Destiny.

M.J met me with a warm embrace at the check-in counter.

'So you made it after all?' He asked surprised.

'Thought you might choose to stay with Destiny after all.'

As I looked down at the ticket home in my hand, I half said to him, and half to myself, 'I don't know. It's not too late yet to go back to her. Is it really possible though?'

Raising an eyebrow, M.J grinned and said, 'well, I don't mean to make things any harder, but I've got an option C for ya mate.'

Signalling for him to go on, he told me, 'well whilst you've been off frolicking with beautiful young women, I decided to sell my ticket for home. I'm not going back after all. I realised I just wasn't quite ready yet. So, I mailed an old friend in Kenya and he's invited me over there. He runs a camp at the base of Mount Kenya. Basically he and a small team help build huts, wells, schools and the like, plant trees, sow seeds to help the locals out, that kind of thing. Apparently he could do with a hand over there, so, that's where I'm off to.'

Looking at him, amazed that even after all these months together he could still surprise me, I didn't realise that my jaw was about to hit the floor even more.

'Well,' continued M.J, 'I mentioned the fact that it's been a life long dream of yours to go do a safari in Africa, and so he's invited you along as well. We can work through the week, and then take the jeeps out on safari on the weekends. You up for one last adventure bro?'

Wow! Fucking hell! Now that's one hell of an opportunity!

Though I suddenly realised a very life changing decision was about to be required. The only option for now was to ask him to give me an hour alone before I could give him a decision, and M.J being M.J, completely understood.

Wandering off into the terminal, pretty oblivious to my surrounds, lost in thought, I eventually found myself sat on a stool in the bar of the Aviator's Club. Ordering a beer, I necked half a glass before sitting back and releasing a long heavy sigh.

The barman looked at me and asked, 'penny for your thoughts?'

'Ah, it's nothing really,' I replied. 'I've just got a bit of a choice to make. Basically I can fly home and take up the job I've spent my whole life training for, getting paid stupidly ridiculous amounts of money for it and never having to worry about finances ever again. Or, I can live out a life long dream by going on safari in Africa with my best friend. Oh, and whilst I'm there, I'd also get to make a difference in this world by building shelters and planting food for the native Kenyan tribesman. Or, Option C, I can fly back down to Christchurch to the woman I love, settle down, grow old and grey together, hold each others hand as we watch our children run around in the sun of summer with smiles on their faces and love in their hearts.'

'Shit,' he let out by accident. 'That's quite some decision to make! What you gonna do?'

'Good question,' I thought.

Then again, it sounded a lot more of a dilemma than it really was. I already knew what I was going to do.

You must forever have the courage and strength to follow your heart in this life. I already had my answer.

But still, that's not the point really is it?

Pouring me a fresh beer as I drained the last dregs of my first, he asked again, 'so, what'll you do?'

Catching his eye, I smiled cheekily and said, 'well, what do you think?'

Printed in the United Kingdom
by Lightning Source UK Ltd.
108696UKS00001B/55-60